AUNT BESSIE SOLVES

AN ISLE OF MAN COZY MYSTERY

DIANA XARISSA

ISBN: 1723483893
ISBN - 13: 978-1723483899

Created with Vellum

For Jack and Maggie.

AUTHOR'S NOTE

Nineteen? How did we get to book nineteen already? In some ways I feel as if I've been writing about Bessie forever, but I also feel as if there are a great many stories left to write.

I hope you are all enjoying your time with Bessie as much as I am. If this is the first Isle of Man Cozy Mystery that you're reading, you should know that the books can all be read on their own, but the characters do change and develop as the series progresses. I always recommend reading them in order (alphabetically by the last word in the title). Bessie first appeared in my romance *Island Inheritance,* although in that title she had just passed away. Unable to let such an interesting character go, I set the cozy mysteries about fifteen years before that series and have been writing about Bessie ever since.

As ever, I've used British and Manx terms and spellings throughout the book. There is a glossary of terms and some notes at the back of the book for readers who are unfamiliar with any of them. Since I've been living in the US for many years now, it is increasingly likely that "Americanisms" have snuck into the texts. I apologize for those and try to correct them when they are pointed out to me.

This is a work of fiction and all of the characters are fictional creations. Any resemblance they share with any real person, living or dead, is entirely coincidental. The Isle of Man is a wonderful and unique place. Any historical sites mentioned within the story are real. The various businesses in the story, however, are fictional and any resemblance that any of them bear to real businesses is also coincidental.

Please get in touch with any questions, comments, thoughts, or just to say "hi." I love hearing from readers. All of my contact details are available at the back of the book.

CHAPTER 1

"Bessie? It's Andrew Cheatham. I understand John Rockwell has spoiled my surprise," the voice in Bessie's ear said.

Bessie grinned. She'd been shocked when John had told her that Andrew was coming to the island for a visit. "John didn't know it was meant to be a surprise."

Andrew laughed. "I didn't really mean it to be, actually, I was just waiting to ring you until after my plans were finalised. Trying to organise eighteen people isn't easy, you know."

"I can't even imagine."

"Yes, well, Helen, my daughter, usually takes care of organising all of us, but since she wasn't particularly interested in visiting the island, she left it all to me. I've had to change the dates three times to accommodate children, grandchildren, and even great-grandchildren who keep insisting on making other plans every two minutes. I've finally decided that enough is enough and given up."

"Oh, dear," Bessie sighed. She'd been looking forward to seeing the handsome man again.

"I haven't given up on visiting. I've just given up on making it a family holiday. I've selected dates that work for me and booked a holiday cottage near your home. Last night I rang the children and told them when I'll be away. If any of them want to join me, they're welcome, but I'm not waiting for them to decide. I shall be there on the tenth."

Bessie glanced at the calendar. "As soon as that?" she exclaimed.

"Yes, as soon as that. I've a conference in London later in the month, and I want to get over while the weather is still good, or at least as good as it ever is over there."

"The weather isn't that bad," Bessie laughed. "Especially if you like rain."

"I don't much mind the weather, whatever it's doing," Andrew told her. "It will just be nice to get away. What exactly I'm getting away from is another matter, of course, being that I'm retired and live a life of leisure."

"It's still nice to have a change," Bessie suggested.

"Indeed it is. Anyway, I'm quite looking forward to seeing you again," the man told her.

Bessie found herself blushing like a schoolgirl at his words. That would never do, she thought. Andrew was a very nice man, but they were both far too old for anything like a romance. "It will be nice to see you again, as well," Bessie replied.

"I've a cold case I want to go over with you and John Rockwell. I believe I know the solution, but I'd like to get some different perspectives on it."

Bessie shook her head at her foolishness. The man wanted to talk to her and John about a cold case. Romance didn't enter into the equation at all. "That sounds intriguing."

"I hope so. I understand John has a case for me, as well."

"He didn't mention it to me, but I wouldn't be surprised if he did."

John Rockwell was a police inspector with the Laxey CID. Andrew had once worked for the police in London. From what John had told her about the man, he'd held a very important position there. Bessie knew that he'd written several training manuals on investigative techniques. She was sure that both men would enjoy spending time talking about their work.

"So I shall see you in a few weeks," Andrew said before he ended the call.

Bessie put her phone down and looked at the calendar again. She'd need to get her hair cut before his arrival, she decided. After putting a small star on the calendar to remind her of the date, something that she knew was completely unnecessary, she went back to the book that she'd been absorbed in when the phone had rung.

"He's arriving tomorrow," Bessie told her friend Doona a few weeks later. "It seems to have crept up on me rather quickly."

"It will be nice to see him again," Doona replied. "He was wonderful when we had all of that trouble across."

Bessie nodded. Andrew had been helpful, especially to Doona, when she and Doona had found themselves caught up in the middle of the murder investigation of Doona's second husband when they'd been on holiday in the UK. Andrew had been staying in the cottage next door to theirs and he'd quickly become a good friend at a very difficult time.

"I didn't realise you'd stayed in touch," Doona added.

Bessie shrugged. "We haven't, really. He rang me once or twice after I got home, but I hadn't spoken to him in months when he rang to say he was coming. When John told me, I honestly thought that Andrew was planning to avoid me on his visit."

"Why else would he visit if not to see you?"

"The island is a beautiful and special place," Bessie argued. "I'm never quite sure why more people don't visit, really." Bessie had lived her entire adult life in the Isle of Man, and she was still fascinated by its unique history and stunning scenery.

"Well, your cottage looks even more spotless than usual," Doona said, glancing around. "You can come and clean my house if you've nothing else to do."

Bessie shook her head. "I hate cleaning. I do it regularly so there's never very much to do at any one time, but if someone invented a self-cleaning house I'd move into it in a heartbeat."

"You'd miss your little cottage."

"But not cleaning it. You wouldn't believe how much sand I have to sweep up every day." Bessie's small cottage sat right on Laxey Beach. She had incredible views of the sea, and a long beach to stroll along whenever she wanted, but sand was a constant problem.

"I'd love to live on the water," Doona told her. "It would be totally worth it."

"So buy a house on the water," Bessie suggested.

Doona shrugged. When her second husband, whom she'd been trying to divorce, had died, he'd left his entire estate to Doona. She'd already inherited more money than she was comfortable with, and she was finding it difficult to spend. "We'll see."

"Do you think my hair is too short?" Bessie asked.

Doona studied her friend's short grey hair. "It looks a tiny bit shorter than normal, but not too short," she said after a moment.

"Yours looks better that colour," Bessie said.

Doona had tried dying her hair red for a few months, but she'd now gone back to a nice medium shade of brown with a few blonde highlights scattered through it. Bessie thought it suited Doona much better than the red had.

"Thanks. I simply couldn't get used to the red," she sighed. "John hated it, too, although he was too polite to tell me so."

Bessie hid a grin. She was convinced that John and Doona were perfect for one another, but they were taking their time reaching the same conclusion themselves. That Doona cared what John thought of her hair was a good sign, however. "I have Victoria sponge for pudding," Bessie announced as she got to her feet.

Doona quickly cleared away the dinner dishes, setting them in Bessie's sink while Bessie cut them each a generous slice of cake.

"This is wonderful," Doona said after her first bite. "I've been avoiding sweets."

"I did notice that you've lost more weight."

"Not much more. Mostly I've just been really busy, but I've been trying to avoid eating things that aren't worth the calories, like cheap chocolate or packet cakes. Your homemade cakes are a different story, though. I don't know why my cakes never taste this good."

"I've a few years more experience," Bessie suggested, not even hinting at how many years that actually might be. She'd stopped counting birthdays at sixty, preferring to simply think of herself as being in her later middle age. Doona, on the other hand, was in her forties, which made the pair unlikely close friends.

"And I hardly ever bake, and then I get frustrated when I do try something and it doesn't come out right," Doona admitted.

"There are always bakeries. Knowing how to bake cakes isn't something women need these days, really."

"It's still a useful skill to have," Doona replied. "For men or women."

"Andy Caine is a much better baker than I am."

Doona nodded. "Just hearing his name makes my mouth water," she laughed.

Andy was a young man who had just gone back to the UK to finish culinary school. He credited Bessie with everything he knew about baking and puddings, but Bessie knew that his talent had taken him past her skill level some time ago. She was pretty sure everyone on the island was looking forward to the restaurant he was planning to open when he finished school.

After pudding, Doona did the washing up, while Bessie tidied the kitchen for the ten thousandth time that day. It wasn't like her to fuss over things, but for some reason Andrew's arrival was causing her some anxiety.

"What are your plans for tomorrow, then?" Doona asked as she drained away the washing-up water.

"Andrew will be arriving around one. He's hiring a car at the airport and driving up to Laxey from there. Once he's checked into his cottage, he's going to come over."

"And then he's going to take you out for a fabulous dinner?"

Bessie laughed. "We haven't talked about dinner yet. We haven't talked about anything past his arrival. He's going to be on holiday. I'm sure the last thing he wants to do is worry about making plans."

"I know he and John are meeting on Saturday afternoon. John has a cold case he wants to discuss with Andrew."

"And Andrew said he has one he wants to talk about with me and

John. I hope we don't end up talking about crime the entire week he's here. Of course, he may not be planning to spend more than a couple of hours with me, anyway."

"I'm sure he's going to want to spend as much time with you as he can," Doona predicted.

"My goodness, I'd forgotten how lovely you are," Andrew said the next afternoon when Bessie answered her door.

Bessie blushed as the man pulled her into a hug. She'd forgotten quite how handsome he was, really, with his military-like bearing. He was bald, but it suited him, and his brown eyes seemed to twinkle with happiness, in spite of everything they must have seen during his years with the police.

"It's lovely to see you, too," she said as he let her go. "Do come in."

"But what is your cottage called?" he asked, pointing to the small sign by her door.

"Treoghe Bwaane," Bessie replied. "It's Manx for widow's cottage."

The man repeated the words. "My first Manx language lesson," he laughed as he followed Bessie into her cottage.

"Oh, I can do better than that," Bessie suggested. "Moghrey mie, although it isn't morning, is it? Fastyr mie, then."

"Fastyr mie," the man repeated. "What have I just said?"

"Good afternoon," Bessie explained.

"And perhaps that is enough Manx for today," Andrew laughed. "I can't properly claim jet lag as it was such a short flight, but I am feeling a bit, well, out of my element, I suppose."

"I thought you told me that you'd been to the island before," Bessie said as she ushered the man through to her sitting room.

"Oh, yes, but during the war, which was a great many years ago. I was only here for a very short space of time and there was a war on. I didn't have time to see the sites or anything. I don't even think I knew then that the island had its own language."

"Have a seat. Would you like a drink?" Bessie offered.

"Something cold would be wonderful," the man replied. "It's surprisingly warm for September."

"It is, at that," Bessie agreed. "You relax and I'll get you a fizzy drink."

"Perfect."

When Bessie walked back into the room a moment later, Andrew was working his way through one of her bookshelves. "I'm sorry. I couldn't resist," he said sheepishly.

"Don't be sorry. I do the same thing when I have the opportunity. You can learn a lot about a person by examining his or her bookshelves."

"Assuming they have books."

"Do some people not have books?" Bessie asked. "I can't begin to imagine."

Andrew smiled and dropped back into a chair. "No, neither can I, but my wife and I were both avid readers and we were fortunate enough to instill the same love of reading into all three of our children. The grandchildren are all great readers, too, and I'm already working on the great-grandchildren, even though they are a bit young to actually read by themselves."

"I still can't imagine what it's like having as much family as you do," Bessie told him. "My sister had ten children, but she's on the other side of the Atlantic, so I've never actually met any of them."

"Ten children? I can't imagine that. Three were quite hard work, even if my wife did do nearly all of it."

"You're of a generation where that was expected," Bessie suggested.

"Oh, yes, of course, but when I see how much more my sons and then my grandson does at home, I can't help but think things are moving in the right direction. Of course, my grandson's wife has a much better job than he does and is much more successful. It's only fair that he does his share at home, too."

"I met a man the other day who is a stay-at-home father. His wife is a doctor who is frequently on call, so it just makes sense for him to be at home so that she never has to worry about finding someone to look after their baby. He told me that he loves it, as well."

"Good for him. It's a very different world to the one we grew up in, isn't it?" Andrew asked.

"Yes, very much so, and it seems to be changing more and more rapidly every day. All of this computer technology is fascinating. I don't know what you're thinking about doing while you're here, but you'll see a big difference if you visit the two main museums on the island. The Manx Museum is far more traditional, with display cases and the like. The House of Manannan is completely different. There are recreated prehistoric structures and interactive displays and more there."

"I'd like to see both," Andrew said. "I'd be delighted if you could accompany me around the island, as well. I had hoped to make more plans with you in advance, but, well, things didn't work out the way I'd hoped."

"Is everything okay?"

"I've just had a few health issues lately, that's all. Part of the reason why my children didn't want to come to the island was because of my health. They didn't want me to be so far away from my doctors, in case I needed them."

"Oh, dear. I am sorry," Bessie said.

"It's all to do with getting older, that's all," Andrew said with a wave of his hand. "But the children kept nagging so much that I wasn't sure I was coming until I was actually at the airport. Now that I'm here, I can't believe I ever considered not coming."

"It's a beautiful island."

"Yes, and when I first got home after we met last year, I did a lot of research into the things to do on the island. Then I got busy and, well, ill, and I never did finish my list of things I wanted to see. You'll have to help me with that, if you have the time."

"I'm more than happy to help," Bessie assured him. "Are you mostly interested in historical sites or would you like to visit the wildlife park or play golf?"

"I used to play a lot of golf, but I've more or less given it up now. It's sad how quickly my game deteriorated when I couldn't play for a few months. I'm not that interested in going back and working hard just to get back to the same level of mediocrity that I was at before I fell ill."

Bessie grinned. "I've never really understood golf. It seems a lot of fuss and bother when you could just have a nice walk."

Andrew nodded. "I'm coming to see it that way as well. So maybe no golf, but I do love zoos and wildlife parks, so yes to that, please."

"As I'm fascinated by history, I tend to drag visitors around the historical sites," Bessie told him. "Don't let me bore you, though."

"Now that you've told me about the two museums, I'd quite like to see them both."

"As they're quite far apart, it's probably best to do them on two separate days. There are other things to see and do in both Douglas and Peel, of course."

"Isn't there a castle in Peel?"

"There is, although to be fair, it's mostly the ruins of a castle. There aren't any habitable structures left. Castle Rushen is in much better shape."

"So two museums and two castles. What else?"

"The wildlife park will take up one morning. There are other things to see in Castletown, as well, when you are there."

"It sounds as if a week isn't going to be enough to see everything," Andrew said.

"If you've any interest in the history of mining, the Laxey Wheel is worth a visit."

"I suppose it's too much to ask, but would you be available to act as my tour guide for any or all of my stay?"

"I don't know about all of your stay, but I can certainly spend some time with you," Bessie said, feeling slightly flustered.

"Wonderful. Let's start with dinner tonight," Andrew suggested. "Where can we get excellent food?"

"I can suggest several places. There's a wonderful little Italian restaurant in Laxey, Douglas is full of great places to eat, and there's a nice café in Lonan that serves sampler plates for dinner and pudding."

"Sampler plates?"

"The chef puts together a plate with three or four small portions of different dishes every day. Sometimes it's all Italian food, or chicken dishes, or whatever he wants to prepare. The puddings all follow a theme as well."

"I wasn't thinking of a café for my first night here, but now I'm awfully tempted. Is Lonan far away?"

"Not at all, especially not if you are used to driving around London."

Andrew grinned. "That's a good point. The drive from the airport to here was shorter than my daily commute was in London a few years ago. Your island is lovely and compact."

"I can't imagine living in London, although I grew up in Cleveland, which is a fairly large city. Once I bought my little cottage, though, I found I truly felt at home."

Andrew glanced around at the snug and comfortable sitting room. "I can see why. Your cottage seems to suit you perfectly. The views are incredible, as well."

"I'm rather spoiled by the views," Bessie agreed.

"I feel lucky to have them myself, if only for a week. I'm afraid I shall quite miss my little holiday cottage when I get back to London."

"You'll have to come back here again soon, then."

"I'd like that. We'll have to see what the doctors say, though. They weren't happy about this trip, although I did get permission in the end."

Bessie frowned. She wanted to know more about the man's health issues, but there was no polite way to ask.

"But back to dinner," Andrew said. "I'm rather worn out from flying and then driving up here in an unfamiliar car. I think I need to go and have a short nap. Shall I come back around five to collect you? Is that too early for you to have dinner?"

"Not at all. We'll still have a short drive to Lonan, but hopefully being early will mean we won't have any difficulty getting a table."

"Do they take bookings?"

"No, but I've never had to wait too long for a table. It actually surprises me how busy they get, as they are rather out of the way, but the food is incredibly good."

"I shall be back at five, then," Andrew said. He rose to his feet as

Bessie stood up. She escorted him back through the kitchen to the door.

"As it's a lovely afternoon, I think I shall take a short walk on the beach," she told the man.

"It is a nice day for a walk, but I'm afraid I'm too tired to appreciate it right now."

Bessie walked Andrew to his cottage, which was the third in the row beyond Bessie's. "If you do visit again, ask for the cottage next to mine," she suggested as he unlocked his door. "Then you'll only have neighbours on one side."

"And I'll be closer to you," Andrew added with a smile. He bowed and then went inside.

Bessie continued on down the beach, walking past the holiday cottages. They all appeared to be occupied, even though it was September and the summer season was over. Bessie could hardly blame Thomas and Maggie Shimmin, the owners of the cottages, for trying to keep them full for as long as possible, though. They'd had some difficulties in the past few months, and the last cottage in the row was still out of service while they tried to work out what to do with it. Very few people wanted to spend their holidays in a cottage where someone had been murdered.

A short distance further down the beach, Bessie passed the stairs to Thie yn Traie, a huge mansion that stood on the cliff above the sand. Someone had been murdered there recently, as well, but Bessie's friends George and Mary Quayle hadn't said anything about not wanting to stay in the house. To be fair, George would have happily sold the house, even at a loss, but he knew that Mary loved it and Mary wasn't going to let a little thing like a murder get in the way of her happiness. As the sun was shining and the beach was quiet, Bessie kept on walking.

A short while later, she found herself approaching the row of new houses that had been built on the beach about a year ago. Bessie thought about turning around, but then she spotted a familiar face on one of the patios.

"Good afternoon," she greeted Grace Watterson.

"Bessie, what a lovely surprise," Grace said. She sat up in her chair and then struggled a bit getting to her feet. When she hugged Bessie tightly, Bessie smiled at the size of the girl's tummy.

"That baby is getting awfully big," Bessie said as Grace released her.

"He is, although I'm just assuming it's a boy because I feel as if I'm eating for six or seven, rather than two," Grace laughed.

"The baby is taking after his father, then," Bessie teased.

Grace nodded. "Although Hugh is getting so nervous about the baby's impending arrival that he isn't eating nearly as much as he normally does."

"You aren't due until December, are you?"

"Mid-December. I hope the baby comes a little early, though. I don't want him or her to have to live with a birthday right around Christmas."

"He or she doesn't have much choice, though," Bessie pointed out.

Grace laughed again. "I know, and it will be fine, whatever happens. I just think it will be nicer for him or her to have a birthday some weeks before things get crazy."

"I'm sure he or she will arrive when ready and not before. But how are you feeling?"

"Fat and fed up, really, but I shouldn't say that. Pregnancy is meant to be magical and amazing, and it does feel incredibly miraculous, but I'm also tired all the time, my legs and back ache, and I haven't slept properly in months."

"Oh, dear, and you have some way to go yet."

"Indeed. Poor Hugh is having to put with a lot these days," Grace sighed. "He's being very good about it all, really. I know I'm incredibly spoiled, as I'm only working a few days a week, just doing supply teaching when I feel up to it. So many of my friends worked full-time right up until their maternity leave started."

"Are you planning to go back to work after the baby arrives?"

"Not for at least two years," Grace said. "It's indulgent, but we can just about afford it as long as we don't have any big expenses. The mortgage is reasonable; we just have to hope that both of our cars keep running."

Bessie glanced at her watch. "I'd love to stay and chat all afternoon, but I'm meeting a friend for dinner. I really must head back."

"Where are you going?"

"The café in Lonan."

"Oh, yummy. I haven't been there in ages. Eating out is not in the budget right now, although I've been tucking away a few pounds here and there to treat Hugh for his birthday. I suspect that café will be his choice when I tell him."

"The food is just so wonderful, and I love not having to choose just one thing but getting to try lots of different things at the same time."

"I really just love the puddings," Grace smiled, a dreamy look in her eyes.

"Ah, yes, the puddings," Bessie agreed.

They both laughed, and then Bessie turned and began the long walk back to Treoghe Bwaane. There were a few people on the beach behind the holiday cottages as Bessie went, but she didn't see Andrew. Back at home, she had just enough time to change into a skirt and light jumper, comb her hair, and add lipstick and powder to her face before someone knocked on her door.

"Andrew, you're right on time," she said brightly as she opened the door. "Did you get any rest?"

"I had a very useful nap," he replied. "It was exactly what I needed. Now I'm ready for a wonderful dinner and maybe a long walk on the beach after that."

"Let me get my bag and we can be on our way." Bessie locked up her cottage and then followed Andrew to his hire car which he had parked in the parking area behind Treoghe Bwaane.

"You're going to have to give me directions," he told Bessie as he started the engine.

"It's very easy to find," Bessie assured him. "You just need to drive up the hill to the main road and then head south."

It only took them a few minutes to reach the main road. Andrew followed Bessie's instructions, and a short while later they were in Lonan.

"This is the café," Bessie told him, pointing to the small building with the very full car park.

"It looks busy," Andrew remarked.

"Yes, I hope we can get a table."

Andrew parked in one of the last spots in the car park and then escorted Bessie to the café's door.

"Ah, Bessie, good evening," Dan Jenkins, the café's owner, called from across the crowded dining room. "I'll find a table for you in just a minute, I promise."

Bessie looked at Andrew and shrugged. From where she was standing it seemed as if there wasn't an empty seat in the room. Three women that Bessie had never seen before were rushing around, delivering drinks and plates of food. Dan was dealing with an angry-looking woman who was waving her arms and shouting.

After a minute, the woman snapped her mouth shut, picked up her handbag, and stormed out of the café. The man who had been sitting at the table with her looked startled and then jumped up and ran after her.

Dan sighed deeply and then turned to Bessie. "Table for two?" he asked with a wry grin.

CHAPTER 2

"Is everything okay?" Bessie asked after she'd introduced Andrew to Dan.

"Everything is fine. The lady just wanted it to be Italian night and it isn't," he sighed. "People seem to think that I should put various sampler plates on the menu so that they can have their favourite whenever they come in. They don't understand that I can't make twenty different dishes every day."

"I never even thought about that," Bessie said. "I mean, it would be lovely if you could put some of the sampler plates on the menu, but I would never expect you do so. What's today's sampler plate, then?"

"I believe you've been here when we've celebrated the chicken," Dan replied. "Today we celebrate the cow."

"Oh, really? Tell me more," Bessie demanded.

Dan laughed. "Our dinner plate offers a small steak and kidney pie, a miniature portion of cottage pie, a tiny helping of spaghetti Bolognese, and an individual beef Wellington."

"Yes, please," Andrew said happily.

"For me as well, but what about pudding?" Bessie asked.

"From cows come milk and cream," Dan replied. "You'll get a small portion of crème brulee, a tiny chocolate fairy cake with a whipped cream centre, a scoop of caramel chocolate chip ice cream, and a few milk chocolate truffles."

"Yes, please, again," Andrew said quickly.

"I hope I have room for all of that," Bessie said. "I can't imagine not trying everything."

"I'll send one of the girls over to get your drink order," Dan said. "I really need to get back to the kitchen. Carol is helping me there tonight, otherwise I'd be in even more trouble than I am."

He dashed away and was almost immediately replaced by one of the waitresses. Once they'd ordered their drinks, Bessie sat back and sighed. "I'm happy Dan and Carol are so successful, for their sakes, but it would be nice to come here sometimes and have the place be less busy."

"If the food tastes anywhere near as good as it sounds, I can't see that happening," Andrew replied.

"It's considerably better than it sounds, and Dan and Carol deserve their success. I'm just being selfish."

"Nothing wrong with that," Andrew laughed.

"But what shall we talk about?" Bessie asked.

"First, we should work out what we're going to do tomorrow. Should we start with the Manx Museum, do you think?"

"I thought you were meeting with John tomorrow afternoon?"

"Oh, heavens, you're right. I'd completely forgotten about that. We're meeting at one o'clock at John's house. Of course, you're welcome to join us, but that does rather limit what we can do in the morning, doesn't it?"

"Maybe you'd like to visit the Laxey Wheel tomorrow? Or you could take a short trip into Ramsey, just to see the town. That wouldn't take more than the morning."

"That sounds good. We could do some shopping and have lunch there before we need to meet John, if that suits you."

"It does," Bessie agreed. "Although I may not be hungry tomorrow if I eat all of this," she added as one of the waitresses delivered their dinners.

"It does seems to be an awful lot of food," Andrew replied, "but I think I'm up to the challenge."

Bessie laughed and then picked up her knife and fork. Neither spoke for some time as they both enjoyed the delicious food.

"I don't think I'll ever want to eat again," Andrew said eventually, as he put down his fork. "Everything was wonderful, though."

"I know, but I can't help but think about the pudding," Bessie sighed.

"Oh, yes, I had nearly forgotten about the pudding. I can't pass it up, even though I'm rather full."

"We can always box it up for you take home," the waitress offered as she cleared their plates. "We can even put the ice cream in a separate container so it doesn't melt all over everything, if you'd like."

"That might be for the best," Bessie said. "I'd like to be able to savour my pudding, and it will be a while before I'll be ready to do that. I don't want to take up one of your valuable tables for that long."

The girl shrugged. "It's always this busy lately. Dan's just too good. He needs to open a bigger place."

"And he might," a voice said from behind the girl. "We have to find just the right place first."

Bessie smiled at Carol, Dan's wife, who'd just come out of the kitchen. "Everything was fabulous, as always," she told the pretty blonde.

"Thank you. I actually helped make a few things today, so I'll even take some of the credit. Now that we have reliable staff out here, Dan's trying to teach me to do more of the cooking. He really is looking around for a larger space, but then he'll need at least one more pair of hands in the kitchen."

Bessie pressed her lips together before she blurted out a rude question. Carol had worked at the café when it first opened, but had cut her hours because she and Dan were planning to start a family. It wasn't any of Bessie's business if they'd put the plan on hold or were having difficulties.

"If you ever decide you'd like to open something in London, let me know," Andrew said. "I'm certain you'd be a huge success there."

Carol laughed. "We moved to the island to get away from living in a big city. We're very happy here, thank you. I know Dan would love having somewhere larger though, if we can find the right location."

"As this is a terrible location and you've been very successful here, perhaps you don't need to worry too much about where your new café is located," Bessie said.

"You could be right. This isn't a great location, but it's been good for us. Anyway, I just wanted to say hello, Bessie, but I must get back to work. Did you want pudding?" Carol asked.

"Only if you can pack mine up to take home," Bessie said. "The celebration of cow was too much food for me."

Carol laughed again. "I did think that Dan went a bit overboard today. We haven't had any complaints, but we have been boxing up nearly all of the puddings for takeaway."

"I'll need mine boxing up as well," Andrew said. "I hope I'll be ready for it in about an hour, or maybe two."

Carol nodded and then disappeared back into the kitchen. A few minutes later one of the waitresses brought their bill and their puddings.

"Put the round container in the freezer as soon as you get home," she told Bessie as she handed her a large bag. "That has ice cream for two in it. The rest should go in the refrigerator until you're ready to eat it."

Andrew insisted on paying for dinner. "While I'm here, dragging you around the island so that you can show me the sights, I will pay for everything," he told Bessie. "Let's not argue about it, okay?"

Bessie wanted to argue, but decided to save it for later. So far he'd only paid for one dinner. That was certainly reasonable enough.

"I hope I don't get stopped for speeding," Andrew joked as he and Bessie made their way back to Laxey. "I want to get the ice cream in the freezer before it melts."

"I'm sure it will be fine. I can't imagine what John would say if you did get stopped."

"My children would go crazy. They'd assume I'd lost my mind and put me into assisted living or something."

"Oh, dear. And people wonder why I'm happy I never had children."

Andrew laughed. "My children mean well, they really do, but they worry about me far more than they should. I'm surprised my mobile hasn't been ringing all evening, really. I thought they'd all be checking up on me by now."

"Is it turned on?" Bessie asked.

Andrew glanced at her and then laughed. "It probably isn't. I switched it off on the plane and I probably never switched it back on. The peace and quiet has been nice, anyway."

Back at Bessie's cottage, Bessie put the ice cream in the freezer and the other two containers in the refrigerator while Andrew turned on his phone. A cacophony of noise burst out of it as soon as it was powered on.

"It appears I may have missed a few calls," he chuckled as he looked at the phone's display.

"Do you need to ring anyone back?" Bessie asked.

"I'll just ring Helen. She'll let the others know I'm okay, and then they can all talk about me for hours while I eat ice cream and chocolate truffles."

Bessie grinned and then filled the kettle with fresh water. A cup of tea would go nicely with their puddings, she thought. She tried not to listen to Andrew's side of the conversation, but he made no effort to lower his voice.

"It's your father. I see from my phone that you rang me twelve times in the last five hours."

"I had to switch it off on the plane and then I got busy with hiring the car and getting checked into my cottage. Then I had a nap."

"I feel fine, stop fussing."

"You know you'd be welcome, but I have plans for every day while I'm here. You'd have to either come along or find your own things to do."

"I'm not giving you my complete itinerary. You don't need it. You can ring me if you want to talk to me."

"I'll try to remember to leave my phone on, but that also means remembering to keep it charged. I won't promise to do both. I can give you Inspector John Rockwell's number if you'd like. You can always ring him if you need to get in touch with me."

Bessie grinned when Andrew pulled a small notebook out of his pocket. It was the exact same type of notebook that John always used. Andrew flipped through it for a minute and then read out a phone number that Bessie recognised as John's office number.

"Don't ring him unless it's an emergency, though. He's a very busy man," Andrew told his daughter.

After he pushed the button to end the call, he shook his head at Bessie. "She's treating me like a small child. I didn't treat her like a small child even when she was one. Okay, maybe when she was very small, but still." He sighed. "I don't know if I'm too upset to enjoy my pudding or if pudding is exactly what I need."

"Why not have a cuppa first," Bessie suggested. "It will soothe you."

After a few sips of tea, Andrew frowned. "It's no good. I need chocolate and ice cream."

Bessie laughed and then pulled the containers out of her refrigerator. "Here you go," she said, putting them on the table. "I'll just put the ice cream into bowls."

When she opened the round container she was shocked by the huge amount of ice cream it held. "This is a lot more than two servings," she told Andrew. "I'll just give us each a scoop for now."

"Maybe two scoops," Andrew suggested.

Chuckling, Bessie spooned two generous scoops into a bowl for Andrew and two slightly smaller ones into another bowl for herself. Then she sat down and opened her box.

"Oh, goodness, how wonderful," she sighed as she looked at the beautifully displayed puddings.

"I'm surprised they held up so well on the journey home."

"Yes, but they look almost too good to eat."

"I'm not having any trouble eating them," Andrew laughed. "While we eat, shall we talk about murder?"

Bessie nearly dropped her spoon. "Murder?"

"I'm sure I told you that I have a cold case I want to discuss with you."

"Yes, you did, but I didn't realise it was a murder case."

"If you'd rather not talk about it, we can talk about anything you'd like," Andrew offered.

"No, we can talk about your case. I was just surprised, that's all."

"Are you sure you wouldn't rather tell me more about the castles and other sites?"

"No, not at all. Those are best discussed when you're seeing them, anyway. Go on, then, tell me about your murder."

"It wasn't even my case," Andrew began. "I wasn't there, in fact, I've never been there. The murder took place in Switzerland at a ski resort, and it really doesn't matter which one, although I'll tell you if you want to know."

"I've never been to Switzerland, so I doubt the name would mean anything to me, even if you did tell me."

"I'll just say that it was a large and popular resort. It still is, for that matter. The investigation was assigned to a man who was more used to looking for lost property or stolen jewellery, rather than investigating murders. Having said that, everything I've learned about the case suggests that he did a competent job with the investigation. He even solved the case and received a full confession."

"I thought you said this was a cold case," Bessie said.

"It isn't really, I suppose. The murder took place about thirty years ago, and the man who completed the investigation subsequently came to London and spent some time working with me. One night we started talking about cold cases, sharing stories about the ones that we'd failed to solve and that still kept us up at night. Towards the end of the evening, he told me about this case. It wasn't properly a cold case, in that he'd received a confession and the alleged killer had gone to prison, but he was still losing sleep over the case, some twenty years after it had happened."

"The wrong person went to prison, then?"

"Maybe, although my colleague didn't seem to think so. There was just something about the case that didn't feel right and he'd never managed to work out what it was."

"Now I'm intrigued. Let me make some more tea while you get started."

"I could do with one more scoop of ice cream if there's any left."

"There's a lot left." Bessie gave them each another scoop of the rich and creamy caramel ice cream before putting the kettle on again. A few minutes later she was back at the table, ready for Andrew to begin.

"It was a dark and stormy night," he said in a mysterious voice.

Bessie laughed. "Really?"

"I've always wanted to say that," Andrew told her. "You've no idea how tempting it was to start some of my police reports in that way, but I was always afraid I'd get into trouble if I actually did it. It would have been just my luck to actually sneak it into one and then end up having to read it out in court or something. Anyway, it truly was a dark and stormy night."

"It's a great beginning."

"Five women had travelled from London to Switzerland for a short skiing holiday in December. One of the women was getting married on New Year's Eve. As I understand it, it was something of a last getaway before the wedding."

"A sort of hen night holiday?"

"Yes, but I don't believe women did hen nights thirty years ago."

"You could be right."

"Anyway, there were five of them. I won't use their real names, to keep things confidential."

Bessie nodded. "Do you know their real names?"

"I don't actually. My colleague never shared them. He worried that I might know some of the people involved. London isn't that big a place, really."

"How mysterious. But perhaps you're simply making the whole story up to give us something to discuss."

"That's an idea. I wish I were clever enough to do that, actually. You may believe me that clever, if you'd like."

"Let me hear the story first. It may not be that interesting," Bessie laughed.

"Right, well, I'll give them all very ordinary names to keep things simple. Let's start with Abby Smith. She was the oldest by a few years, maybe thirty, although she'd have probably denied it. She was undoubtedly the best skier in the group, and it was highly likely that the entire holiday was her idea. She was, well, let's say, the ringleader of the little group."

"What did Abby do for a living?"

Andrew frowned. "I don't think their occupations matter, but all five of the girls were models. Not supermodels who were making millions, but rather more ordinary ones who did a lot of catalogue work and made a decent but unspectacular living at it."

"But you don't think their work had anything to do with the murder?"

"No, I don't."

"No professional rivalry between the girls? Modelling is a very competitive business, isn't it?"

"Yes, but it's less competitive at the level these girls were at. It was thirty years ago, too. For the most part, they were just working while they were waiting to find husbands. They all had family money with which to support themselves. From what I was told, the modelling was more of a hobby than a career for any of them."

Bessie nodded. "So we have Abby, who's the ringleader and an avid skier. Who's next?"

"Betty Jones. She was twenty-five, and she was the young woman who was getting married later in the month."

"Presumably she liked skiing enough to go along with Abby's plans?" Bessie made the statement a question.

"My colleague always got the feeling that most of the women were more interested in keeping Abby happy than anything else. When I say she was the ringleader, she was that and perhaps more. My colleague always felt as if she had some sort of control over the other girls."

"I have a dozen questions about that, but tell me about the rest of the party first."

"Cindy Jones was Betty's younger sister. She was maybe twenty-two or twenty-three at the time. She was easily the most attractive of the women, and she seemed to take her job seriously, unlike the others."

"So if there was any professional rivalry, it was probably between Cindy and someone else."

"Perhaps. Dorothy Johnson comes next. She was also around twenty-five, the same age as the bride-to-be. Her family was new money, something that caused a bit of friction between her and Abby, who was very much old money and rather snobbish about it. Dorothy was only invited because Betty really liked her."

"Oh, my. What an interesting bunch of people."

"Last, but not least, Flora Wright rounded out the party. Again, she was around twenty-five. She was, well, the least successful in modelling. My colleague described her as plain and rather heavyset. What she had in her favour was a father with a great deal of money and a real willingness to spoil his daughter. As I understand it, he paid companies to hire Flora as a model, paying for entire advertising campaigns or catalogues, many of which were never actually released anywhere."

"The poor girl. Perhaps her father should have paid for her to get a good education so that she could find a job doing something that better suited her talents," Bessie suggested.

Andrew chuckled. "My colleague also told me that she was rather thick."

Bessie sighed. "I feel sorry for all of them, and I don't even know what happened next."

"What happened next was that dark and stormy night I mentioned earlier. The girls were staying in a small chalet some distance from the main resort. It was an expensive option, but it came with its own staff to cook and clean for the women. They arrived on a Friday evening and spent the night eating and drinking and laughing together. That's according to the cook and the maid who were charged with looking after them."

"A cook and a maid? How lovely," Bessie sighed. "I'd love a cook. In fact, I'd love to hire Dan to come in and make all my meals from now on."

"Do you think he'd be willing to do it? Maybe he could split his time between your cottage and my flat in London."

Bessie shook her head. "He loves having his own business. My friend Mary Quayle has offered him a job numerous times, at a far more generous salary than I could afford, and he always turns her down."

"I suppose I shall have to go back to ready meals and cold cereal," Andrew sighed.

"But we've wandered away from your story. What happened after a night of eating and drinking?"

"The maid and the cook left the chalet right around two o'clock in the morning. All hotel staff lived in a block of rooms in a separate building behind the main resort building. There was security at the front door and everyone had to check in and out. I believe they were trying to avoid having the staff, um, fraternizing with the guests. Anyway, both the maid and the cook checked into their building about two-fifteen. Around three o'clock a blizzard blew in and began to dump significant amounts of snow on the resort and the surrounding area."

"I've never been skiing, but having grown up in Cleveland, Ohio, I've seen more than my fair share of snow. It's shocking how much can pile up in a short space of time."

"Apparently, they received three feet of snow over the next six hours. Obviously the entire resort was at a standstill on Saturday morning. The snow didn't actually stop falling until nearly midday, by which time something like four feet of snow had piled up across the area. Work crews were sent out to start digging everyone out. When they reached the women in their chalet, though, one of them was missing."

"Which one?" Bessie demanded as Andrew stopped to sip tea.

"Would you like to guess?"

Bessie thought for a minute. "Betty Jones," she said after a moment.

"How did you know?"

"There was just something about the way you talked about her that made me think something awful was going to happen to her," Bessie explained. "It wasn't anything you said, more the way you said it."

Andrew frowned. "And I was trying so hard not to give you any hints."

"Maybe it was just my imagination. I did have a twenty per cent chance of guessing correctly, anyway."

"Well, you were right. Betty was missing and the other girls were frantic. Someone rang the police and my colleague was sent to investigate."

"Poor Betty," Bessie sighed as she got up to make more tea. "You did say this was a murder case, so I can only assume she was the victim."

"Yes, but you're getting ahead of the story," Andrew replied. "My colleague questioned all four of the girls at the chalet. They all told the same story, almost word for word. They'd been drinking together and having a wonderful time until about four in the morning. Then the phone had rung. It was Betty's fiancé. The others sat quietly while Betty spoke to him. There was a screaming row that ended with Betty slamming down the phone and running off to her bedroom. The others decided it was probably bedtime as well, so they all headed upstairs. Each of the four girls claimed to have knocked on Betty's door to check on her before she went to bed. In every case, Betty allegedly told them through the door that she was fine and she'd see them in the morning."

"Not a very heavy door then," Bessie mused.

"No, that was one of the things that my colleague checked. The women would have had to shout pretty loudly, but if the rest of the chalet was quiet, they could have heard one another through the door."

"What happened next?"

"Abby woke up first the next morning. When she discovered that the cook hadn't arrived to make breakfast, she began waking the others to see if anyone was capable of cooking anything. Betty didn't answer her door, so Abby just assumed she was still sleeping. It was only hours later, after Flora had made everyone else breakfast, that Cindy went to check on her sister."

"And found the room empty and the bed not slept in?" Bessie guessed.

"Yes, exactly that. It didn't take the women long to search the entire chalet, but Betty was nowhere to be found. A short while later, the resort staff finally dug a path to the chalet's door."

"What did the fiancé say about the phone conversation he'd had with Betty?"

"He denied ringing."

"But four women heard half of the conversation."

"Except the storm started right around three and by four o'clock the resort's phone lines were all down."

Bessie sat back in her seat and frowned. "All four women lied? But why?"

"An excellent question. I can't tell you the answer to that, but I can tell you that they all stuck to the story, even when confronted by the facts. They all insisted that the phone lines to the chalet were still working at four and that Betty's fiancé had rung, even though he denied it and the resort manager testified in court that the lines were down."

"The chalet didn't have it's own separate line or anything like that?"

"This was thirty years ago. The chalet was lucky to have a phone at all. Even a year or two earlier, guests in the chalets had to walk to the main resort if they wanted to ring anyone."

"We were just talking about how much things have changed. If this happened today, all of the girls would have had their own mobile phones with them. But what happened next?"

"My colleague did a thorough examination of the grounds of the chalet. Everything was covered in a tremendous amount of snow, of course, but that allowed him to check for footprints. Aside from where the resort work crew had dug the opening to the front door, the snow appeared completely undisturbed everywhere else around the chalet."

"But the work crew could have destroyed evidence."

"They all swore that there weren't any footprints anywhere when they'd begun to dig out the chalet. Remember that the girl was only missing at this point. Everyone was concerned with working out how she'd left the chalet."

"If she'd left right after the maid and cook, her footprints would have disappeared under the subsequent snowfall."

"And that was my colleague's theory in the beginning. He began a methodical search of the entire resort. Considering that the other four girls were lying about the phone call, he assumed that nothing they said could be trusted."

"That seems a fair assumption."

Andrew nodded. "As half of the resort staff carried on clearing away the snow, the other half got to work looking for Betty Jones. The entire resort was checked, every chalet was searched, even the cars in the car park were examined. My colleague was starting to consider where the girl might have found a taxi or some other form of transportation at two or three in the morning when he had another idea. He rounded up a few men with shovels and headed back to the chalet."

"Oh, dear," Bessie sighed.

"They dug their way around the entire chalet, in increasingly larger circles. It only took them an hour to find her."

Bessie brushed away a tear. "I can't believe I'm crying over a total stranger who died thirty years ago," she said, shaking her head.

"I think it's kind of you to care," Andrew told her, patting her hand. "I only wish her friends had cared a bit more, but I'm getting ahead of the story."

"She wasn't found far from the chalet, then?" Bessie asked after she'd wiped away one last tear.

"Not too far, maybe a few steps away, in the small garden behind the building. She was lying on her stomach, and at first my colleague thought that maybe she'd simply stepped outside to get some fresh air, unaware of the storm, and had frozen to death."

"But she hadn't?"

"When he turned her over, she had a knife in her chest."

Bessie gasped even though she'd known that something awful was coming. "The poor girl."

"There was no evidence of a struggle, although the snow could have simply hidden any that might have been there."

"Was she wearing a coat?"

"A light jacket that wouldn't have protected her from the cold but did manage to soak up most of the blood, leaving the snow fairly clean around the body."

"I don't understand," Bessie said.

"Neither did my colleague. All he could do was ask more questions, but the more questions he asked, the harder it became. The four women all stuck to their story. Nothing he did or said could convince them to tell the truth."

"Maybe they were all in on it together?"

"It certainly seemed that way and that was my colleague's initial conclusion. There didn't seem to be any other possible explanation."

"I can't think of one, that's for sure," Bessie sighed.

"And then one of the women confessed to killing Betty."

CHAPTER 3

"Which one?" Bessie asked.

"Do you want to guess again? You did so well the first time."

Bessie thought for a minute. "Tell me more about them all first, and then I'll guess. Abby was the leader of the group and the oldest. What else do you know about her?"

"As I said, she came from old money and was something of a snob about it. She'd done some modelling work when she'd been younger, but she'd mostly quit by the time of the skiing weekend. She still described herself as a model, but she hadn't worked in almost a year."

"By choice or because she was getting older?"

"That's a good question, and I'm sorry I don't know the answer to it. I'm sure if she'd been asked, she would have insisted that it was her choice, but there's no way to be certain, not at this late date, anyway. She didn't need to work, though."

"Did she have a boyfriend back in the UK or elsewhere?"

"She did, although from what my colleague could piece together from what the other girls said, either they were having difficulties, or they weren't at all serious, or Abby was more serious than the man in question was. My colleague could never quite pin down anyone to clarify the situation. Abby told him that she and her boyfriend were very close, practically engaged, even."

"And did she end up marrying the man eventually?"

Andrew shook his head. "I don't know the answer to that, actually. I don't believe that my colleague kept track of them after the confession."

"Okay, what did your colleague think of Abby, then?"

"He didn't like her, but he didn't like any of the women. He found Abby bossy and rude. It was evident that she considered herself far superior to nearly everyone else, especially anyone with the police. She was demanding to be allowed to go home within an hour after the body had been found."

"What about Betty? What do you know about her and her fiancé?"

"Betty had had something of a wild reputation before she met the man she was planning to marry. He was the second son of an earl and as such his family didn't approve of Betty at all. He'd been left a great deal of money by an aunt or some other relative, which made him one of London's most eligible bachelors. While Betty's family had some money, it was really only after she started seeing, well, let's call him Albert, that she and Abby became friends."

"And the pair were happy together, planning a wedding?"

"That was generally what people thought, right up until the night Betty died, anyway."

"I thought the phone call from Albert never actually happened?"

"It definitely didn't happen at the time the women claimed it had, but there was some debate about whether it could have happened earlier in the day."

"I thought Albert denied ringing Betty?"

I've read and reread the statements, and his denial was oddly phrased. My colleague noted it as well, but could never work out the significance of the phrasing. What the man said was 'I never rang my fiancée after midnight that night.'"

"Had he spoken to her earlier in the day?"

"We don't know, but we believe so. Remember that my colleague was in Switzerland, being told a particular story. When he rang

London and asked someone there to question Albert, he had very specific questions for the man, all pertaining to the phone call that couldn't have taken place. That was the answer that Albert gave when asked about the call. He wasn't asked anything else at that point and when an inspector visited a second time to ask additional questions, he was referred to the family solicitor."

"That's suspicious."

"Perhaps, but there's no way the man had anything to do with Betty's death. He was definitely in London when she died."

"But he could have paid someone else to kill her, or at least have been the motive behind the killing."

"We've no reason to believe that any of the women would have killed their friend for money. As I said, they were all quite wealthy already. And there was no hint that Albert was involved with any of the others, either. He and Betty were reportedly devoted to one another. He was practically living with her, although he did have his own flat."

"What about her sister? She was younger?"

"Yes, and as I said, she was also the most successful model. She travelled a great deal and was, I was told, a last-minute addition to the party. She was meant to be in Milan for work but changed her plans at the last minute."

"Was she close friends with the others?"

"Not especially, as I understood it. Betty was the popular one, but, as I said, Cindy traveled a great deal."

"Did she have a flat in London, too?"

"No, when she was in London, she stayed with her sister."

"Interesting," Bessie said. "Tell me about Dorothy. You said she was new money?"

"Yes, and that's about all I know about her, aside from the fact that she was Betty's friend and that Abby didn't like her."

"She was also a model?"

"Some of the time. She worked more than Abby did, but not nearly as much as Cindy. Mostly she went to parties and shopped, at least that's the impression my colleague got of her."

"And Flora was plump and only worked when her father was footing the bill?"

"Yes. She was actually the only one of the women that my colleague didn't dislike. He said she was quite sweet, really, and only too aware of her shortcomings in spite of being not very bright otherwise. He felt that she was happy to simply coast through life spending her father's money."

"She doesn't sound very likeable."

"No, not to me, either, but perhaps she was only likeable when compared with her friends."

Bessie nodded. "I forgot to ask. Did any of the other women have boyfriends in London or elsewhere?"

"Cindy, like her sister, had something of a wild reputation. I understand she was involved with a number of men, but none of the relationships were serious. Dorothy had a boyfriend. He was old money, which was another thing about Dorothy that annoyed Abby. I don't know how serious it was, but I know he flew over to Switzerland after the body was found and Dorothy refused to see him."

"How odd."

"There was no way he was involved in the murder. He was in London at a party with friends on the night that Betty died."

"Was Flora involved with anyone?"

"No, at least not at the time of the murder. There were rumours that she'd been spending some time with Abby's younger brother, but both Flora and Abby denied that they were anything more than friends."

"Abby didn't approve?"

Andrew shrugged. "I doubt she would have considered Flora the sort of sister-in-law she wanted, but Flora was from the right sort of family and they were wealthier than Abby's family, so I can't see her saying anything against the relationship, either. It's possible, maybe even probable, that the pair were just friends."

"What about Betty's parents? I assume they flew over when they heard what had happened."

"They didn't, actually. They were on some sort of world cruise holiday or some such thing. Remember that this was thirty years ago, so there weren't any mobile phones. I believe my colleague sent a telegram to the next port on their itinerary, but by the time the message caught up with them, Betty had already been buried and the murderer had already confessed."

"They weren't planning on attending Betty's wedding?"

"Apparently not. I'm not certain if the wedding was planned before they decided to take their cruise or after. From what I've been told, Betty wasn't close to her parents, which may have been a factor."

"Aside from whatever the killer said in her confession, was there anyone at the party who had a clear motive for killing Betty?"

"None that my colleague ever discovered."

"What about means? What do you know about the knife?"

"It was from a set in the chalet's kitchen. The cook had used it during dinner. The maid washed and dried it and put it back in its place in the chopping block before she left."

"Fingerprints?"

"A few smudges that were eventually attributed to the maid and the cook."

"And we don't know anything about opportunity, as the statements the women made can't be trusted," Bessie sighed.

"No, they can't. They were obviously lying, and it seems clear that they all had equal opportunity."

"Maybe they were all working together?"

"It's one possibility, certainly, but it's difficult to find a motive that would make the four women work together to kill the fifth. They were meant to be there celebrating Betty's engagement, after all."

"I could almost understand it if Abby had been the one who'd died," Bessie said thoughtfully. "If she was as bossy and awful as you say she was, anyway."

"She was, or at least that's what my colleague thought."

"But he didn't like any of the women, correct? Except maybe Flora."

"You're right. He didn't like any of them."

"I'm going to guess that it was Cindy who confessed."

Andrew looked startled. "You're right, but how did you know?"

"I didn't know, but it seemed the most likely answer. Sisters fight all the time. I have a sister, I should know. They'd been drinking, as well."

"They had, and quite a lot. Betty's blood alcohol content was well over the drink drive limit when she died."

"What happened after Cindy confessed?"

"The other girls still stood by their statements. Cindy stated that she went to talk to her sister after the others were all in bed and that she and Betty started arguing. They moved downstairs to avoid waking the others and eventually went outside because things were getting so heated. Cindy claimed that Betty grabbed the knife on the way out of the chalet and started waving it around and screaming at her. There was a struggle and Betty ended up dead."

"Was there any evidence at the scene to support Cindy's version of events?"

"Any signs of a struggle had disappeared under the snow," Andrew sighed. "The body didn't have any injuries consistent with a physical altercation, either, aside from one stab wound to the heart."

"What about bruises or anything on Cindy?"

"She didn't appear to have a scratch on her. As they were both wearing coats and gloves, it was deemed possible that the extra padding helped protect Betty from bruising, although the coroner couldn't be certain."

"Did Cindy say what the fight was about?"

"Nothing and everything was how she summarised it. She said she went in to make sure Betty was okay after the argument with Albert. Then, when she asked Betty what she and Albert had been fighting about, Betty went crazy. From there it degenerated into a screaming row about everything either sister had ever done to upset the other over the past twenty-odd years."

"If the case was solved, why was your colleague still talking about it after so many years?"

"Because there was always something about the case that he didn't feel was right. The women insisted on standing by their story about the phone call, for one thing. Cindy even included it in her confession."

Bessie sat back in her chair. There was something about the story that didn't quite fit, but what was it? She had a theory, but she wasn't sure she wanted to share it with the man. He'd been a senior police inspector in London. The last thing she wanted was for him to laugh at her, and her theory seemed rather far-fetched.

"You've had an idea," Andrew said, staring at her.

"Maybe, but it's an odd idea."

"I'd love to hear it. Maybe an odd idea is exactly what we need."

"Are you still in touch with your colleague?"

"I am. He retired last year, but we still email one another once in a while. I'd love to share your thoughts with him, if they seem at all reasonable."

"You may be able to squash my idea in a second. It may not have even been possible."

"Now I'm really intrigued. My colleague was certain that no one from outside the chalet could have killed Betty, if that's where you're going, though."

"It isn't," Bessie replied. "If my crazy idea is right, then the murderer is probably the person who confessed."

"Go on, then, share your idea," Andrew urged her. "I promise not to laugh, even if you suggest space aliens or an orangutan who climbed down the chimney."

Bessie laughed. "I don't think my idea is that odd, but I'll offer it as a question, rather than an idea. Is your colleague absolutely certain that it was Betty who died?"

"What do you mean? You don't think there was another woman at the party who was killed, do you?"

"That's an idea, actually. Maybe there were six women at the party and the sixth woman was killed…" Bessie trailed off. "I could get lost chasing after that thought, but my idea was that maybe it was Cindy who was murdered and the others all lied about it. Is that possible?"

Andrew sat forward and rested his elbow on the table and his chin in his hand. He stared straight ahead at nothing. Bessie could only assume that he was busy thinking. After several minutes, he sat up straight and looked at her. "I've been through everything my colleague told me about a dozen times in my head and I can't find anywhere your idea doesn't fit. He arrived at the chalet and was told that Betty was missing. When he found the body, he would have simply assumed it was Betty. I'm sure her sister made a formal identification, one he wouldn't have thought to question."

"It was just an idea," Bessie said. "From what you told me, I couldn't see all of the women lying for Cindy's benefit, but they were all close to Betty, so maybe they were willing to lie for her."

"I still don't understand why they lied about the phone call."

"Maybe they didn't lie about the phone call. Maybe they lied about the timing of the phone call. Maybe Albert rang earlier in the evening."

"If he had, the maid and the cook would still have been there."

"Maybe they were never asked about phone calls before they left."

"But surely they would have mentioned it if they'd overheard a screaming row?"

"Maybe there wasn't any row. Maybe Albert called and they talked and everything was fine," Bessie suggested.

"I don't understand."

"I'm not sure that I do, but Albert said he didn't talk to his fiancée after midnight, right?"

"Yes, that's right."

"Maybe he rang back later, after midnight but before the storm brought the phone lines down. Maybe he talked to Cindy instead of Betty."

"I'm not following you."

"You said Cindy had a wild reputation, that Betty and Albert were practically living together, and that Cindy stayed with her sister whenever she was in London. It doesn't seem much of a stretch to consider that perhaps Cindy was having an affair with Albert."

"He was her sister's fiancé."

"I'm sure she wouldn't have been the first woman to sleep with her sister's fiancé," Bessie said.

Andrew shook his head. "I'm feeling rather overwhelmed," he admitted. "I never questioned the identity of the body and now that you've mentioned it, it seems almost too obvious. The parents were away and unreachable. By the time they were contacted, their one daughter had confessed to killing the other. As I understand it, they refused to visit Cindy once she went to prison."

"So if she did switch places with her sister, no one ever found out."

"Why would she switch places with her sister, though?"

"I don't know the answer to that, but she must have had a reason. Was one sister worth more than the other?"

"That's an interesting question, actually. And the answer is yes. Cindy was more successful in her career, but their grandmother didn't approve of some of the work she'd done. Apparently, she'd done a few lingerie shoots that Grandmum had felt were too racy. When she passed away, about a year before the skiing holiday, she left the bulk of her fortune to Betty."

"So Betty was wealthier," Bessie frowned. "That seems to contradict my theory."

"Betty left her fortune to Cindy, but she was deemed ineligible to inherit because she'd murdered Betty. The contingency in Betty's will stated that if Cindy was unable to inherit, the money would all go to charity. There was a bit of a court battle where Albert attempted to get his hands on the estate, but the will had actually been drawn up after he and Betty had become engaged, so he lost his fight."

"What charity?"

"What do you mean?"

"I mean, what charity was the beneficiary of the will? Is it possible that Betty set it all up somehow so that she could inherit her own fortune back?"

Andrew frowned. "I'm going to have to talk to my colleague about that," he said. "But that suggests that considerable planning went into all of this."

"You said the pair hadn't been engaged for very long, which made me wonder about her rewriting her will so quickly. Surely she'd have wanted to write another one after she and Albert were wed, so as to make her husband her heir."

"You'd think so, wouldn't you?"

"What happened to Cindy, then? I assume she went to prison for murder."

"She went to prison on a lesser charge. The courts took into consideration her insistence that it was Betty who'd brought the knife outside and her testimony about the struggle. She was also very convincing when she told the courts that she couldn't possibly have had any reason for wanting her sister dead. I believe she tried to sell them the idea that Betty was suicidal after her fight with Albert and that she was simply trying to get the knife away from her sister rather than trying to stab her."

"And the courts believed her?"

"She went to prison for seven years in the end."

"But she was barred from inheriting her sister's estate?"

"Yes, although I'm going to have to check on that. I seem to recall my colleague saying something about her voluntarily refusing the estate considering the circumstances."

"I'm really curious about the charity now."

"And if it's legitimate, we'll both be disappointed."

"I may be completely wrong, though," Bessie reminded him. "When you talk to your colleague, he may say that he confirmed the corpse's identity and it was really Betty."

"I'm still curious about the charity, and also what happened to Cindy after she left prison. She had a considerable amount of her own money anyway. I'm not sure our version of events explains why everyone lied, though."

"Perhaps the original plan didn't include the confession," Bessie suggested. "If Cindy hadn't confessed, she might never have been caught."

"So why did she confess?"

"Guilt? Or maybe she felt as if she had to for some reason. Maybe she felt that was the best way to keep her parents away?"

"I'm not sure if we're getting any closer to solving this or just adding to the confusion," Andrew sighed. "You've certainly given me something completely different to consider, anyway." He glanced at the clock. "And on that note, I think I shall head for home, or for what passes for home at the moment. I won't go to bed before I've sent a quick email to my colleague, though. I wasn't going to bring my laptop, but my daughter insisted that I have it. Now I'm glad I do."

"Find out what happened to the other women, too," Bessie suggested. "I'm curious now about all of them."

Bessie let the man out and then shut the door behind him. She didn't really think that she'd solved his thirty-year-old cold case for him, but it had been an interesting puzzle and she was quite pleased with the idea that she'd offered. At least Andrew hadn't laughed in her face when she'd suggested it.

Although her mind was racing, Bessie fell asleep as soon as her head touched the pillow, and she slept soundly until four minutes past six. She allowed her internal alarm five minutes on either side of the hour, so she was satisfied with that. The sun was coming up after she'd showered, dressed, and had a light breakfast, and it looked as if it was going to be a lovely day.

As Bessie headed out for her morning walk, she tried to decide how to casually walk past Andrew's cottage. She didn't want to stare at the windows as if she were trying to spot the man, but equally, she didn't want to be looking at the sea, which might make him think she was ignoring him. She was relieved to see all of the cottage's curtains were tightly drawn as she crossed the beach. Walking briskly, she reached Thie yn Traie quickly and continued on for a short while. She was meant to be meeting Andrew at half eight, which gave her plenty of time for a long walk.

Mindful that she and Andrew were planning to walk around Ramsey before lunch, Bessie headed for home before she felt tired. Andrew's curtains were still drawn, which saved her from having to worry about looking or not looking, but also made her worry that he'd overslept. She decided to shelve her worries and read a book. As was typical, she quickly found herself lost in the story, and when

Andrew knocked on her door around nine, she was surprised to see how late it was.

"I was miles away," she said apologetically as she let the man in.

"And here I was, worried about being a few minutes late," he laughed.

Bessie grabbed her handbag and quickly checked that she had everything. "I'm ready to go," she told him.

"Excellent. I know just what we can talk about while I drive."

Bessie locked up her cottage and followed the man to his hire car. Surely it was too soon for him to have heard back from his colleague about the cold case? It didn't take long for Bessie to direct Andrew onto the main road. "You haven't heard back from your colleague already, have you?" she asked once they were properly underway.

"I have, actually. As I said, the case has been bothering him for years. I sent an email last night before I went to bed and I had a reply this morning."

"And?" Bessie demanded when Andrew fell silent.

"Sorry," he chuckled, "and he was startled by your suggestion, but he couldn't immediately refute it. He admitted that he never questioned the dead woman's identity as he had four witnesses identify the body. I believe he's rather annoyed with himself now, seeing as how he knew the women were lying about other things, but he never gave it any thought."

"What about the cook or the maid? Didn't either of them say anything?"

"I gather the women hadn't been there long enough for the cook and the maid to know which woman was which. The two sisters also looked very similar. My colleague sent me copies of their passport photos and I don't think I would have been able to tell them apart."

"And neither had ever had her fingerprints taken for any reason or anything like that, I suppose."

"Not that my colleague was aware of, anyway. He's going to go back through all of his case notes again for what he reckons will be the millionth time and see if he can find anything that disproves your theory. He's also going to start trying to locate the four women. He'd really like to question them again. It's always possible that they would be more honest with him now that so much time has passed."

"I don't know about that, but it would be interesting to know what they're all doing now."

Bessie directed Andrew into the small car park near the large bookshop. "This is the best place to park for shopping," she told him.

"Where shall we start?" he asked after they'd climbed out of the car.

"Are we shopping for anything special?"

"Not really," Andrew laughed. "Unless you need something?"

"Not at all, but I always like to visit the bookshop."

"Bookshop it is," he said. He offered his arm and Bessie took it with a grin. Inside the shop she stopped to inhale. It smelled of paper and ink, with some hint of scented candles from the gift section of the shop mixed in. Bessie loved the scent.

"It's bigger than it looked from the outside," Andrew said.

"They have a wonderful selection."

"Just point me towards the nonfiction and look for me in half an hour."

Bessie laughed and then did as he'd asked. She wandered off to the mystery and thriller shelves and immediately began making a small pile of titles she couldn't resist.

"We really should be going," Andrew said about an hour later.

Bessie jumped and looked up at him. She was sitting on the floor going through the books on the very bottom shelf. "What time is it?"

"It's gone ten and we still have the rest of the town to explore," he told her.

"My goodness, the day is getting away from us, isn't it?" Bessie exclaimed. She got to her feet and then brushed off her trousers. "I've found several books for my collection, though."

"I found four or five myself. There were several others that looked interesting as well. I had to force myself to put some of them back, though. I don't have room in my suitcase to take back more than a handful of titles."

They made their way to the tills and then dropped their bags of books in Andrew's car. "And now where?" Andrew asked.

"Let's just wander up the main shopping street," Bessie suggested. "We can pop into any shop that looks interesting."

Bessie was surprised when Andrew pulled her into the toyshop. "I need to bring back a few things for the grandchildren, well, the younger grandchildren, and my great-grandchildren as well," he explained.

Nothing on the shelves looked anything like what Bessie remembered playing with in her childhood. Everything in the shop seemed to be made of brightly coloured plastic. It was only after she'd looked around for some time that she finally found a box of wooden blocks. They were painted lurid colours, but at least they were made of wood.

She shook her head and then went in search of Andrew. He was standing in front of a huge display with a sign that read "Fashion Dolls" above it.

"I'm afraid I'm going to buy one of these," Andrew told her as she approached. "Which one do you think is the prettiest?"

Bessie looked at the dolls, with their implausible figures and their inflated lips, and sighed. "I don't think any of them are pretty. Maybe a cuddly toy instead?"

"I'm under strict orders to stop buying cuddly toys. I tend to give them to the kids for everything." He picked up a doll in a tiny red swimsuit. "This is the one my daughter said to get. Apparently it's very popular with the under-sixes."

"Why?"

Andrew laughed. "I have no idea, but I should probably do as I'm told anyway."

Bessie watched as Andrew selected sets of plastic bricks, more dolls, and some sort of electronic block that made a range of annoying sounds whenever anyone touched it. The total at the till shocked her.

"That didn't come to as much as I'd feared," Andrew said as they walked back out into the sunshine.

"It didn't?"

"Toys are very expensive, especially the popular ones."

"Again, I'm glad I never had children."

"Maybe we should get some lunch," Andrew suggested a short time later. "We want to make sure we're back in Laxey in plenty of time for our meeting with John."

There were a number of small cafés along the street. The pair chose one at random and were shown to a table right away.

"They do excellent soups," Bessie told Andrew.

"It's too nice a day for soup," he replied. A moment later he put his menu down with a sigh. "I'm going to try some soup. It just sounds too good to pass up."

With lunch ordered, the pair sipped their drinks and chatted about nothing much while they waited for the food to be delivered. After a few bites, Andrew put down his spoon.

"You were absolutely right. This is delicious," he told Bessie. "Thank you for suggesting soup."

"I've never had one here that wasn't good. I think the leek and potato is my favourite, though."

"I should have asked you that, shouldn't I?" Andrew laughed. "But if it's your favourite, why am I having leek and potato while you're having tomato?"

"Because tomato sounded good today."

"Would you like a bite?" he offered.

Bessie hesitated. "Would you like to try mine?"

"That's why I offered," Andrew admitted.

When both bowls were completely empty, Andrew insisted on paying the bill. As the soup wasn't terribly expensive, Bessie didn't argue. At some point she'd have to take a stand against the man's insistence on paying for everything, but that was a discussion to have at home, not in the centre of Ramsey.

They made their way back towards Andrew's car, but he stopped in front of an ice cream shop before they'd reached the car. "How about a scoop or two for pudding?" he asked.

"I don't know," Bessie said.

"I'm having some. I'm on holiday, after all," Andrew told her. "You may as well have a small scoop. It will help cool down the soup in your tummy."

Bessie laughed and then followed the man into the shop. She ended up with two scoops, one vanilla and one strawberry. They sat together on a bench and ate their ice cream before walking back to the car.

"That was a real treat," Bessie told Andrew as he started the engine. "I never get ice cream like that."

"You should. Life's too short to walk past an ice cream shop without stopping," he told her.

"I'd weigh twenty stone if I stopped at every ice cream shop I saw," Bessie argued.

"But it would be worth it."

Bessie laughed and then shook her head. She'd never had a problem with maintaining her slender figure, but perhaps that was because she rarely ate ice cream and never got it from an ice cream shop in the middle of the day.

CHAPTER 4

"Inspector Cheatham, it's nice to see you again," John Rockwell said when he opened the door to them a short while later. "Please come in."

Andrew stepped back and let Bessie enter first. John's house was a remodelled fifties bungalow. It wasn't huge, but it was comfortable. It had been a while since Bessie had been there and she was surprised to see how much John's children had taken over the place. There were piles of things everywhere and none of them seemed to be John's things.

"I'm sorry about the mess," John said, looking slightly embarrassed. "The kids seem to just leave everything wherever it falls."

"I remember it well," Andrew laughed, "and then they grow up and leave home and you actually miss the mess."

"I can believe that," John said.

Bessie knew that the children were due to move back to Manchester later in the month. When she'd first met John, he and his family had just moved to the island, where he'd been offered his job with the CID. His wife, Sue, hadn't liked the island, and she'd recently been reunited with a former boyfriend, one she'd never stopped loving. While Sue and John had tried to find a way to make their marriage work, after a year on the island Sue had returned to Manchester and filed for divorce. With John's consent, she'd taken the children with her, but now they were having an extended visit to the island while Sue was honeymooning with her second husband, the man she'd left John to be with.

"When are Sue and Harvey back?" Bessie asked.

"It's now going to be mid-October," John sighed. "The kids are staying in school here until she's back and we can talk everything through. I'm already arguing that she should let them stay here for the rest of the school year. I hate the thought of them having to go back and forth so much."

"What do Thomas and Amy think?" was Bessie's next question.

"At the moment, they both want to stay here, too, but they are both struggling a little bit with school since things are different here to Manchester. I wish, I mean, it's really..." John trailed off and looked at the ground.

"I know. It's really hard, but it will all work out in the end," Bessie said soothingly.

"How old are the children?" Andrew asked.

"Thomas is fifteen and Amy is thirteen," John replied. "They're both out having fun with their friends today, even though I'm sure they both have homework to get done."

"It's Saturday. Let them have some fun today and then crack the whip tomorrow," Andrew suggested. "Although you probably shouldn't take advice from me. I was the fun parent. My poor wife had to be the one who cracked the whip all the time."

"I was the fun parent when Sue and I were together. Now I'm the only parent when the kids are here and that isn't any fun for anyone," John said. He shook his head. "I'm sorry. It isn't like me to complain."

"No it isn't, and it's long overdue," Bessie said firmly. "Sue is being selfish and she's put you in an impossible situation."

"Who's Sue?" Andrew asked in a loud whisper.

Bessie and John both laughed. "Sue is my former wife and the mother of my wonderful children," John explained. "She just remarried and is on a honeymoon trip with her husband, an oncologist.

They thought it would be, um, interesting to spend their honeymoon in a developing country helping people in need."

"Interesting, maybe, but not very romantic. Her new husband seems to be a bit of an idiot," Andrew said.

John laughed again. "I would never say such a thing about the man, but you may believe what you like. Anyway, they left in July and were meant to be back by the middle of September. The kids were going to move back to Manchester and stay with Sue's mother for a few weeks until Sue and Harvey returned. The return date keeps getting pushed back further and further, though, and the kids don't really want to go and stay with Sue's mum anyway."

Bessie hated the frustrated look that she could see on her friend's handsome face. John was only in his forties, but the stress of the current situation seemed to be taking a toll on him. His bright green eyes looked tired and she was sure she could see more grey in his brown hair than normal.

"It will all work out in the end," she said soothingly.

"I certainly hope so," John replied, 'but let's go into the sitting room and relax. I promise there's less mess in there. I cleared off the couches and everything."

The sitting room was spacious and comfortable. Bessie sank into an overstuffed chair while Andrew settled onto one of the couches.

"Does anyone want tea or coffee or something cold?" John asked.

"We just had lunch and ice cream," Bessie replied. "I won't want anything else for hours."

"I'm fine as well," Andrew said.

John nodded and then dropped onto the other couch. "I asked you here to tell you about a cold case," he told Andrew. "I was hoping to reopen the investigation into it, but I've not been given permission to do so."

"Why not?" Bessie asked.

"Our resources are stretched thin at the moment for one thing, and it isn't really my cold case, either, for another. The murder took place in Ramsey, which is outside my jurisdiction," John explained.

"Whose case is it, then?" Bessie wanted to know.

"Technically, it now belongs to Carl Clague. When it happened, Patrick Kelly was working CID there, but he's now working in the drugs and alcohol unit and Carl has taken over in CID," John said.

"I'm sure Carl wouldn't mind if you wanted to solve one of his cold cases for him," Bessie replied. She'd met the man during a recent murder investigation. He was charming and kind, and nearing retirement. There was no way he was going to be upset if John started a new investigation.

"He would probably be delighted, but the chief constable doesn't want anyone working on cold cases until we get our staffing numbers back where they should be," John explained.

"But you can still tell us about the case," Andrew suggested. "Maybe Bessie will have a brilliant idea about it like she did with my cold case."

"Did she, now? Maybe you should go first, then. I can't wait to hear about Bessie's brilliant idea," John said.

Andrew cleared his throat while Bessie blushed and stared at the floor. "It was a dark and stormy night," Andrew began.

Bessie laughed and then sat back and listened as Andrew recounted the story for John. When he was finished, John asked a number of questions, most of which Bessie thought were much smarter than the ones she'd asked.

"And Bessie had a brilliant idea," John mused. "Bessie usually thinks outside the box. All I keep coming back to is the idea that the four women couldn't be trusted, but I can't seem to work out why they all lied about the same thing, even when it was proven that they were lying."

"Ready to hear Bessie's bright idea?" Andrew asked.

John shook his head. "Let me leave all of that ticking over in the back of my mind while I tell you about my cold case. Then while you and Bessie are puzzling over it, I can think more about yours."

"That sounds a fair deal," Andrew said.

"My case only happened about five years ago," John began. "A woman called Jeanne Stowe was found dead in her flat in Ramsey."

Bessie gasped. "I remember the case," she told the others. "As you said, it wasn't that long ago. I would have said just a few years, really, but it could have been five, I suppose. It was the talk of the island for weeks, but as far as I know no one was ever arrested. I had never been involved in a murder investigation when it happened. I followed the case in the local paper, of course, but I didn't do any more than that."

"Maybe you could try tapping a few of your sources now, then," John suggested. "It's the sort of case that should have been solved but wasn't."

"Tell me the whole story," Andrew said. "From the very beginning, please."

John sat back and shut his eyes. "Jeanne was thirty-seven. She lived alone in the flat that she'd purchased after she and her husband, Kenny, divorced. He kept the house in Douglas that he and Jeanne had purchased together."

"And from what I can remember, he had another woman moved into the place before Jeanne was fully moved out," Bessie added.

John nodded. "He and Jeanne had divorced because Kenny's girlfriend had fallen pregnant. From what Kenny said to the papers, Jeanne didn't want children and Kenny realised that he did. He and Jeanne were already talking about separating when Kenny started seeing Sandra Oliver. She fell pregnant almost immediately, and that sped up the divorce proceedings. According to Kenny, it was all friendly, though."

"I remember Jeanne's closest friend told a different story," Bessie said.

"That would have been Mabel Lloyd. She gave an interview to the paper in which she claimed that Jeanne had been devastated when Kenny asked her to leave. Mabel's version had Jeanne struggling with infertility. Mabel told the papers that she was sure that Kenny had killed Jeanne," John told them.

"How long before Jeanne's death did the divorce happen?" Andrew asked.

"About three years," John said. "Which was one of the reasons why Kenny was never taken seriously as a suspect. He and Jeanne were divorced and he and Sandra were living together. Inspector Kelly couldn't come up with any possible motive for Kenny or Sandra."

"Was it possible that Kenny was seeing Jeanne again behind Sandra's back?" Andrew asked.

"He was working full-time and going to school at night. Besides that, he and Sandra had a toddler and a new baby. Inspector Kelly didn't think the man had time to cheat on Sandra," John replied.

"Before we get too caught up in the suspects, take me through the crime scene," Andrew requested.

Bessie sat up a little straighter. This was information about which she knew nothing. The papers hadn't said anything about the crime scene.

John nodded. "None of this can leave this room. Officially, it's still an open investigation, and we never released any information about the crime scene."

Bessie and Andrew both nodded before John continued.

"Jeanne was found in her bed. She'd taken a massive overdose of several different drugs, mostly various sleeping pills and painkillers. She even left a note of the 'I can't take it any more' variety, but there were a number of problems with the setup as suicide. For one thing, someone had taken away all of the medicine bottles."

"That was sloppy," Bessie remarked.

"Inspector Kelly assumed that at least some of the bottles may have been prescribed for the killer, who took them away as his or her name was printed on the label," John explained.

"That makes sense, but surely if someone went to the trouble to make it appear to be suicide, they'd be smarter than that," Bessie argued.

"Well, in this case they weren't. There were no bottles, and there was no glass of water or even an empty glass on the bedside table. The bedroom door was locked, but it was a simple push lock that could have been set before the door was shut. The door to the flat was also locked, but it was self-locking. The deadbolt wasn't on."

"You're going to have tell us how the body was found," Andrew said.

John sighed. "I'm going about this all wrong. I've read about the case so much that I'm jumping around and skipping important things. Let me try starting at the very beginning, when the police were first rung."

"That's a good idea," Andrew said.

"The police were rung on October 18th, which was a Tuesday, around ten o'clock in the morning. Jeanne hadn't turned up for work on Monday, which wasn't like her. Her supervisor rang her flat and didn't get any answer. She wanted to ring the police on Monday, but was persuaded to wait twenty-four hours. When Jeanne didn't appear on Tuesday, the woman rang 999," John told them.

"What was the supervisor's name?" Andrew asked.

Bessie hid a grin as she noted that Andrew had pulled out a note-book and started taking notes. Clearly old habits died hard.

"Amanda McBride," John replied.

"And where did Jeanne work?" was Andrew's next question.

"For Ramsey National Bank," John replied. "It was only open for about five years. I'm sure Bessie can tell you more about it, if you're interested."

"I am," Andrew replied, looking at Bessie.

"I believe it opened in the early nineties," Bessie said, trying to think. "It closed about two years ago."

"It closed in ninety-six," John interjected.

"Okay, three years ago," Bessie grinned. "It was started by a local who'd had a disagreement with the island's main bank and decided that he could do it better himself. He started out with about a dozen customers, nearly all of whom were his friends or family, but the bank did manage to grow slowly over the years."

"What went wrong?" Andrew asked.

"I don't know that anything went wrong," Bessie told him. "It was a very small operation, really, with only a handful of employees. The man who started it fell ill and no one else in his family wanted to take over running a bank. I believe he ended up selling the entire operation to the same bank that he'd argued with in the first place."

Andrew laughed. "There's irony there, somewhere, but as far as you know, the bank was legitimate and no one lost money when it was sold?"

"As far as I know, yes," Bessie replied. "I had a few friends who banked there, but only a very few. It only had the one office, which wasn't the most convenient setup. My friends would have let me know if they'd lost money when it shut, though, and none of them ever complained."

"And what did Jeanne do at the bank?" Andrew asked John.

"She was a customer service associate," he replied. "They only had two of them and they both worked full-time hours. Amanda McBride was their supervisor, and she also had to cover for their lunch hours and breaks and things."

"And who told her not to report Jeanne's absence on the Monday?" was Andrew's next question.

"Amanda's supervisor, the bank's vice-president. He was Nick Grant, and his father was the man who'd started the bank," John said.

"The father was called Jefferson," Bessie added. "It's an unusual name, at least in this country. I believe his mother was an American or something."

"I don't know about that, but he was called Jefferson. He left the island after the bank was sold due to his health. He and his family are settled in Australia now, I believe."

"Nick went with him?" Andrew asked.

"Yes, he did. Jefferson and his wife, Julie, went, along with Nick and his wife, Heather. Nick and Heather didn't have any children, at least not when they lived on the island," Bessie told him.

"Any idea why Nick didn't want Amanda to ring the police straight away?" Andrew wanted to know.

"In his statement, he said that Jeanne had been known to be late from time to time and he didn't want to involve the police in what he'd assumed was simply an employee problem. He claimed that Jeanne had been increasingly unreliable over the past three or four months."

"And did Amanda concur?" Andrew asked.

"Not exactly. She did admit that Jeanne had been late a few times, but she insisted that Jeanne had been having problems with her car and that that was only reason why she'd been late a handful of times. For what it's worth, Inspector Kelly checked and Jeanne's car had been in for repairs three times in four months," John said.

Andrew nodded and then turned to a new page in his notebook. "Okay, so the police were rung on the Tuesday and someone went to Jeanne's flat, correct?"

"That's correct. Amanda didn't even talk to Nick on Tuesday. When Jeanne didn't arrive as expected, she rang the police. A constable went to Jeanne's flat and found the door locked. When he reported that to his supervisor, someone rang Amanda back. Amanda then rang Mabel and asked her to meet the police at Jeanne's with Jeanne's spare key," John said.

"How did Amanda know Mabel?" Bessie asked.

"Mabel was listed on Jeanne's paperwork as her emergency contact," John explained. "I'm not sure if Amanda and Mabel had ever met before that day. I can go back through the notes later to check, if it seems important."

"So Mabel arrived at the flat with a key and the constable was still there?" Andrew checked.

"That's right. It must have been a slow crime day in Ramsey," John said. "The constable stayed at the flat and waited. I should add that Mabel wasn't all that far away. She worked for one of the cafés in the town centre. According to the police report, it only took her seven minutes to get to Jeanne's flat once she was contacted."

"Walk me through what the constable did, please," Andrew said.

"Mabel unlocked the door and the constable entered the flat. He reported that there was an unpleasant odor that was noticeable as soon as he'd entered. Suspecting what it was, he sent Mabel out of the building and rang for reinforcements. He then waited for Inspector Kelly to arrive. The inspector was able to force open the lock on the bedroom door."

"I'd like to see the crime scene photos," Andrew told John when he'd finished.

"I wish I could show them to you, but I don't have access to them. I can probably get Carl to share them with me, but I'd rather not ask him unless we have reason to believe that we'll be able to contribute something to the investigation," John replied.

"You said that Jeanne was lying on the bed, and that she'd taken an overdose of several medications. Was she meant to be taking any prescription medications herself?" Andrew asked.

"No, although she did have some bottles of over-the-counter drugs in her bathroom. Mabel told the police that she'd never seen Jeanne take anything stronger than over-the-counter headache tablets and that she only took those when she had a migraine," John said.

"I would have thought she'd have some sort of prescription for migraine," Bessie said.

"Mabel said that they were infrequent and that Jeanne preferred over-the-counter drugs because she worried about addiction," John told her.

"And the bottles in her bathroom still had tablets in them?" Andrew asked.

John nodded. "Jeanne had some of the same drugs in her system as were in her bathroom, but all of the bottles in the bathroom still had at least some tablets in them. We've no way to know how full they were before that day, of course."

"Fingerprints? Neighbours who heard voices? Signs of a struggle?" Andrew listed his questions.

"No signs of a struggle. Inspector Kelly suggested that she was already in bed when someone forced her to swallow the tablets," John said.

"How do you make someone take tablets?" Bessie asked.

"Perhaps by drugging them in the first place," Andrew suggested. "Maybe she was drinking with someone and that someone managed to slip Jeanne a sleeping tablet or two. When she started to get drowsy, her companion may have even helped her get ready for bed. Then he or she simply had to keep giving her more and more tablets, perhaps assuring poor Jeanne that each one would help to make her feel better."

Bessie shuddered. "What an awful scenario."

"It seems a likely one, though," John told her. "There are ways to physically force someone to take tablets, but there were no signs on the body that anything like that had been done. If the killer had left a few bottles on the table, the case may have been ruled suicide."

"What about the note?" Andrew asked.

"It was definitely in Jeanne's handwriting, at least according to the experts," John told him. "As I said, it basically said that she simply couldn't take it any more. There was no hint of what was wrong, however, and none of Jeanne's friends or coworkers could suggest anything that might have driven her to take her own life."

"What about her fertility issues?" Bessie wondered.

"Mabel suggested that, but Inspector Kelly didn't find any evidence that the woman had fertility issues. He had a look at her medical records and there was nothing in them to suggest that she'd ever consulted a doctor about them, anyway," John said.

"No one could suggest any other reason why she might have killed herself?" Andrew asked.

"No. Everyone that the inspector spoke with said pretty much the same thing. She was a hard worker who was friendly and compassionate. I already told you that Nick Grant was unhappy with her being late occasionally, but she was in no danger of losing her job over the matter and as far as the inspector could determine, the car had finally been repaired properly." John sighed. "As unlikely as suicide seemed, though, no one could imagine any reason why anyone would have murdered her, either."

"Tell me more about her," Andrew requested. "She and her husband had been apart for three years. Surely there were other men in her life after him?"

"Right after she and Kenny separated, she started seeing a man called Ron Adams," John said. "They were only together for a few months, and from what Mabel had to say it wasn't a particularly happy relationship, but it was over at least two years before Jeanne died."

"Unhappy in what way?" Bessie wanted to know.

"Mabel just said they fought a lot. The man was questioned as well, but he was living in Peel by that time, and there was no evidence that he'd been in touch with Jeanne after their relationship had ended," John told her.

"And someone else came after Ron?" Andrew asked.

"Yes, within a few months of ending things with Ron, Jeanne started seeing a man called James Poole. They were together for about a year. According to Mabel, things were getting serious, but then Mr. Poole's mother fell ill. She lived in Brighton and Mr. Poole ended up moving back there to be with her," John said. "According to Mabel, Jeanne was disappointed that the relationship ended, and maybe had entertained some hopes of moving with Mr. Poole, but in the end it was a friendly enough split."

"And that was still a year or more before Jeanne died?" Bessie checked that she was following the time line.

"Yes, about that. As far as Mabel knew, Jeanne remained single after that," John said.

"That's hard to believe," Andrew said. "I mean, from what you've told us, the woman moved from relationship to relationship with only small gaps between them. It would be unusual for her to then remain single for over a year, wouldn't it?"

"Maybe she was having trouble finding someone," Bessie suggested. "She was getting older, getting to an age where most men are already married to other women, maybe?"

"So maybe she was involved with a married man," Andrew suggested.

"If she was, they were very discreet," John told him. "Obviously, Inspector Kelly looked at Nick pretty closely. He couldn't find any evidence of anything between the pair."

"So who were the main suspects?" Andrew asked.

"Inspector Kelly never managed to develop anything like a short list of suspects," John sighed.

"Means, motive, opportunity?" Bessie wondered.

"The various drugs that were found in Jeanne's system were all fairly typically prescribed sleep aids. It wasn't so much what she was given, but the quantity and variety of what she was given that killed her. But it wouldn't have been difficult for the killer to save a few pills here and there from every prescription he or she was given, and that seems most likely to have been what he or she did, actually," John said.

"Did any of the suspects admit to being prescribed any of the drugs?" Bessie asked.

"I believe all of them admitted to having tried at least one of the drugs," John told her. "As I said, they were typical sleep aids, and at the time there was a doctor in Ramsey who seemed inclined to prescribe them for just about everything."

Bessie nodded. "Yes, I remember him. He did tend to give out sleeping tablets as if they could cure everything from the common cold to cancer. Several of my friends visited him regularly and ended up with quite a stockpile of different tablets. I never once thought about the dangers of them."

"Inspector Kelly determined that everyone connected with the case had access to at least some of the different drugs that were found in the body. Some of them could have been obtained illegally or could have been stolen from family members or friends, as well. The inspector treated the case as if everyone had the means to commit the crime," John explained.

"I hope that doctor is no longer practicing medicine," Andrew said.

"He is not," John told him. "There was talk of an investigation, but he retired and moved to Spain before it took place."

"What about opportunity? When did Jeanne actually die?" Bessie asked.

"I believe I told you that the body was found on Tuesday. The coroner had difficulty establishing a time of death, but he believed she died on either Friday evening or early Saturday," John said.

"That's a pretty big range," Andrew sighed.

"It is, yes. The inspector couldn't determine that anyone had a solid alibi for the entire period," John said.

"So everyone had the means and the opportunity and we have no idea of the motive," Bessie summarised.

"Yes, that's correct," John said. "When you put it that way, it seems quite hopeless, really."

"It's never hopeless, but it is complicated," Andrew said. "A lot of time has passed, as well, which is unfortunate. It sounds as though several of the key witnesses have left the island."

"Which is why the chief constable doesn't want the case reopening," John said. "He'd much rather I focus my efforts on other things."

"But he can't stop me from poking around," Andrew replied with a grin, "and I'm sure Bessie will help. Won't you?"

Bessie smiled. "If that's your idea of a fun thing to do on your holiday, I suppose I don't mind helping."

"It is actually exactly what I like to do on holiday," Andrew told her. "We'll have to find ways to meet the various suspects that seem natural, though. It would be probably be best if we didn't tell anyone that I used to be a police inspector, as well."

"I can tell you how to find Mabel and Amanda," John said. "They're probably your best place to start."

"Where can we find them, then?" Andrew asked.

John flipped through his notebook. "Amanda works for the Ramey branch of the island's largest bank. She's a loan specialist now."

"Maybe it's time to think about taking out a loan to do some improvements on my cottage," Bessie mused.

John grinned. "Mabel waits tables at a café in Port St. Mary. I'm sure you'll be able to find an excuse to visit her there."

"Which café?" Bessie asked.

John told her and Bessie frowned. "It wouldn't be my first choice for a meal in Port St. Mary, or even my second or third," she said.

"Maybe we could just go for tea and a slice of cake or something," Andrew suggested.

"I suppose so," Bessie said, "but only because you want to talk to Mabel. I would never take anyone there otherwise. I've no idea how they even stay in business, really. The last time I ate there, which was a great many years ago now, it was truly dreadful, and from what I hear it hasn't improved any."

"Now I'm looking forward to visiting," Andrew laughed. "If only to see if it truly is as bad as you say it is."

Bessie shook her head. "You'll be sorry that you said that," she predicted.

"After you've spoken to the two of them, we should meet again and talk everything through," John suggested. "I'm doing some investigating on my own, just checking to see where the people who've left the island are now. I don't know if it matters, but I'd like to know more about Jefferson and Julie Grant and their son, Nick."

"I'm with you on that," Andrew said. "Nick is the one person I'd most like to interview, actually, but I'm not sure a trip to Australia is in the cards, at least not right now."

"Have you ever been?" John asked.

"Yes, a few times," Andrew replied. "I was first sent there during the war, but I went back for a few international conferences and the like. My wife and I even had a holiday there once. It's a very different country, and an incredibly beautiful one."

"I'm not sure I'd like the heat, "John said.

"I'm quite sure I wouldn't like the spiders, snakes, and crocodiles," Bessie said firmly.

"You don't see a lot of them in the cities," Andrew told her. "If I do end up going to talk to Nick Grant, I'm going to insist that you come with me."

Bessie only just stopped herself from refusing immediately. A trip to Australia was something that needed more than just a moment's thought.

"But let's get back to your cold case," John said, nodding at Andrew. "I have a few questions for you."

CHAPTER 5

"Go ahead," Andrew invited.

"Who identified the body?" John asked.

Andrew exchanged glances with Bessie. "Her sister," he said.

"Is it possible that the dead woman wasn't Betty Jones, then?" John asked. "We know the women lied about the phone call. Could they have lied about the victim's identity as well?"

"It's a possibility," Andrew admitted. "One that never occurred me, I'm ashamed to say. Bessie picked up on the same thing."

"I think that may have coloured how you told me the story," John said. "If the body wasn't Betty's, though, whose might it have been?"

"Bessie's idea was that it was Cindy who was murdered and that the women agreed to identify the body as Betty's for some reason," Andrew told him.

"I'm not sure I understand why Cindy confessed, whether she was actually Betty or not," John said.

"That's just one of the many questions that remain unanswered," Andrew told him. "I'm checking into the money that Betty left behind to see where it went. I know that it was meant to go to charity, because Cindy was unable to inherit, but I'm trying to work out exactly which charity benefitted."

"It isn't that difficult to set up a charity," John suggested, "but if she'd done that before she faked her own death, that suggests a great deal of planning went into it."

"It does, yes," Andrew agreed. "I've suggested to my colleague that he try to track down Cindy Jones. She was released from prison years ago, of course."

"I'd like to know what happened to the other women, too," John said. "If the body really was Cindy's, that suggests that Betty killed her and then assumed her identity. I've no idea why she would have done that, but that seems like the most likely scenario, from what you've told me."

"I'd never once considered the idea until Bessie suggested it, but now that it's out there, I have to agree with you. I couldn't imagine why anyone would have killed Betty. She was on holiday with her friends, celebrating her engagement. Cindy was far less popular with the other women. That doesn't mean they wanted her dead, but she seems a more likely victim than Betty, anyway," Andrew said.

"Let me know what your colleague tells you about all of the women," John requested. "I find the case intriguing."

"Oh, I'll let you know," Andrew assured him. "I have a feeling things could get interesting."

The pair chatted for a few minutes about police work in general while Bessie listened. She couldn't help but feel as if she'd have been a good police inspector, had she been given the opportunity. Perhaps that was only because of all of the murder mysteries she'd read over the years, though. Maybe she was simply always looking for red herrings and unlikely solutions.

Bessie was starting to get a bit restless when they all heard a loud crashing noise. John winced and then got to his feet.

"What have I said about that front door?" he shouted.

"Sorry, dad," Amy said as she dashed into the room. She gave John a quick hug that wiped the angry look off his face instantly. "I'm just passing through from Jen's house to Kate's and I wanted to grab a bite to eat really quickly."

"There's plenty of food in the kitchen," John told her. "I went shopping this morning."

"You're the best," Amy said as she rushed away.

"And that was Amy," John said to Andrew in an apologetic tone.

"She's lovely," Andrew replied. "She must resemble her mother."

"Yes, she does," John agreed as a series of emotions flashed across his face.

"Dad, can I eat the ham in the package you wrote 'do not eat' on?" Amy's voice called from the kitchen.

John rolled his eyes. "That's for my lunches this week," he shouted back.

"I think Bessie and I should get out of your way so that you can protect your ham," Andrew laughed. "I promise, it gets better."

John nodded. "I'm still getting used to having them here. I know I'll miss them when they move back to their mother's." He walked Bessie and Andrew to the door where Bessie gave him a hug before she followed Andrew back down the short stretch of pavement to Andrew's car.

"It's later than I realised," Andrew said before he started the engine. "It's nearly time for dinner. Where would you like to go?"

"I've no idea," Bessie replied. "What sounds good to you?"

"Lunch seems to have been a long time ago and we only had soup. I think I'd like something more substantial for dinner."

"We had ice cream, too," Bessie pointed out.

"Does that mean you aren't hungry?"

"No, actually, I'm really hungry now that you've mentioned it," Bessie admitted.

"So, where can we get a good and filling meal?"

"Assuming you don't want to drive all over the island, there's a nice café in Laxey or a good fish and chips shop," Bessie told him.

"I don't mind driving elsewhere, but if the café in Laxey is good, let's go there."

"It's near the Laxey Wheel, and I'm sure the owner will appreciate the business."

"Will he?"

"She will," Bessie said. "She's a lovely woman called Jasmina who moved over here from Devon. She met a man on the Internet, you see, and he turned out to be something less than advertised. Doona and I have been trying to eat at her café at least once a week. She does great food, and she's already rid herself of the man for whom she relocated to the island."

"Good for her. Now I'm looking forward to dinner. Of course, I'm always looking forward to food. I hope she does puddings."

"She does excellent puddings."

The tiny café only had room for twelve customers around its three tables at any time. Bessie and Andrew walked up to the door just as Jasmina was unlocking it.

"Hello, Bessie," the short, plump woman said. "I'm a bit late opening today, but I'll tell you all about that later."

Bessie introduced her to Andrew and then they followed the woman into the tiny building.

"Sit anywhere," Jasmina said, waving a hand. "The cooker isn't working properly again, but I can do sandwiches and toasties, and I put a big pot of beef stew on this afternoon. It won't take but a few minutes to warm through, if you fancy it."

"That does sound good," Andrew said. "Although I'm hungry enough to eat just about anything."

Jasmina laughed. "My kind of customer," she said.

Bessie and Andrew settled into chairs at the table furthest from the door. Jasmina disappeared behind the counter to get their drinks. A moment later the door opened and a group of teenagers flooded in.

"Mum, we're here," one of the girls shouted.

"That's Jasmina's daughter," Bessie whispered. "Her name is Tamazin."

"There are more of them then there are chairs," Andrew noted.

"Maybe we should go," Bessie said with a frown.

"Don't shout. We have customers," Jasmina said as she swept back into the room. She put Bessie's and Andrew's drinks on their table and then winked at Bessie. "I just have to deal with this lot, if you don't mind waiting a moment."

Bessie shook her head. She didn't mind. In fact, she was curious what the children wanted.

Jasmina was in and out of the kitchen in a flash, returning with a large box. "Right, box lunches for fifteen. I hope that's enough," she said.

"It's perfect. Thanks, mum," Tamazin said, taking the box from her mother.

"I think I should take that," one of the boys said.

"I'll let you. Not because I think you're stronger than me, but if you're dumb enough to want to carry it, I should take advantage," Tamazin laughed.

"There are cold drinks in the bottom of the box, too," Jasmina said. "I expect you home by midnight."

Tamazin rolled her eyes. "Yes, Mum, I know."

The group made their way back out of the room, leaving it suddenly feeling much more spacious. Bessie smiled at Jasmina. "It looks as if your daughter is making friends."

"Yes, she definitely is," Jasmina grinned. "She's refused to even consider going back to Devon, which is just as well, as I'm starting to really like the island."

"I'm glad to hear that," Bessie said.

"And I've even met a rather nice gentleman," Jasmina added. "I'm taking things slowly, after the unfortunate experience I had with Richard, but so far he seems lovely."

"It's a small island. I wonder if I know him," Bessie said.

Jasmina blushed. "I suspect you probably do, as the island is so small." She glanced back and forth, as if checking that they were still alone, before taking a step closer to Bessie. "His name is Henry Costain. He works for Manx National Heritage. He's been working at the Laxey Wheel all month, which is why I was late opening. I was over chatting with him and I forgot about the time."

Bessie grinned. She knew Henry well and she was pleased to hear that he and Jasmina had become friends. As far as Bessie knew, Henry had been a lifelong bachelor until a short time back. He'd started seeing a woman called Laura sometime before Christmas, but the relationship had ended when she'd moved back to the UK. Perhaps Henry and Jasmina would have better luck. "I do know Henry. He's a lovely man," Bessie told her.

"I think so, too, although he's quite shy with women, isn't he? I'm glad he's taking things slowly, but I am starting to wonder if he just wants to be friends, rather than anything more," the woman replied.

"I don't believe he's been in very many relationships," Bessie replied. "If you aren't sure how he feels, you could try asking him."

Jasmina blushed. "I'm not sure I could do that, but I'll think about it. But what would you like to eat?"

Andrew and Bessie both ordered the stew, and when it came it was just as delicious as Bessie had expected. While they were eating, two groups of four came in and took up the other tables. When another group of three arrived, there was nowhere for them to sit.

"I can do you some takeaway boxes," Jasmina suggested to them.

"We'll wait," one of the women said. "We've heard you do the tastiest sandwiches on the island."

Jasmina grinned. "I don't know about that, but I do my best."

The little group went back outside to wait. Andrew looked at Bessie. "Maybe we should get our pudding in takeaway boxes," he suggested.

"That's probably a good idea," Bessie agreed. "I won't be hungry for mine immediately, anyway. This stew is very filling."

When Jasmina came over to clear the table a few minutes later, they asked her what they could get for pudding.

"I have a Victoria sponge, a chocolate gateau, or a jam roly-poly," she replied. "I baked them all this morning between the breakfast rush and the lunch crowd."

"You do seem to be busier every time I come in," Bessie said.

"I'm getting more and more word-of-mouth advertising," the woman said happily. "I'm actually looking around for a larger space, but everything is terribly expensive. Richard rented this for me for six months. That was all he ever did for me, really, but that's another matter. Anyway, I have a few months left on the lease so I need to work out what I'm going to do soon. If I can't find anything larger, I suppose I could stay here for another six months, but we'll see."

"I'll have the chocolate gateau," Andrew told her, "but box up our puddings and we'll take them home. You need the table."

"Are you sure?" Jasmina asked. "I don't want you to feel as if you have to leave."

"I'm not ready for pudding yet, but I don't want to miss out on a slice of your chocolate gateau," Bessie said. "Box them up and we'll get out of the way."

Jasmina looked as if she wanted to argue, but someone at one of the other tables called her name and she had to rush away. When she came back a few minutes later, she had their boxes and their bill.

Andrew took the bill before she could even put it down.

"Perhaps tonight should be my treat," Bessie suggested as Andrew pulled out his wallet.

"I said I was buying while I was here," he reminded her. "As I would pay considerably more than this for a single cold sandwich in London, you mustn't feel the least bit guilty."

Bessie didn't argue, as she knew Jasmina's prices were very low. They would probably go up if the woman moved to a larger location, but Bessie knew people would pay more for the woman's excellent cooking. She had argued with Jasmina about her pricing more than once, but the woman always insisted that she needed to build up her business before she started charging more.

Outside, the group of three had been joined by a group of four who were also, presumably, waiting for a table. A small cheer went up as Bessie and Andrew walked out of the building.

"What did you have?" someone shouted at them.

"Beef stew, and it was excellent," Andrew told him. A few people cheered again.

"I hope you didn't get the last of the chocolate gateau," someone else said.

Bessie glanced at Andrew, and he smiled at her. "No worries. I'll protect your pudding."

Bessie laughed. "I'm sure there's plenty for everyone," she said to the crowd. Just in case she was wrong, she picked up her pace, though. Andrew followed her to his car.

"You were nearly running there," he said as he started the engine.

"I was afraid Jasmina might come out and tell them she was out of chocolate gateau."

"Maybe we should have John step up his patrols here. I'd hate for a fight to start over a slice of cake."

"Jasmina said she just baked today. Things should be okay for tonight."

"I certainly hope so," Andrew laughed.

As it was still early, Bessie suggested a drive along the coast road. They drove in silence for several minutes before Andrew pulled off the road and stopped the car.

"This view is amazing," he sighed. "I'd love to have a house that looked out on this view."

"There are several houses on the cliff above us," Bessie pointed out. "I don't know if any of them are for sale, though."

"My children would have a fit if I moved to the island."

"Do they visit you in London often?"

Andrew laughed. "No, not at all. But they all plan to visit quite regularly, and talk about visiting nearly all the time. They're all just incredibly busy with their lives, you see."

Bessie bit her tongue. It wasn't her place to comment, really.

"Can we walk for a bit here?" Andrew asked.

"Of course we can. There's a public footpath alongside the road."

They both got out of the car and walked over to the path that was nearly at the water's edge. "Which way should we go?" he asked.

"It's probably best to go that way," Bessie said, gesturing. "I think the tide is still coming in. The path in the other direction may get covered before the tide has finished."

They walked in silence for a few minutes, simply enjoying the view. After a while, Andrew reached over and took Bessie's hand. She almost pulled her hand away, but then decided that it was pleasant strolling along hand in hand. Bessie felt as if she could walk forever, but after twenty minutes or so Andrew stopped.

"We should turn around. I'm getting tired quickly."

"Of course," Bessie agreed.

The walk back to the car took longer as Andrew walked more slowly. When they finally reached it, Andrew sat in the driver's seat for several minutes, seemingly catching his breath. "I'm sorry about that," he told Bessie eventually. "As I said, I've been having some problems with my health. I'm meant to be walking. The exercise is good for me, but I forget that I can't simply walk forever. I get tired much more quickly than I should."

"I'm sorry that you haven't been well. I hope all of the sea air will do you some good," Bessie replied.

"I'm sure it already has. That and the wonderful company," Andrew said, glancing at Bessie.

She was glad the sun was setting as she could only hope he couldn't see how much she was blushing from the compliment.

"But we need to get back and have our puddings," Andrew exclaimed. "I nearly forgot about my gateau."

When they reached Bessie's cottage, Andrew pulled into the parking area next to it. "As my cottage is quite close, I may just leave my car here, if that's okay with you," he told Bessie. "The car park for the cottages is considerably busier than this."

"Of course you can leave your car here," Bessie assured him.

They made their way into Bessie's cottage where she switched the kettle on straight away. "I shall want tea with my pudding," she said.

"Tea sounds wonderful."

A few minutes later they were sitting together at Bessie's table with tea and their boxes from the café. Andrew took a few bites of his gateau and then sighed. "This is incredible. I need to holiday here more often."

"You know you're always welcome," Bessie said. She felt herself flushing again and quickly focussed on her cake. "This was worth defending," she told Andrew after she'd eaten the last bite.

"As was mine," he sighed, "but now we must walk on the beach to work it off."

"I think we'd probably have to walk to Douglas and back in order to work off all of that cake," Bessie laughed. "I'm always happy to walk on the beach, though."

Darkness had fallen while they'd been eating, but the moon was large and bright in the clear sky. Lights in the holiday cottages helped to show them their way as well. Bessie headed for the sea first and then turned at the water's edge to walk along the wet sand. Andrew took her hand again as they went.

"I'm sure the sea air has restorative properties," he said after a short while.

"I credit it for my long and healthy life," Bessie replied.

They walked as far as Thie yn Traie before turning around. Bessie found herself watching Andrew closely, worried about his running out of energy, but he seemed fine. When they reached his cottage, he stopped.

"Maybe we should go inside and check my email," he suggested. "There may be something there from my colleague in Switzerland."

"Oh, yes, let's," Bessie agreed. She hoped he'd have a reply and that it would be interesting.

At first glance the cottage didn't really look occupied. Andrew was obviously keeping most of his things in the cottage's bedroom. There was a spare pair of shoes near the front door and a raincoat hanging on the hook behind the door, but otherwise there was nothing to suggest that anyone was staying there.

"Have a seat," he told Bessie. "I'll just go and get my laptop."

Bessie sat down on the couch and frowned. The furniture in all of the cottages looked considerably more comfortable than it actually was. Andrew was back a moment later. He sat down at the small dining table and opened his laptop. Bessie crossed to him and sat in the chair next to his.

The small machine clicked and whirred for what felt like several minutes before anything happened. Bessie waited patiently while

Andrew did what he needed to do. After a minute, he looked over at Bessie.

"I suppose I'd consider this bad news, really," he said. "My colleague has tracked down the woman I've been calling Abby. She died in a skiing accident about twenty years ago."

"He's sure it was an accident?" was Bessie's first thought.

Andrew nodded slowly. "It happened in Canada. The police there were convinced that it was an accident, anyway. My colleague is going to ask them for a copy of the full report, but he doesn't want to suggest in any way that they were negligent or anything, so he's treading very carefully."

"What about the other women?"

"He hasn't found any of the others yet."

"And where was Cindy when Abby died?"

"He doesn't know that, either. She was out of prison by then, of course, but she could have been anywhere in the world."

"What about the charity?"

"He doesn't know anything about that. It was a UK charity and he didn't feel any need to investigate it. He never even found out the name, so I shall have to start by looking for Betty's will to find out that detail. I know just the person to do that, fortunately. If you'll pardon me for a minute, I'll send an email."

"You have Betty's real name?"

"I do. My colleague was kind enough to share it in his reply. I won't tell you, though, if you don't mind."

"I don't mind," Bessie assured him. While he was typing, she tried to think what Abby's death might mean. It may have genuinely been an accident, of course, but she was highly suspicious of accidents, especially under the circumstances."

"Abby was on a skiing holiday in Canada?" Bessie asked when Andrew was finished sending his email.

"That's what my colleague said."

"She wouldn't have been alone," Bessie mused. "That's a long way to go for a holiday, as well."

"She had plenty of money and probably quite a few friends who would have been happy to go with her."

"I wish we knew more about that holiday."

"I do, too, but hopefully we'll get more information tomorrow. I'll send my colleague a long list of questions, but he can only tell me what he can learn from the Canadian authorities, of course."

"He should concentrate on finding Cindy," Bessie said. "I can't help but think that she's the key to the whole case."

"I'm inclined to agree with you, and I believe my colleague would agree as well. From what he said in his email, finding Cindy isn't proving all that easy, though."

Bessie sighed. "So now we just have to sit back and wait."

"Unfortunately, yes, at least for that case. We still have John's murder to solve, though."

"I haven't forgotten, but your case intrigues me more."

"I'm flattered, but I'm quite interested in the death of Jeanne Stowe, especially as it appears that no one had a motive."

"If I've learned anything from all of the different cases I've been involved with over the past year and a half, it's that motives for murder can spring from just about anywhere. Besides that, they often don't make sense to anyone other than the killer."

Andrew nodded. "You're right, of course, but from what I've seen of John Rockwell, he's good at his job. There's something about this case that's bothering him, which suggests to me that something was missed the first time around. I think talking to the various, um, witnesses could prove interesting."

"I'm happy to talk to anyone and everyone. If nothing else, it will help fill in the time while we wait for your colleague to get back to us."

"I should give him a name, too," Andrew laughed. "We keep calling him my colleague, which is sounding more and more awkward every time I hear it. Let's call him Lukas, as I had another Swiss colleague called that."

"We could probably use his real name. I'm highly unlikely to ever meet the man," Bessie suggested.

"I'd rather not. I know I spent too many years working with MI5 and MI6 on different operations, but I prefer to keep things as anonymous as possible whenever I can."

"You've had an interesting life."

"I have, really, and most of it I can't discuss," Andrew laughed. "I can tell you a few stories, if you'd like to hear them. I'll change all of the names, of course."

"Of course," Bessie laughed.

They moved over to the couch and sat together. Andrew told Bessie stories for hours, stopping to make tea after a short while and then continuing until Bessie was struggling to keep her eyes open.

"I'm boring you," Andrew said as Bessie yawned.

"Not at all," she replied quickly, "but it's getting late and I'm nearly always in bed before now."

"I should get you home, then. Tomorrow is another day."

"And I shall be up at six, no matter what time I go to bed."

"I usually set my alarm for seven, but I nearly always wake up well before it. I'm not great at sleeping these days, really. Maybe the sea air here will help with that as well."

"I hope so, for your sake," Bessie said. She rarely had difficulty sleeping, but she'd heard enough horror stories about insomnia to worry about it anyway.

Andrew insisted on walking Bessie back to her cottage. "I'll just check that everything is okay," he said when they reached it.

"Everything will be fine," Bessie told him. "You may stick your head in the door if you really want to, but that will be more than enough checking for tonight."

Andrew walked quickly through the ground level of Bessie's cottage. "I won't go upstairs," he told her. "You know where I am if you need me."

"I do, indeed," Bessie agreed.

"What are we doing tomorrow, then?" he asked in the cottage doorway.

"Maybe we should find out about a loan," Bessie suggested. "If Amanda McBride is free to discuss the matter, that is."

"And then we could have lunch in Port St. Mary," Andrew suggested. "I'll leave it up to you to decide where we eat."

"I suggest we have a big lunch somewhere before we head to the café where Mabel works," Bessie replied. "I think it would be best to go there for pudding or ice cream only."

"If they do ice cream, I'll be happy."

"You only think you'll be happy," Bessie muttered.

"What time shall I collect you?"

"The bank opens at nine, but it's only a short drive from here," Bessie told him. "We actually drove past it today when we went into Ramsey."

"I'll collect you at about quarter to nine, then. I'd suggest we meet earlier and go somewhere for breakfast, but I'm going to try to stick to the diet my doctor gave me, for breakfast, anyway. Porridge and fruit is just about all I can eat."

Bessie made a face. "I'd rather eat cereal, I think."

"I can have cereal, as long as I chose from a very short list of incredibly healthy cereals. Luckily for me, I actually like porridge."

"I hate it, but I wouldn't mind the fruit part."

"It's my favourite part, too. Anyway, I'll see you around half eight, quarter to nine."

"I'll be ready to go," Bessie promised.

She let the man out and locked the door behind him. It was past her usual bedtime, but she suddenly felt rather wide awake. There were bookshelves all around the cottage, and it took Bessie several minutes to locate the book that she wanted. One of her friends had once gone on a skiing holiday and she had brought Bessie back a book full of glossy photos and glowing descriptions of various ski resorts around the world.

After getting herself ready for bed, Bessie climbed under the duvet and switched on her bedside lamp. She flipped through the pages, stopping when she reached the section on Switzerland. Page after page of gorgeous pictures of snowy white mountains were followed by brief guides to the different resorts. Bessie wondered whether Andrew would tell her which ski resort the women had been staying at when Betty died. She read all of the short resort descriptions, shaking her head at the level of luxury offered by some of them. She couldn't imagine holidaying at a chalet with its own chef making gourmet meals three times a day, but clearly other people enjoyed such things. When she was done with Switzerland, she opened the book to the section on Canada.

It was a much larger section, and Bessie could feel her eyes drooping as she tried to work her way through the list of resorts. After a few pages, she gave up and put the book on her bedside table. Switching off the bedside light, she snuggled down under the duvet and fell asleep.

It was freezing cold and Bessie couldn't seem to get warm. There was a fire in the corner of the room, but there were too many people between Bessie and the fire for her to feel its warmth. As Bessie tried to push her way through the crowd, she could hear people shouting her name. When she stopped to listen, though, she realised that they were shouting "Betty" and not "Bessie." She gasped and then sat up in bed. Her clock told her that it was nearly six and time to get up anyway.

CHAPTER 6

Bessie showered and got dressed and then headed out for her morning walk. After a brisk stroll past the holiday cottages to Thie yn Traie and back home again, she made herself a light breakfast. As she reached into the cupboard for some cereal, her hand hovered near the porridge. She really didn't like it, but she tried to force herself to eat it once in a while, as she knew it was good for her. Pulling the box down, she found that it was now out of date. Sticking it back in the cupboard, she pulled down her favourite cereal and poured it into a bowl. Throwing away the porridge box would have meant adding it to her shopping list, so she simply ignored it for the day.

All of the curtains at Andrew's cottage had been tightly closed when she'd walked past. At half eight Bessie began to pace around her kitchen. She was worried about the two meetings that she and Andrew had planned for the day. Pretending to need a loan in order to see Amanda McBride felt wrong, but Bessie didn't know how else to arrange to see her. Getting into the woman's office wouldn't be difficult with their plan, but she couldn't imagine how Andrew was going to bring the conversation around to Jeanne Stowe's death without upsetting Amanda and getting them both thrown out of the bank. At least I keep my money elsewhere, Bessie thought.

She didn't want to think too much about the café in Port St. Mary, either. Her last visit there had been so unpleasant that she'd vowed never to go back. It was possible that the food had improved since then, but she hadn't heard anything to suggest that it had. She barely knew Mabel Lloyd, but she was pretty sure that Mabel wasn't the unpleasant woman who had waited on her all those years ago, at least. Again, Bessie couldn't imagine how Andrew would bring up the murder case without causing a scene.

At quarter to nine Bessie checked her hair one more time in the mirror. She didn't usually put much thought into her appearance, but she did feel as if she should make a little bit of an effort while Andrew was visiting. Chiding herself for being foolish, she picked up her handbag and opened the front door of her cottage. Andrew was nowhere in sight. After a moment's hesitation, Bessie walked out of the cottage and locked the door behind her.

There was a large rock on the beach behind Treoghe Bwaane. At high tide the base of the rock was covered in water, but now the tide was out, so Bessie walked to the rock and settled on top of it. From there she could watch the sea and also keep an eye out for Andrew. By nine she was starting to get worried. Maybe he's usually late, she told herself. He'd been late the previous day, after all. When her mobile phone began to ring, she jumped. Of course, the phone was in the bottom of her handbag and it took her ages to dig it out.

"Hello?"

"Ah, Bessie, it's Andrew. I hope you haven't decided to take off for Ramsey without me?"

"No, not at all. I'm just sitting on the rock behind my cottage enjoying the lovely day."

"Excellent. I'm sorry to say it, but the incredible sea air did wonders for my insomnia. I slept like a baby, right through my alarm clock. I haven't slept this well in a great many years, but now I'm afraid I'm terribly late."

"I'm glad you slept well. Come over when you're ready. You are on holiday, after all. You should be allowed to sleep late."

"But we have a murder to investigate," Andrew countered. "I'll be over as soon as I can get myself through a shower and into something decent."

"I'll be on the rock behind the cottage."

Bessie dropped her phone back into her bag with relief. She hadn't realised how worried she'd been about the man until he'd rung to say he was okay. And he'd had a good night's sleep, which was great news. If only she could say the same.

Less than half an hour later, Bessie spotted Andrew rushing towards her. She climbed down off the rock and walked up the beach to meet him.

"I'm so sorry," he said as he swept her into a hug.

"It's fine," she assured him. "We didn't make an appointment or anything, after all."

"But we did. I told you that I would collect you at quarter to nine. Now it's nearly ten. I'm embarrassed."

"You shouldn't be. It's all the fault of the sea air."

Andrew laughed. "You could be right about that. I'm feeling incredibly energetic today. Let's go and question some suspects."

"You know we aren't allowed to question them, exactly," Bessie said as they walked towards the man's car.

"Oh, I know. I shall be incredibly discreet, even as you discuss a loan or some such thing," he assured her. "Have you decided what you're going to say?"

"I was hoping that you might have some suggestions."

"I was a police inspector. I never had to justify why I was asking questions," Andrew said with a grin. "This is going to be quite interesting, I think."

The drive into Ramsey didn't take nearly long enough for Bessie. She was still trying to make up her mind about what she was going to say as Andrew pulled his car into the car park.

"Ready?" he asked, looking over at Bessie.

Bessie shook her head. "I've no idea what I'm going to say."

"Let's go. You can make it up as we go along."

Feeling entirely out of her element, Bessie followed the man out of the car. They were crossing the car park when the door to the bank swung open. Bessie recognised the woman who walked out the door.

"Amanda?" she called.

The tall, thin woman stopped and stared at Bessie. "Yes?" she said.

"It's Bessie Cubbon," Bessie said as she stopped in front of Amanda. "I was just coming in to see you. Are you having a break?"

"I'm, yes, er, I mean, sort of," the woman stammered. "Why did you want to see me?"

"Oh, I was just thinking about adding another addition to my cottage, but I wasn't sure about financing. You seem upset. Is everything okay?" Bessie asked.

"Not really, but it isn't anything you need to worry about. If you go inside and talk to Bev, she'll make you an appointment to see me. I'm afraid it will have to be later in the week, though," Amanda told her.

"That's fine. There's no rush," Bessie replied. "Are you sure you're okay?"

Amanda shook her head. "You've been involved in a lot of murder investigations, haven't you? When does it stop? When I can I finally stop thinking about it? When will they finally arrest someone so that I can sleep at night?"

Bessie patted the woman's arm. "What's happened?"

"The local paper today had an article about Jeanne in it," Amanda told her. "It was just delivered to the bank and everyone made sure to point it out to me. According to the paper, the police are thinking of reopening the investigation. The woman has been dead for five years. They never should have closed the investigation, should they?"

"They haven't," Bessie assured her. "Unsolved murders are never closed, but sometimes they reinvestigate cold cases. Maybe they'll try talking to the witnesses again, hoping that someone might remember something more this time around."

"I don't remember anything more," Amanda said, her eyes filling with tears. "I didn't know anything last time, anyway. I barely knew the woman."

"Would you like to go somewhere and talk about it?" Bessie asked.

"No, I mean, I don't want, that is, maybe," the woman replied. "If I can just talk and not have to answer any questions."

"Whatever you want," Bessie said soothingly.

Andrew put a hand on her arm. Bessie looked at him and then shrugged. "This is my friend Andrew," she told Amanda. "He's just visiting the island from across."

"It's nice to meet you," Amanda replied unenthusiastically. "There's a café across the road that does tea and coffee and biscuits. Let's go there. I won't promise that I'll say anything, but I think I'd like some company right now."

"I can go and find something else to do for a while," Andrew offered.

"No, you're more than welcome," Amanda said. "It isn't as if you'll even know who or what we're talking about, anyway."

Bessie and Andrew exchanged glances as they followed Amanda across the road. The café was small and badly lit, but it was also empty, something for which Bessie was grateful. They settled at a table near the window that gave them a little bit more light.

"What can I get you?" a woman shouted from behind the counter at the back of the room.

"Tea for three, and a plate of biscuits," Andrew called back.

"It'll be a minute or two," the voice replied.

"Or ten or twenty," Amanda said under her breath.

"I haven't seen you in years," Bessie said, wondering if she'd met the woman more than once or twice before. "How have you been?"

"Not good," Amanda replied with a shrug. "I feel as if I haven't slept or eaten properly since Jeanne's death. I feel as if I'm constantly waiting for the police to arrest someone, but they never do."

"Who do you think killed her?" Bessie asked bluntly.

Amanda blinked and then sighed. "That's the question, isn't it? I'd always thought it was Nick, but the police didn't stop him from moving away, so I'm probably wrong."

"Why Nick?" was Bessie's next question.

"Because he didn't want me to ring the police. He kept saying that

Jeanne was just being irresponsible, even though she was usually very good about letting me know if she was going to be late. I only rang the police on the Tuesday because Nick wasn't at the bank. He had a meeting in Douglas, so I went ahead and rang the police before he got into Ramsey. He was quite cross with me when he found out, but by that time the police had found Jeanne's body." Amanda shuddered and then blinked back tears.

Bessie dug around in her handbag for a tissue and passed it to the other woman. "If it wasn't Nick, who else might have killed her?" she asked after a minute.

"Kenny, maybe," Amanda suggested. "There was no love lost between those two. When Jeanne first started working at the bank, she was furious with the man. That mellowed slightly over the years, but she was still terribly bitter about their split."

"But why would he have killed her?" Bessie wondered.

"Maybe he got tired of her harassing him."

"She was harassing him?" Bessie was surprised.

"Oh, not to the point where the police were involved or anything, but she kept doing little things that I'm sure were making his life miserable."

"Like what?" Bessie demanded.

"She'd ring him and ask him to come over and help her with things around her flat, like changing light bulbs or repairing dripping taps. He always did it, too, because he felt guilty about keeping what had been their home together."

Bessie frowned. John hadn't mentioned any of this. "I'm surprised his second wife didn't complain."

"Sandra? I met her a couple of times. Back then she still thought Kenny was the best thing that had ever happened to her. I think if you talk to her today, you'll get a different answer, but at the time she was head over heels in love. I remember her telling me that she thought it was sweet that he was still looking after Jeanne. I know she felt guilty about coming between them, as well, even though she didn't even know Jeanne existed until after she'd fallen pregnant."

"I didn't know that," Bessie exclaimed.

"Oh yeah, Kenny was a real prince. He started seeing Sandra behind Jeanne's back and never bothered to tell Sandra that he was married. Goodness knows how long that might have gone on if Sandra hadn't fallen pregnant and forced the issue."

"But Jeanne was still getting Kenny to help her around her flat?" Bessie checked.

"Yeah, when she was between men, at least," Amanda said.

Before Bessie could reply, the waitress walked over with her tray and unloaded their tea and biscuits. Andrew was quick to help himself and settle back while Bessie took a sip of tea and tried to think of her next question.

"Jeanne had other boyfriends after Kenny, then?" was what she finally came up with.

"Oh, yes. Jeanne didn't like being on her own. She was with some guy called Ron almost immediately until he got tired of her demands and moved himself to Peel to get away from her."

Bessie was starting to think that Amanda hadn't like Jeanne very much. "And after Ron?"

"After Ron was someone called James. He stuck around for about a year before he managed to find an excuse to move back to the UK."

"She sounds as if she's a difficult person," Bessie said, trying to sound diplomatic.

"She was very difficult, but she worked hard and that was all that I cared about, really. I didn't enjoy listening to her talk about the men in her life, but she did enjoy telling me about them."

"What about after James?" Bessie asked.

"I don't know. I'm sure there was someone because she wasn't ringing Kenny every few days to change her light bulbs, but whoever it was, she didn't talk about him."

"Do you know why not?" Bessie wondered.

"At the time I assumed he was married. At first I thought maybe she'd gone back to Kenny and was seeing him behind Sandra's back, but I think she'd have told me if that were the case. After her murder, I started to think that maybe she was seeing Nick and that he'd grown tired of her demands and killed her."

"I suppose that's one possibility," Bessie said.

"It's the only one that makes sense, although the police didn't see it that way. They never arrested anyone."

"If it wasn't Nick that she was involved with, who else might it have been?" Bessie asked.

Amanda shrugged. "Jeanne could meet men anywhere. If she were here now, she probably would have found a man in this empty room. I never quite understood how she did it, but we'd be sitting somewhere having a cuppa and suddenly a man would start talking to her. Even when she was married to Kenny, she seemed to have men trying to talk her into going out with them all the time. They never seemed to last very long once they got to know her, but that was another matter."

Bessie glanced at Andrew. They were certainly finding out a lot about Jeanne Stowe. "But you don't know if she was actually involved with someone when she died or not?"

"Like I said, I'm sure she was, but I don't know who. Jeanne didn't like being single. I could never understand that. I'm very happy on my own."

The woman didn't look particularly happy, but Bessie didn't comment. "And you still think Nick had something to do with Jeanne's death?" she asked instead.

"Who knows?" Amanda sighed. "Five years ago I would have said yes, definitely, but the police never arrested him, so there mustn't have been any evidence against him. Maybe it was a random stranger. That happens sometimes."

"Did Jeanne take random strangers home with her?" Andrew asked.

Amanda looked startled at the question and then took a sip of tea. "Maybe, once in a while. I'm not actually certain. We weren't all that close, really. I mean, she told me about the various men in her life, the ones that she was with for any length of time, but whether she participated in one-night stands, well, I simply don't know the answer to that."

"Was she the type to do so?" was Andrew's next question.

Again Amanda took a sip of tea before she replied. Clearly something about this line of questioning was making her think about her answers. "I don't like to speak ill of the dead," she said after a moment. "As I said, Jeanne was a hard worker. She had some car trouble once in a while, which made her late, but beyond that she was reliable. Having seen how men behaved around her, yes, I do think that she might have participated in one-night stands from time to time, though. She had a different moral code to mine, I'm sure of that."

Andrew nodded and looked at Bessie. "If you think of anything that might help with the investigation, you should ring Inspector John Rockwell at the Laxey station," Bessie told the woman. "I don't know if the case is being reexamined or not, but John is very good at his job."

"I thought Inspector Kelly was in charge of the investigation," Amanda said.

"He's working in Douglas now in the drugs and alcohol unit. Inspector Clague in Ramsey is officially in charge of Jeanne's case. You could talk to him if you'd prefer. John is a friend of mine, that's all," Bessie explained.

"I know who he is and I know about your connection with him," Amanda replied. "It's been all over the papers for the past year."

Bessie flushed. "They don't always get everything right," she said softly.

Amanda shrugged. "The whole idea of the case being reopened upset me when I first heard about it, but it would be wonderful if someone could actually find the man or woman who killed Jeanne. As I said, I haven't slept properly since her death. I even thought about moving away, maybe to Peel or even up north, just to get away from it all."

"Remember anything you can tell the police would help," Bessie said.

Amanda nodded. "And now I must go home and have a good cry, I think," she said, getting to her feet. She opened her handbag and pulled out her wallet.

Bessie waved a hand. "Tea is on me," she said firmly.

"Are you quite certain?" Amanda asked, looking surprised.

"I am, yes. You've had an upset. Buying you a cuppa and a few biscuits is the least I can do," Bessie replied.

"Well, thank you," Amanda said. She put her wallet back in her bag and headed towards the door. "Yes, thank you," she repeated herself, glancing back at Bessie before she pushed open the café's door.

As the door swung shut behind Amanda, Bessie looked at Andrew. "That was interesting."

"It was indeed. We've learned a great deal about Jeanne, not least that Amanda didn't much like her or approve of her lifestyle. Obviously, John couldn't share what Amanda said in her original statement, but I suspect she told us more today than she told Inspector Kelly five years ago."

"I suspect you're right. I don't think she would have told him how she really felt about Jeanne, especially not right after the woman's untimely death."

Bessie took a biscuit and bit into it. Making a face, she put it down quickly.

"Yeah, they aren't great," Andrew whispered, "but I ate three of them because my breakfast seems to have been a long time ago."

"We should go and get some lunch somewhere, then," Bessie suggested. "Although it is a bit early for lunch, really."

Andrew grabbed another biscuit from the tray and then stood up. As he did so, the waitress wandered out from the kitchen. "All set?" she asked, handing Andrew the bill.

"Yes, thanks," he replied. He glanced at the slip of paper and then pulled some money out of his wallet. "That's fine, thank you," he told the woman as he handed her the money.

"Oh, my, well, thank you, sir," the woman replied.

Bessie raised an eyebrow and then stood up and followed Andrew out of the café. "That must have been a very generous tip," she suggested as they reached the car.

"It was, yes. I can afford it and she seemed as if she could use something to make her smile."

Bessie couldn't argue with the man. She slid into her seat and fastened her seatbelt as he climbed in beside her.

"Where are we going now?" he asked.

"How about lunch in Castletown?" Bessie suggested. "We may even have time for a short tour of the castle if you'd like to see it. I'm sure the café in Port St. Mary is open all day."

"It's open until six, and more importantly, Mabel works from one to six today," Andrew replied. "I rang this morning while I was waiting for my porridge to cook."

"What reason did you give for wanting to know when Mabel would be there?"

"I didn't give a reason, I just asked."

"I never would have thought to do that," Bessie told him.

"I'm rather used to simply asking questions and getting answers. I was with the police for a long time, remember?"

Bessie laughed. "And I'm just a nosy middle-aged woman. There is a difference."

Andrew smiled at her. "And yet you did wonderfully well getting information from Amanda just then."

"She was angry about the story in the paper. She just needed someone to talk to, and I happened to be there at the right time."

"Let's hope that Mabel has seen the article and is feeling similarly loquacious about it."

Bessie directed Andrew out of the car park and onto the mountain road that led to Douglas. As they went, she pointed out various points of interest.

"This road is a part of the TT Course," she said as they drove around a hairpin bend. "I assume you know all about the TT."

"It's a motorcycle road race, isn't it? I've heard of it, but I never really thought about what that meant. The bikes race on actual roads, then?"

"Oh, yes. The course is about thirty-seven miles long and goes from Douglas, across the centre of the island, and then around to Ramsey, across the mountains, and then back into Douglas. We can drive past the grandstand if you'd like to see it."

"If it's on our way, maybe, but let's not go out of our way. I'd really rather see the castle if we can find the time."

"It isn't out of our way, really," Bessie told him. "In fact, it's probably the fastest way to get through Douglas and head south."

"Castletown is near the airport, right?"

"Yes, that's right."

"So I may have driven right past the grandstand on my way to Laxey when I arrived."

Bessie laughed. "You may have. I'm not sure what route you took on your way north."

"The man at the car hire place gave me a map and I followed it. I probably should have left it in the car, but I think it's sitting on the table in my cottage right now doing me no good whatsoever."

"As long as I'm with you, you won't need it," Bessie assured him. "Even though I don't drive, I know the island well. Watch out here for trams."

"Trams?"

"This is the Snaefell Mountain Railway line," she told him as they passed over the bumpy tracks. "It's an electric railway that takes passengers from Laxey to the top of Snaefell, the highest peak on the island."

"Which one is Snaefell?" Andrew asked as he pulled his car over to the side of the road.

Bessie pointed out the railway line that could be seen snaking up the side of the mountain.

"It doesn't look taller than the other mountains," Andrew said.

"It is, though. You can see seven kingdoms from the top of Snaefell, if the weather is clear."

"Can you? Seven? England, Scotland, Wales, Ireland, and the Isle of Man. I'm missing two."

Bessie laughed. "You've missed the Kingdom of the Sea and the Kingdom of Heaven," she told him.

"And can you really see them all?"

"On a very clear day, yes, but there aren't very many clear days."

"So maybe I won't worry about getting to the top of Snaefell, at least not on this trip."

"I haven't been up there in years," Bessie told him. "Whatever the weather, there's a little café. It isn't a bad way to spend a few hours, if you have the time. Of course, I'd suggest the castles and museums are a better way to spend your time, but it is your holiday."

"I'm happy with castles and museums. Maybe the next time I come over we can take a tram up Snaefell."

"That sounds good," Bessie said. She hadn't realised that the man was planning another visit, but she was enjoying his company, so she wouldn't complain if he did come across again one day. She wasn't certain that his family would be as excited by the idea, but that was his problem, not hers.

Bessie pointed out a few more landmarks as they made their way towards Douglas. "And there's the TT Grandstand," she pointed out.

"They start and stop here? On what appears to be an ordinary piece of road?"

"It is an ordinary road most of the year," Bessie told him, "but it's also the start and finish of the TT."

Andrew shook his head. "I'm going to have to find out more about the TT. Now that I've seen some of the course, I'm fascinated by it all. Are we going to be driving on more of the course?"

"Not really. We need to head south now."

"Well, I remember this part of my journey from the airport," Andrew said a short time later. "All I kept thinking was how lovely the island is."

"I hope you said hello to the little people," Bessie said. "Wave now as we go over the bridge."

Andrew glanced at her and then raised a hand as Bessie waved. "Should I ask?"

"That was Fairy Bridge. You must always wave or say hello to the little people as you go over the bridge or else you'll have bad luck."

"Do people actually believe that?" Andrew demanded.

"I don't know if we all believe it or if we simply don't want to tempt fate," Bessie laughed. "It only takes a moment to wave, so why not?"

Andrew looked as if he wanted to argue, but after a moment he grinned at her. "Since I waved nicely, do I get extra good luck?"

"I certainly hope so."

"And there's the airport," Andrew said a few minutes later. "I have a rough idea where I am now, but everything south of here will be new to me."

"Castletown isn't hard to find. There are plenty of signs, and once you get close you'll be able to see the castle."

As they approached the island's former capital, Bessie directed Andrew down a side street and then into a small car park. "I find this is the best place to park for the castle," she told him. "We can walk over and take a look and then get some lunch. If you want to take the time, we can even go around the castle, either before or after lunch."

"Let's see how it looks from the outside."

They had only just gone around the corner when Andrew sighed. "I have to go inside. It's too wonderful to miss."

"Before lunch or after?"

"I'm starving, but maybe we should do it straight away. If I'm hungry, then I won't be as inclined to linger. I'd like to be at the café in Port St. Mary by two at the latest. I've arranged to ring Lukas at five and I'd rather do that from my cottage than anywhere else."

Bessie nodded. "Let's go, then. There is a lot to see, but I've seen it all hundreds of times. We can speed through most of it."

That was her plan, anyway, but it quickly became obvious that Andrew wasn't going to speed anywhere. As Bessie looked at her watch for the tenth time, he sighed.

"I'm really sorry, but I can't rush past all of this amazing history," he told her from in front of one of the castle's large display boards. "I really should have been a historian instead of a policeman."

"I don't mind, but I don't want you to be late for your phone call later."

"Yes, I know. It's my own fault. Maybe we could come back here again another day?"

"We can do whatever you want," Bessie assured him.

The assurance seemed to speed him up slightly, but it was still nearly two o'clock when they finally made their way out of the building and into the castle grounds.

"We don't have time to walk around the grounds, do we?" he asked.

Bessie shook her head. "Not if you want to get lunch and then talk to Mabel and still be back in Laxey for five."

"Maybe we should just get lunch at the café in Port St. Mary," he suggested.

"The last time I ate there the food was dreadful," Bessie reminded him.

"Yes, I know, but maybe it's improved? Or maybe we could just get something light like a toasted teacake or something and then make up for it at dinner time?"

Bessie was starving, but she was also sympathetic. She could hardly blame the man for being so enamoured of Castle Rushen that he'd taken his time admiring the place. "Let's go and see what they even have to eat," she suggested. "I'm sure we'll be able to find something on the menu that will keep us going for a few more hours."

The drive from Castletown to Port St. Mary didn't take a terribly long time. "I haven't been down here in a long time," Bessie said as they went. "I have a few friends who live down this way. I don't visit them as often as I should."

"It's rather a long way from Laxey," Andrew suggested.

"It feels as if it is, anyway. I'm sure it isn't as far as one side of London to the other, though."

"No, you're right, it isn't. Now, where am I going?"

Bessie navigated through the streets of Port St. Mary, eventually directing him into a small car park. "The café is only a few doors away. Let's just hope Mabel is in the mood for a chat."

CHAPTER 7

"I should have expected you, shouldn't I?" Mabel Lloyd demanded as Bessie and Andrew walked into the café. At least that was who Bessie assumed the woman was. It had been years since she'd seen the woman, and those years had not been especially kind to Mabel. While the woman had always been plump, she was larger now than Bessie remembered. Mabel was wearing thick glasses and an unflattering pink dress. Her brown hair was now more grey than brown and it was piled into a messy bun on the top of her head.

"Expected me?" Bessie echoed as she glanced around the empty café.

"Yeah, what with your friend Inspector Rockwell reopening the investigation into Jeanne's death and all. He sent you down here to snoop, didn't he? You'll ask me a bunch of rude questions and then you'll tell him everything I said. He can compare that to the statement I made five years ago and then decide that I'm lying and arrest me," Mabel suggested.

Bessie shook her head. "No one sent me down here to snoop. I'm showing a friend around the island and we thought we'd stop for a tea break, that's all."

"A friend? He looks like police."

"I was police," Andrew said with a small bow. "But I'm long retired. I'm Andrew Cheatham. It's a pleasure to meet you."

"Yeah, likewise," the woman drawled. "If you can find an empty table, take a seat."

Bessie and Andrew exchanged glances. Andrew crossed to a table near the wall and slid into a seat. Bessie sat down across from him.

"The menu is on the board," Mabel said, gesturing towards a chalkboard on the wall.

Reading through the list of options made Bessie's stomach growl. Andrew chuckled. "I'm hungry, too, but I'm not sure I want to eat anything in here," he said in a low voice.

Bessie glanced around at the sticky table and the cracked and peeling wallpaper on the wall next to them. "Maybe just a slice of cake or some biscuits," she suggested.

"Get the Victoria sponge," Mabel advised. "We buy that from a shop in Douglas. Everything else is homemade and I wouldn't recommend it."

A dozen questions sprang to Bessie's lips, but she bit her tongue and looked at Andrew.

"Sure, two slices of Victoria sponge and two cups of tea, please," he said after a moment.

"Won't take more than a minute," Mabel said before disappearing into the kitchen.

"She was expecting you," Andrew said quietly.

"I suppose I'm getting something of a reputation on the island," Bessie sighed.

"We can use that in our favour, though. Now that she's brought it up, we can ask her about the case."

"I just don't want her thinking that I'm going to run right back to John with everything she tells me."

"But you are."

"Yes, I know, but, oh, never mind." Bessie sighed and rested her head in her hand. As soon as her elbow touched the table she realised her mistake. When she pulled her arm back, she didn't want to look at her now sticky elbow.

"Should I start the questioning when she comes back, then?" Andrew asked.

"I will. It will seem more natural coming from me," Bessie said, after a moment's thought.

"Assuming she ever comes back," Andrew added, looking at his watch.

They chatted for twenty minutes about the castle they'd just toured before Bessie lost her patience. "They only have to slice two pieces of cake and boil a kettle," she complained. "What could possibly be taking so long? We're the only people here."

"Maybe Mabel decided she didn't want to talk to us, so she's hiding in the kitchen until we leave," Andrew suggested.

"Well, as far as I'm concerned, she can have her wish," Bessie snapped. She got to her feet and headed for the door. Andrew was only a few steps behind her when the kitchen door suddenly swung open.

"Running out without paying the bill?" Mabel demanded.

"We didn't get served anything that needs paying for," Bessie replied tightly.

"But I have your cake and tea right here," Mabel told her, nodding towards the tray she was carrying. "I would have been faster, but the kettle kept shorting out."

Bessie looked at Andrew and he shrugged. Clearly the decision to stay or go was hers. She looked at Mabel and then sighed. "We don't have much time," she told the woman as she crossed back to her seat. "Maybe you could join us for a minute, though. Now that you've brought it up, I'd love to hear more about that murder case you mentioned."

Mabel narrowed her eyes suspiciously. "Now that I've brought it up? Are you trying to tell me that you don't know anything about Jeanne's murder?"

"No, not at all. Obviously, I remember hearing about it when it happened, but that was five years ago, and you were right at the centre of the case. As Andrew said, he used to be with the police. I'm sure he'd enjoy hearing the story while we eat."

Mabel passed around their tea things and cake plates, looking thoughtful. When her tray was empty, she put it on a nearby table and sat down next to Bessie. "Sure, why not," she said. "I'll tell you about the case. I'll expect a big tip for my time, though."

"That's fair enough," Andrew said. He took a sip of tea and then settled back in his seat.

Bessie smiled at Mabel. "Why don't you just tell us about Jeanne? How long were you two friends?"

"Not all that long," Mabel said with a shrug. "She was working for that bank in Ramsey and I was working at the café across the street. We got to talking one day when she was having lunch with some guy. They'd had a fight and he'd walked out, you see. She was kinda upset, so I took her in the back room and let her cry on my shoulder."

"That was kind of you," Bessie said. She took a sip of the lukewarm, weak tea and then picked up her fork. How bad could the cake be?

"We both had bad luck with men, me and Jeanne," Mabel said. "I was on my second husband back then and she was in the middle of her divorce. That Kenny broke her heart and then he killed her, I'm sure of it."

"Why would he kill her?" Bessie asked. She still hadn't worked up the nerve to try the cake. When she looked up, she saw that Andrew was watching her closely, his own cake still untouched.

"Because he's a horrible person. He broke Jeanne's heart, but that wasn't enough for him. He had to murder her as well. I know he found Jeanne annoying, because she rang him once in a while for little favours, but he'd been married to her when he got another woman pregnant. In my book that made him responsible for her when she needed help."

"But he didn't agree?"

"Oh, I don't think he minded much. No, it was that girlfriend of his that minded. It wasn't bad enough that she'd seduced him and managed to get him to get her pregnant. She used to carry on something awful whenever he went over to help out poor Jeanne, as I understand it, anyway."

"But you never thought that she might have killed Jeanne?"

"Oh, no. She wouldn't have had the nerve. I reckon she just nagged Kenny into it. Not that he would have needed much nagging, mind. Like I said, he was tired of her and all of her demands."

"It's all terribly sad," Bessie said. "What about other men in Jeanne's life? Could any of them have wanted to kill her?"

"Oh, I doubt it. She had a few short relationships after she and Kenny split, but she never really got over Kenny, as far I could tell. Whenever another relationship ended, she was quick to ring Kenny and get him around for something, that's for sure. Although, once I met Howard, she started ringing him instead."

"Howard?" Bessie echoed.

"Yeah, my third husband. I reckon he's going to stick around, too. It only took me three tries to find a good one."

"When did you start seeing Howard?" Bessie asked.

"Oh, a few months after my second divorce. I met him at ShopFast in the frozen food aisle. He was buying some frozen pizzas and I asked him which ones were best for just one person. He said maybe we should just share one, instead of both of us eating alone. We've been together ever since."

"And he was friendly with Jeanne?" was Bessie's next question.

"Oh, aye, because she was my dearest friend, you know? She used to ring him up to help her with little projects around her flat when she couldn't reach Kenny or whatever other guy she was seeing at the time."

Bessie finally gave in and forked up a bit of cake. "And you didn't mind?" she asked before she put the bite in her mouth.

"Mind? Why would I mind? Like I said, Jeanne was my dearest friend. I usually went with him, and we'd take care of Jeanne's little problem and then have a few drinks together, or whatever."

Bessie swallowed the surprisingly edible bite. "And you and Howard are still together?"

"We got married, didn't we? Not long after Jeanne passed, actually. Howard was pretty shaken up by her death, and he decided he wanted to make our relationship more official. We've been living happily ever after ever since."

Bessie took another bite of cake while her mind raced. John hadn't mentioned anyone called Howard. Was it possible that the man was missed during the initial investigation, or had he been eliminated from suspicion? She looked over at Andrew, who was just now cautiously trying his cake. "Did Howard have any theories on who might have killed Jeanne?" she asked Mabel.

"He was with me. He always reckoned it was Kenny. He'd seen Kenny shouting at Jeanne more than once, same as me."

"What about Jeanne's job? Was there anything about her job that seemed odd?"

"Besides her boss, you mean?" Mabel asked.

"Her boss?" Bessie repeated.

"That woman, Amanda McBride. She was a snobby witch, although I'd spell it with a b if I had to spell it."

"Really?" Bessie said.

"Oh, yes. She used to shout at Jeanne something terrible whenever Jeanne was even a minute late. Jeanne had some car trouble for a few weeks and the woman nearly let her go because of it. My Howard ended up taking Jeanne into work a few times to help her out. It was awful."

"What about Nick Grant?" Bessie asked.

Mabel smiled. "Ah, he was gorgeous, was Nick. I'd have liked to get to know him better, but he was already married and not the type to spend time with a woman like me, anyway. I always thought Jeanne could have had a chance with him, but she always said she wasn't interested."

"And he was married," Bessie said.

"Yeah, but that wouldn't have stopped him from going after Jeanne if she'd given him any encouragement. I mean, he wasn't going to leave his wife or anything, but I'm sure he'd have been good for a few nice presents, and maybe a holiday somewhere fancy as well."

Bessie bit her tongue and then decided to finish her cake instead. It wasn't anywhere near the best Victoria sponge she'd ever eaten, but it wasn't terrible, and she was hungry. She washed it down with another sip of the unpleasant tea and then looked at Andrew. He'd finished his cake as well.

"I don't suppose we should take up any more of your time," he said to Mabel. "If you remember anything about Jeanne or her death, you should ring the police and let them know."

"I remember everything about Jeanne, but I told the police all of it when it happened. I hope the police aren't going to start asking questions again. It was very upsetting the first time and I don't fancy doing it all again."

"They'll only ask questions because they want to work out what happened to Jeanne," Bessie told her. "You do want them to find her killer, don't you?"

"Yeah, of course I do, but, well, maybe after all this time it would be better if they just left things alone."

The café door swung open. A tall man who looked around fifty stood in the doorway. He was wearing dirty jeans and a stained T-shirt. His hair was plastered to his head and he looked as if he needed a shower. He glanced at Bessie and Andrew and then focussed on Mabel. "We need to talk," he said curtly.

"Yeah, sure, honey," Mabel said, jumping to her feet. "We can talk in the kitchen. Paul is on his break."

"I'm going to guess that that was Howard," Bessie whispered as the pair left the room.

"That seems a safe guess," Andrew replied. "I wonder why John didn't mention him when he told us about the case."

"I didn't like him."

"I'd like to learn his surname."

Bessie nodded. That was something to ask Mabel when the woman returned. Several minutes ticked by with no sign of either Mabel or the man. "Maybe we should check on Mabel," Bessie said eventually.

"That might be a good idea," Andrew replied with a frown. He got to his feet and headed for the kitchen door. Just before he reached it, it swung open.

"Mabel asked me to give you this," the man told Andrew, handing him their bill. "She isn't feeling well. She's gone to lie down before the dinner rush."

"Is she okay?" Bessie demanded, getting to her feet.

"She's fine. Just tired, that's all," the man said. "You can pay me," he added with a smirk.

"I'm Inspector Andrew Cheatham," Andrew said in his most serious tone. "And you are?"

"Just helping out Mabel by getting you to pay your bill," the man replied.

"I'm happy to pay the bill. I just want to be sure that Mabel is okay," Andrew told him.

"She's fine. Like I said, she's gone home to lie down. She'll be back here in an hour or so. You can check on her then."

"I think I'd rather check on her now," Andrew replied.

The man shook his head. "I'm sorry, I get that you're a policeman and all, but I don't understand what the problem is. I came to talk to my wife about a private matter and she got upset. I sent her home and told her that I'd take care of her customers. Why are you giving me such a hard time about this?"

"We're just worried about Mabel," Bessie interjected. "She was already upset when you arrived. We were talking about Jeanne Stowe's death."

"Jeanne Stowe?" the man sounded surprised. "I haven't heard that name in over five years, I'm sure. She was Mabel's closest friend. No wonder she was upset when I got here. Why were you talking about Jeanne?"

"There was an article in today's paper about her murder. Apparently, the police might be reinvestigating the case," Bessie replied.

"That would be good news. I'm sure Mabel would love to see the killer found and locked up. She's never really forgiven herself for not being with Jeanne that night," the man told her.

"Why would she have been with Jeanne that night?" Bessie asked.

"They were meant to be going out for a meal, but, well, Mabel and I hadn't been going out together for long and I asked her to have dinner with me instead. Mabel rang Jeanne and cancelled their plans at the last minute so that she could be with me. When the body was found, Mabel was really afraid that it was going to turn out to have been suicide. She would have blamed herself," the man explained.

"You knew Jeanne. Who do you think killed her?" Bessie tried the question.

"Me? I've never really given it much thought," the man replied. "When it happened, I was really busy trying to help Mabel get through it. Who killed Jeanne? It's a good question. Mabel always insisted that it was Kenny, but I don't know about that. I never thought he was strong enough. He didn't even have the nerve to stand up to her and tell her to stop ringing him all the time. I mean, he would tell her to stop, but then the next time she rang, he'd drop everything and rush over to help her. I still don't know why that girlfriend of his put up with it."

"Maybe she killed Jeanne," Bessie suggested.

"I like that idea," the man said with a grin. "Kenny divorced Jeanne for Sandra, but even that wasn't enough, so Sandra killed her. It would make a great plot for a television show, but I don't think that's what really happened. Sandra was worse than Kenny, really. She never could stand up to either of them. She hated Jeanne for making Kenny rush around to help her, and she hated Kenny for going. I think if she were going to snap and murder someone, it would have been Kenny, though."

"What about other men in Jeanne's life?" Bessie asked.

"Well, there were certainly plenty of them," the man laughed. "I mean, she'd barely left Kenny and she was already seeing some guy called Ron. They had lots of problems, though. Then she was with James for a while. He was a good guy, but they still fought a lot. I found out all of this later, of course. I didn't start seeing Mabel until only a few months before Jeanne died. She'd already ended things with James by that time, but I got to hear all about him, Ron, and Kenny. Jeanne used to spend a lot of time at Mabel's flat complaining about her exes."

"Whom was she seeing just before she died?" was Bessie's next question.

"I don't know if she was seeing anyone or not. I think she was more or less just playing the field, not getting serious about anyone at that point," he replied. "She said something one day about some guy from her office. Rick or Nick or something like that."

"Did she now?" Andrew asked.

"Yeah, she did. It wasn't like she was seeing him, but more like she'd been with him, if you know what I mean. But she wasn't exactly the shy and retiring type when it came to men. She slept with just about every one of my friends when she met them."

"I didn't catch your name," Andrew said.

"Oh, sorry. I'm Howard, Howard Miles. Mabel and I have been married for a few years now, but she still uses her maiden name. I suppose after two divorces she decided that was easier than changing things again."

"Could you give me the names of these friends of yours who were involved with Jeanne, as well, please?" Andrew asked.

Howard looked startled and then shook his head. "I don't want to get my mates into any trouble, you know. I mean, they're all married men now, and some of them were married back then. They don't need to be caught up in an old murder investigation."

"If they were involved with the victim, they should have been questioned when Jeanne was killed," Andrew told him.

"It wasn't like they were actually involved with her, though, I mean not long-term or anything. Jeanne was just, well, she liked men a lot and she was really good at attracting them. She was really demanding once she got her hooks into a guy, though. I'd seen that firsthand and I warned my mates before I introduced them to her. They all just had a little fun and then let it go, if you know what I mean."

Bessie shuddered. She felt sorry for Jeanne, but she simply couldn't understand the woman's behaviour. No one deserved to be murdered, though, no matter what.

"The police can speak to your friends very discreetly," Andrew said. "Their wives won't even have to know."

"I'll have to think about that," Howard said. "You can talk to Max, though. Max Rogers. He's single and he'll probably think it's funny, being questioned about an old murder case. He and Jeanne got real friendly real fast and then split up within like a week. There's no way he'll be able to help with the investigation, but that's true for all of my friends."

"I appreciate that name, anyway," Andrew said. "One of my colleagues from the Ramsey station will probably be in touch to get more."

Howard flushed. "I'd really rather not, that is, I can't..." he trailed off and sighed. "I'll talk to my friends. Maybe some of them will come forward on their own now that they know the case is being reopened. It wasn't that many guys, anyway, maybe three, and I gave you Max's name."

Andrew nodded. "And now I just need a word with Mabel and we'll be on our way."

"With Mabel? I told you, she's gone home," the man protested.

"You must live close by, then," Andrew suggested.

"Yeah, we do. But I don't want you bothering Mabel. She needs to rest for a bit before she comes back to work."

Andrew exchanged glances with Bessie. When the man had first walked out of the kitchen, Bessie had been convinced that he'd done something awful to Mabel, but now that they'd talked for a while, she was feeling less certain. As the trio stood and stared at one another, the door to the kitchen swung open again.

"Are you still here?" Mabel demanded. "You haven't been bothering Howard about Jeanne, have you? The poor man comes to talk to me about something and you start badgering him about Jeanne?" She crossed the room to Howard and put her arms around him. "Are you okay?" she asked.

"I'm fine. They're still here because they were worried about you," he told her.

"Worried about me? I went home to get my headache tablets and grab a bite to eat. Worried about me? What did they think had happened to me?" Mabel asked.

"I think they thought I hit you or something," Howard said.

Mabel laughed. "He knows better than to try that. I'd hit him back and he'd be well sorry."

Howard laughed. "Don't I know it." He turned to Andrew. "As you can see, Mabel is absolutely fine."

"I'm sorry, but in my line of work we see a lot of domestic abuse. I was just exercising an abundance of caution," Andrew told him.

"It's fine. I suppose I should be grateful that the police look after people. Anyway, now that you know that Mabel is fine, maybe you'd like to get back to your investigation and we'll get back to our lives."

Andrew nodded. He pulled out his wallet and took out a handful of notes. After handing them to Mabel, he turned and offered Bessie his arm. She took it and the pair made their way out of the café. Neither spoke as the walked back to Andrew's car and climbed inside. As Andrew pulled away from his parking space, Bessie glanced back at the café. Mabel appeared to be crying in Howard's arms.

"That was interesting as well," Andrew said once he'd found his way back out of Port St. Mary.

"It certainly was. I didn't like Howard at all at first, but he grew on me," Bessie admitted.

"Yes, and he and Mabel seemed quite happy together, really. I almost felt bad for thinking that he'd done something to her in the kitchen. But only almost. I'm not sure I believed anything he said, anyway."

"I wondered if he and Jeanne ever got together," Bessie said. "If she was as generous with her favours as he suggested, I mean."

"Mabel did say that Jeanne rang him all the time to do little jobs around her flat. Mabel didn't seem to be jealous, but I'm not sure why she wasn't."

"I would have been, in her place," Bessie said after thinking about it for a moment.

"We'll have to share everything that we've learned with John," Andrew said. "I think we should do it soon, as well."

"I'll ring him and see if he's available tonight," Bessie suggested.

"Maybe I can persuade him to bring pizza or something with him when he comes over."

"I was just going to suggest stopping somewhere on the way home for something. I'm starving over here."

"But you have your phone call to get back for," Bessie reminded him.

"I know," he sighed, "and I'm looking forward to talking to Lukas. I'm just hungry."

"On a positive note, the Victoria sponge wasn't bad."

"No, it was certainly edible, but it didn't really feel as if it were an indulgence, either. When I eat cake, I want to feel guilty afterwards."

Bessie laughed. "I know what you mean, but maybe you don't feel guilty because we didn't have any lunch."

"Maybe. Why don't you ring John and see if he can meet us at your cottage at half five. If he can bring food, any food, I'll be in his debt forever."

"I'm sure he'll be agreeable, if he isn't busy." He wasn't busy, and by the time Bessie put her mobile back in her bag, everything was arranged.

"John will be at Treoghe Bwaane with pizza, garlic bread, and something for pudding around half five. He's going to invite Doona and Hugh to join us as well," she told Andrew.

"It will be nice to see Doona again," he replied. "I feel as if I know Hugh because I've heard so much about him. It will be nice to finally meet him."

The drive back across the island seemed to take forever, mostly because Bessie was watching the clock the entire time. As they were heading back to Laxey rather than Ramsey, Bessie had Andrew take the coast road.

"The scenery is enough to make anyone want to live here," he sighed as they rounded a bend. The sea seemed to stretch out endlessly in front of them for a moment before the road curved back around.

"I love it, but I especially love the view from my cottage."

"You're spoiled," Andrew laughed. "I've only been here a day and

I'm already madly in love with the view from my cottage. I don't even want to think about going back to London where I look at other blocks of flats on all sides."

"I can't even imagine," Bessie sighed. "I know I'm quite spoiled, but I didn't realise that when I bought my cottage. Would you believe I didn't even think about the view? The cottage was just about the only thing I could afford because it was tiny and a bit run-down, even then. I probably paid a few pounds extra for the location, being right on the sea, but that wasn't as much of a thing in those days. Lots of houses and cottages were right on the sea, or so it seemed."

"How old were you when you bought it?"

"Eighteen, and only just eighteen," Bessie told him. "I'd been forced to leave the man I loved in the US and move back to the island with my parents. When he tried to follow me, he didn't survive the sea journey. Before he'd left for the island, he'd written out his will, and in it he left me his entire fortune. It wasn't much, really, but it was enough for me to buy my cottage."

"I'm sure we've talked about this before," Andrew said. "You said you'd never held down a paying job, didn't you?"

"That's right. My advocate invested my inheritance for me and somehow managed to generate a small income from what was left after I'd bought Treoghe Bwaane. In the early years, I struggled and I often thought about finding work, but I hadn't any good qualifications and there weren't many jobs in Laxey. Not driving was another complication. Anyway, women didn't really work in those days, especially not once they were married. It all worked out though, over time. Now that I'm getting older, there's almost too much money. I indulge myself with books and all the expensive chocolate truffles I want, and my advocate assures me that my heirs will still be left with something."

"If I'm not being too personal, who are your heirs?"

"My sister's family is all in the US. I shall be leaving my money to whoever is still around when I go," Bessie told him.

"I hope someone wants your cottage. It should stay in the family."

Bessie shrugged. "It will be up to them what they want to do with everything. I don't worry about it as I won't be around to know."

Andrew pulled into the parking area behind Bessie's cottage with just a few minutes to spare.

"Go and ring your friend," Bessie told him. "I'll put the kettle on. By the time you're finished, John should be here with the pizza."

"I certainly hope so," Andrew called over his shoulder as he rushed towards his cottage.

Bessie let herself into Treoghe Bwaane and looked around her cozy kitchen. Her heirs would be crazy to keep this place, she thought as she refilled the kettle with fresh water.

CHAPTER 8

John and the pizzas arrived first. Bessie gave him a hug with her mouth watering. "I hope the others get here quickly," she told the man. "I didn't get much lunch and that smells wonderful."

"Doona is bringing pudding," he replied as he set the pizza boxes on Bessie's counter.

"That probably means something chocolate," Bessie said happily.

Doona arrived a moment later with a large box of chocolate fairy cakes. "I thought about getting a few other flavours, but you can't go wrong with chocolate," she said as she handed Bessie the bakery box.

Hugh was only a minute behind Doona. Bessie had him bring a chair from the dining room into the kitchen, and then he and John shuffled all of the chairs around the table to make room for it. Bessie found herself studying the young man as he moved things around the small space.

In her eyes, he didn't look much older than fifteen, although now that he was married with a child on the way she fancied that he looked more mature. She'd known him for most of his twenty-something years, and as she remembered it, he'd always wanted to be a policeman. He'd had something of a reputation for being lazy when he'd been younger, but under John's tutelage he was working harder than ever. His brown hair nearly always looked as if it needed cutting, and today was no exception.

"I expected Andrew to already be here," John commented as he sat down in one of the chairs.

"He had to ring someone," Bessie explained. "Actually, he had to ring his colleague in Switzerland, the one with the cold case that we discussed."

"Really? I hope he manages to learn more about the case. I found it fascinating," John replied.

While they waited, Bessie quickly told Doona and Hugh about Andrew's case. "I'm sure I'm leaving things out, but that's a rough outline of the story, anyway," she said when she was finished.

"I'm not sure I understand why it's a cold case," Doona said. "Surely if the killer confessed and went to prison, the case is solved."

"Andrew's friend, Lukas, never felt as if the case was properly solved," Bessie explained. "He always felt as if he'd missed something."

"We all have cases like that," Hugh said. "There isn't much you can do about them, really. We don't have time to keep investigating cases that are closed."

"Bessie had an interesting theory about Andrew's case, though," John said.

A knock in the door interrupted the conversation. Bessie opened it and Andrew rushed inside. "I'm terribly sorry that I'm so late," he said. "Lukas simply can't be brief."

"It's fine, but let's get our plates filled before anything gets cold," Bessie suggested. She quickly introduced the man to Hugh before passing around plates.

A few minutes later the five were sitting around the table with food and cold drinks. After her first few bites, Bessie began to feel more like herself again. "This is really good," she told John. "Where did it come from?"

"A new place that just opened across from the station," he told her. "The constables are going to love it."

"Me, too," Doona said.

"While we were waiting for you, I told Doona and Hugh about your cold case," Bessie told Andrew.

"And I was just going to tell them about Bessie's theory," John said. He took a sip of his drink and then told the others what Bessie had suggested.

"So Betty killed Cindy and then pretended to be her, but we don't know why," Doona mused. "There definitely seems to be more to the case than meets the eye."

"And I just talked to Lukas. I told Bessie earlier, but he tracked down Abby. She was killed in a skiing accident in Canada about ten years after Betty's murder. Tonight he told me that he's found Flora."

"I hope she's okay," Bessie said.

Andrew shook his head. "She died in a car crash in Belgium about a year after Abby's death," he told her. "Lukas is going to request a copy of the police report, but at the moment he doesn't have any reason to suspect that it was anything other than an accident."

Bessie sat back in her chair and stared at the man.

"I don't really like coincidences," John said. "He hasn't been able to find Cindy?"

"No, but he's stepping up his efforts to locate her. He doesn't believe in coincidences, not like this, anyway," Andrew replied.

"Why would Cindy want to kill the other three women?" Doona asked.

"Maybe because they're the only ones who know who she really is?" Hugh suggested.

"But she went to prison for killing her sister. Would she really be in that much more trouble for impersonating her?" Bessie wondered.

"A lot will depend on what was in Betty's will," Andrew said. "I have a friend in London working on finding that for me."

"I hope he finds Dorothy soon. If she is still alive, maybe she'll be willing to talk once she finds out the others are all dead," Bessie said.

"That's what Lukas is hoping for, but he isn't optimistic. He's going to email me as soon as he learns anything, though," Andrew replied.

"And he's certain there wasn't a sixth person staying at the chalet and that there wasn't any way anyone could have managed to sneak in, either?" Hugh asked.

"He's fairly sure that there were only five guests and that no one else arrived that evening. If they did, they bypassed the resort and went straight to the chalet, which would have been difficult. The chalet was on the resort's grounds and the entire complex is fenced. The only way to reach the grounds is by walking through the resort first. After midnight, there was meant to be tight security," Andrew explained.

"So maybe someone from one of the other chalets or the resort itself came to visit," Doona suggested.

"According to Lukas, the possibility of that is remote," Andrew told her. "He's going back through all the statements, though, just in case he missed something. Remember that the storm came in very quickly and didn't let up for many hours. If someone else was visiting the chalet, he or she probably would have been stuck there until the chalet was dug out."

"Bessie, you're going to have to ring all of us every time Andrew hears anything," Doona said.

"I think I can manage that," Bessie laughed.

When everyone was stuffed full of pizza and garlic bread, Doona cleared the table and then brought out the box of fairy cakes. Bessie made tea to go with pudding and then they all settled in again.

"Time to talk about my case," John said. "The one I'm not officially investigating."

"You need to tell Dan Ross that," Bessie said, referring to the reporter with the local paper. "I haven't actually seen today's paper yet, but apparently there's an article in it about the case being reopened."

"Is there?" John said, sounding not at all surprised. "I wonder how that happened."

Bessie narrowed her eyes at him. "You didn't give the story to Dan Ross, did you?" she demanded.

"As I've been specifically told not to reinvestigate the case, that wouldn't have been wise, would it?" John asked.

"You didn't answer the question," Bessie pointed out. "You told Dan about the case to see if you could start people talking, didn't you?"

John shrugged. "As I'm not officially investigating anything, putting a story like that into the local papers might help to get the case a bit of attention. I can assure you that I haven't spoken to Dan Ross in weeks, however."

Bessie considering the carefully worded denial and then shrugged. "You're right about the story getting some attention," she told him. "We talked to Amanda and Mabel today and they were both wound up about the whole thing."

"Tell me everything from today," John replied.

Bessie took John back through the day, having Andrew help her as she tried to remember everything that was said. When she was finished, she took a sip of tea and then ate her fairy cake, feeling she'd earned it.

"You've already learned things that don't appear in Inspector Kelly's notes," John said. "Under the circumstances, it might be wise for me to speak to both women myself, and to Howard, although I may have to do so with Carl's cooperation. I must say, they've painted a rather different picture of Jeanne than I got from Inspector Kelly's notes."

"Was Howard mentioned anywhere in the case file?" Andrew asked.

"I'm going to have to have Carl go through it and check. I believe there was a brief mention of the man as Mabel's boyfriend. I don't think there was anything there to suggest that he was someone who made frequent visits to Jeanne's flat, either with or without his wife," John replied.

"I think a chat with Max Rogers could be instructive," Andrew said, "and with Jeanne's two former boyfriends, if they can be found."

"Ron is still in Peel," John told him. "I'm working on tracking down James Poole."

"We were going to go to Peel tomorrow, weren't we?" Andrew asked Bessie. "Where does Ron work?"

"He's an estate agent," John replied.

"Maybe I should be looking at houses, then," Andrew suggested. "The island is truly lovely, and I'd love to live here, really."

"We can visit Ron and then go around Peel Castle," Bessie suggested.

"We seem to have a plan," Andrew nodded.

"You'll never guess who just found a job with Manx National Heritage," John said.

"Who?" Bessie asked.

"Sandra Oliver," John replied. "As I understand it, she's currently working in the gift shop at Peel Castle."

"How incredibly convenient," Bessie said.

"Is the island truly this small or are we just having good luck?" Andrew asked.

"It's a bit of both, I think," Bessie replied.

"When you told me about the case, you said everyone had the means and the opportunity," Hugh said. "Should we try talking about motive, then?"

"That's the problem," John told him. "From what everyone has said, no one seems to have had any motive for killing the woman."

"Kenny did," Doona suggested. "Everyone has agreed that Jeanne used to ring him up and get him to do little jobs around her flat. Maybe he simply grew tired of the demands."

Bessie found a piece of paper and wrote Kenny's name at the top of it. "It seems a fairly flimsy reason for killing someone. I mean, why couldn't he simply refuse to keep helping?"

"Guilt," Doona said. "He felt terrible for the way he'd treated her, so he felt as if he had to keep helping her, until it all finally got to be too much and he killed her."

"If he felt guilty about leaving her, surely he'd have felt even worse about killing her," Hugh suggested.

"Maybe he didn't mean to kill her, maybe he just wanted her to leave him alone for a short while. Maybe he was hoping she'd sleep for a few days or something," Doona said.

"I think, having looked at the lab report, that whoever drugged her wanted her dead. They didn't just slip her a few extra sleeping tablets. They gave her a whole chemist's shop full of medications," John said.

"I think Kenny should be at the top of the suspect list," Doona said firmly.

"He is, at least on the top of my list," Bessie said, holding up the sheet of paper with only one name on it.

Everyone laughed. "More fairy cakes, anyone?" Doona asked. It didn't take her long to persuade them all to have a second cake.

"I'd add Sandra to the list, and put her fairly high up,' Hugh said once Doona had sat back down. "If anything, she had more reason for wanting Jeanne dead than Kenny did. She was at home with two small children while Kenny was running over to Jeanne's to change light bulbs."

"Who doesn't change their own light bulbs?" Doona asked. "I mean, I'm not any good at DIY, but I can change a light bulb. I can't imagine ringing an ex and asking him to come over and do it for me."

"Maybe the light bulb thing was an exaggeration," Bessie said.

"I certainly hope so. If it wasn't, I can certainly see Sandra wanting to kill the woman," Doona replied.

"I'm going to reserve judgment on her until after we've met her tomorrow," Andrew said. "I'd say she definitely belongs on the list, though."

Bessie added the woman's name under Kenny's.

"What about Amanda McBride? She sounded as if she didn't like Jeanne," Hugh said.

"I got the feeling that she didn't like Jeanne much, but that she appreciated that Jeanne worked hard," Andrew said. "At least when her car was running, she did."

"Maybe Amanda had a secret crush on Kenny or some other guy with whom Jeanne was involved," Doona suggested.

"I got the impression that Amanda doesn't have much time for men, generally," Bessie told her. "I may have misread her, of course."

"I'd agree with Bessie on that, actually. If Amanda killed Jeanne, it wasn't over a man," Andrew said.

"Does she go on the list or not?" Hugh asked.

"Everyone needs to go on the list," Andrew told him. "She should probably go near the bottom, though."

Bessie added the woman's name about halfway down the sheet of paper. "What about Mabel?" she asked.

"Mabel was harder to read," Andrew said with a frown. "I think if she'd found out that her husband was having an affair with Jeanne, she would have killed her, but she didn't seem to have had any suspicions in that area."

"Which was odd, really, as she told us that Jeanne attracted men easily and that her husband was often at Jeanne's flat, ostensibly helping her out. Surely she must have put two and two together at some point," Bessie said.

"Perhaps she simply trusts her husband," Hugh suggested.

"Having met him, I wouldn't trust him," Bessie said. "He struck me as the kind of man who would cheat if he thought he could get away with it."

"Again, I'd have to agree with Bessie. Howard seemed untrustworthy in every way," Andrew said.

"Do you really think that she'd kill her closest friend over a man?" Hugh asked.

Bessie looked at Andrew and then nodded. "Howard is her third husband. She said something about finally finding one that was worth keeping. I'm not sure how far she'd go to keep him, but I think it's a possibility."

"If I were her, I'd have killed Howard," Doona said.

"But Jeanne had something of a reputation for being almost irresistible to men," Bessie pointed out. "He could have insisted that it wasn't his fault."

"If you knew your friend was irresistible to men, would you let your husband go and spend time alone with her?" Doona demanded.

"They weren't married yet, of course," Bessie said thoughtfully. "I believe if I were in Mabel's shoes, I'd have wanted to keep Howard and Jeanne apart. I'll put Mabel on the list under Kenny and Sandra, and I'll put Howard there, as well."

"What was his motive?" Hugh asked.

"Maybe he was having an affair with Jeanne and she threatened to tell Mabel," Doona suggested. "Or maybe he was just tired of being sent over to change light bulbs and wanted it to stop."

"Or maybe he was going around and helping her and she wasn't having an affair with him," Hugh said. "Maybe he was the one guy she turned down. That would make him angry, especially if she was sleeping with all of his friends."

"We don't have any evidence to suggest that she was sleeping with anyone," John pointed out.

"And maybe his friends were bragging about sleeping with her but they really weren't," Doona added. "Men can be like that."

Hugh nodded. "Anyway, he goes on the list. What about this Max Rogers?"

"We know nothing about him, aside from his name," John said. "At this point, I suggest he goes at the very bottom of the list, right above person or persons unknown."

"We know he was friends with Howard five years ago," Bessie said as she added his name to her list. "And that he may have had a fling with Jeanne. Is there any way you can track him down?"

"I'll do some discreet digging," John told her. "Or rather, Hugh will. It will be good practice for him. I'll let you know if we find him."

"What about the former boyfriends for whom we have names?" Bessie asked. "I'm looking forward to meeting Ron Adams tomorrow. Where does he fall on the list?"

"Somewhere near the middle, I would suggest," Andrew replied. "We know he and Jeanne had a relationship and we've been told it was volatile. He'd be higher on the list if they hadn't split up years before Jeanne's death."

"And James Poole?" Bessie wondered.

"If he truly was living across when Jeanne died, it's hard to imagine a motive for him," Hugh said. "I'm sure Inspector Kelly checked to make sure he wasn't on the island at the relevant time."

"I'm not certain that he checked," John replied, "but I'll see what I can find out."

"We haven't mentioned Nick Grant," Bessie said suddenly. "He was

Amanda's first choice. As she worked with the man, she must have known him well."

"From everything you've said, it seems as if he and Jeanne might have had an affair," Doona said.

"That was one thing that Inspector Kelly tried to pin down. He couldn't find any evidence that they ever saw one another outside of the office," John said.

"But they could have been very discreet," Hugh said. "If they were having an affair, she might have threatened to tell his wife."

"Did Inspector Kelly look at the bank's accounts at all?" Bessie asked.

"I don't believe so," John replied. "There was no reason to suppose that the murder had anything to do with Jeanne's job."

"What if Jeanne had discovered that Nick was stealing from the bank in some way?" Bessie asked. "That might have been an even stronger motive for murder."

"We've no evidence to suggest that anyone was stealing from the bank," John said. "It was all wound up years ago without any hint of anything criminal having ever happened."

"I still think it's worth someone taking a look," Bessie said. "I'd really like to talk to Nick Grant, as well."

"A trip to Australia it is," Andrew said. "I won't tell my children we're going. They can find out when we return."

"I'm not sure I'm ready to jet off to Australia," Bessie gasped.

"I've been working on tracking Nick down," John said. "I don't think anyone will have to go down under to find him. It appears the family moved back to the UK in the past year."

"All of them?" Bessie asked.

"Yes, Jefferson and his wife, Julie, and Nick and his wife, Heather," John replied.

"Did any of them get into any trouble while they were away?" Hugh asked.

"I've sent a request to the police in Australia, requesting that information," John told him. "I've not heard back yet."

"What about Jefferson?" Doona wondered. "Did he ever spend any time at the bank? Could he have been having an affair with Jeanne?"

"He was over seventy when Jeanne died," John said. "I'm not sure that Jeanne would have been interested, even if he was."

"I never heard any hint that he cheated on Julie," Bessie said. "He and Julie were quite prominent in the island's high society for many years, and I never heard a whisper of scandal attached to either of them. Nick and Heather were a different matter."

"Go on, then. What did they get up to?" Andrew asked.

"There were rumours of affairs on both sides," Bessie told him. "I never heard anything definite, and I can't recall any of the names with which either of them were linked, but I definitely remember hearing that he was seeing someone behind her back, and that she was cheating as well. I believe they'd originally planned to stay on the island and keep the bank running when Jefferson decided to leave, but then decided to go as well, perhaps as much to avoid the gossip as anything else."

"Maybe both Nick and Heather should be on the list, then," Hugh suggested.

"I'll add them, but I'm going to put Nick higher up than Heather," Bessie replied.

"As he may have had a professional or a personal motive, that seems fair," Andrew said.

"Although, if Nick was stealing from the bank, Heather may have known about it. She may have been willing to kill to protect her husband and/or their money," Doona suggested.

"Add Jefferson and Julie, too," Andrew said, "but at the very bottom."

Bessie complied. "Jefferson was mostly retired by that time," she said thoughtfully. "I don't know that he was spending much, if any time, at the office. Still, it was a small company. He must have known Jeanne."

"Is there anyone else to add to the list?" Doona asked.

Bessie looked at the paper on the table in front of her. "It seems quite a long list, really," she said. "I hope that's everyone."

"We don't have names for Howard's other friends, the ones that he said had flings with Jeanne," Andrew pointed out.

Bessie added two lines to represent the unknown men. "Is that everyone?" she asked.

"Except for person or persons unknown," John said. "What's significant is that it is already a longer list than the one from which Inspector Kelly was working. As I said, I don't recall much mention of Howard, and there certainly isn't any mention of Max Rogers or any other men who had short-term relationships with Jeanne in the last year of her life."

"And everyone had the means and the opportunity?" Doona questioned.

"Jeanne was given a large number of sleeping tablets along with a variety of other medicines and some alcohol," John told her. "While some of the drugs required a prescription, they were all common enough to be considered available if someone was determined to get his or her hands on them. Many of them would have been easy to acquire."

"I can't even get sleeping tablets from my own doctor when I'm having trouble sleeping," Doona said. "How did someone manage to stockpile a bunch of them?"

"Are you okay?" Bessie asked, feeling concerned.

Doona nodded. "I really wanted them back when Charles and I first split up years ago," she explained. "My doctor offered me one tablet at a time. I decided not to bother."

"Maybe he was worried that you were suicidal," Bessie said gently.

Doona shrugged. "I wasn't, but I was pretty devastated. Now that it's all behind me, I'm glad I never tried sleeping tablets, though. I got through it and I'm stronger for it."

"To get back to your question," John said, "Jeanne was given many tablets, but there were several different types. It's possible that someone was given only a few tablets from any one doctor, but that they were able to get a few others from another, and so on. It's also possible that they found an illegal source for what they wanted. I understand that an illegal prescription drug ring was discovered on the island not long after Jeanne's death."

Bessie nodded. "I remember that. One of the chemists in the Ramsey shop was selling one or two tablets out of every shipment. He might have continued to get away with it if he hadn't become greedy and started stealing more and more of the shop's inventory."

"What about opportunity, then?" Hugh asked. "Surely we can eliminate at least one or two people who couldn't have done it?"

"Because the exact time of death couldn't be determined, it was difficult for Inspector Kelly to pin down alibis for anyone for the entire block of time when Jeanne might have died," John explained. "Even James Poole, who was living across at the time in question, could have just about made it over to the island, killed Jeanne, and returned home before the next time he can be proven to have been anywhere."

"So where do we go from here?" Hugh asked.

"You're going to try to track down Max Rogers," John said. "Very discreetly, though. Unless Howard has rung him and told him that his name has been given to the police, he won't know we're looking for him. I'd rather he didn't find that out until I know a great deal more about him."

Hugh nodded. "I'll do my best," he promised.

"Bessie and I will talk to Ron and Sandra tomorrow, or at least that's our plan," Andrew said. "Maybe we can track down Kenny as well."

"Sandra may be able to tell you how to find him," John said. "He isn't working at the same place where he was when Jeanne died, and he isn't living in the same house, either."

"Sandra should know where he is," Bessie said. "I just hope she's willing to talk to us. From what Mabel said, I don't think she and Kenny are still together."

"I don't think they are, but he is still the father of her children. She may be willing to lie to protect him," John warned her.

"Have you tried talking to Inspector Kelly about the case?" Bessie asked.

John shook his head. "I was going to, once I received official approval to reinvestigate, but when the chief constable told me that I wasn't to do so, I cancelled my meeting with the man. I'd rather the chief constable not know that I'm still doing some checking into the case."

And Inspector Kelly would tell the man, that was for sure, Bessie thought. "What about Carl Clague?" she asked. "Have you talked to him about it?"

"I have. We had lunch together yesterday and went over the case file. He wasn't involved in the initial investigation, though, so he wasn't able to do much more than make a few suggestions based on his years of experience," John told her.

"I think that's all we can do for tonight, then," Andrew said. "Bessie and I will continue to do what we can while you try to find us more, um, witnesses to interview. If they are all as forthcoming as the three we met today, maybe we'll be able to crack this case before I head for home."

"I doubt they'll all be that forthcoming," Bessie said. "At least one of them killed Jeanne, after all."

"Yes, but that might make someone even more talkative," Andrew suggested. "Maybe he or she is feeling confident, having managed to get away with it for the last five years."

"Let's hope," John said as he got to his feet. "And now I should get home and see if my house is still standing. The kids each had a friend around. Those four teenagers have probably eaten everything in the house."

"Take the rest of the pizza and fairy cakes to them," Bessie suggested.

"We always let Hugh have the leftovers," John replied. "He's a growing boy, after all."

"I think I'm done growing," Hugh said with a grin. "Take everything for your kids. I'm eating too much lately as it is. For some reason, whenever Grace gets a craving, I get it, too. We've been living on ice cream and mince pies all week."

"Mince pies?" Doona echoed.

"Yeah," Hugh flushed. "Grace started craving them, so she made a batch, and now we both can't stop eating them. I think she bought every jar of mincemeat she could find, though. We'll probably run out soon and have to wait until closer to Christmas for the shops to get mincemeat back in stock."

"By which time she'll probably be craving something else," Andrew laughed. "My wife craved all manner of things when she was pregnant with our children. After the first we were both less indulgent of the cravings, though. With a baby in the house, we didn't have the time to rush out to the shops every time she wanted something different."

Hugh shrugged. "I'm not sure if we'll have any more. This one is proving very stressful."

"I thought the same. They get easier," Andrew assured him. "Maybe not on your wife, but on you."

Bessie and John packed up the leftover food while Doona and Hugh took care of the washing-up. With a flurry of hugs, they all headed out, leaving Bessie alone with Andrew.

"I'd love to go for a long walk on the beach tonight, but I'm afraid I'm rather tired," he said as Bessie sat back down next to him. "I think the sea air is proving almost too good for me. I feel as if I'm going to sleep well again tonight."

"I hope you do. Tomorrow sounds as if it's going to be an interesting day."

"It does indeed. I'm looking forward to it. Two more witnesses and another castle should keep us busy for much of the day, anyway. Then I'd like to take you somewhere nice for dinner."

"You've already spent too much money on me," Bessie protested. "Let me buy dinner tomorrow night."

Andrew shook his head. "I'm just old-fashioned enough to feel as if I should pay when I'm with a lady. And I can certainly afford it. My ungrateful children will be inheriting quite enough money as it is."

Bessie wanted to argue, but she couldn't work out exactly what to say. As the silence between them began to stretch, she sighed. "Let me cook for you one night, then," she suggested.

"Maybe, later in my holiday, if we find the time," Andrew replied evasively.

Bessie let it go at that. She'd have to find a way to make it happen. Andrew stood up and headed for the door. Bessie followed.

"I'll just walk you back to your cottage and then continue on for a bit," she said. "It's too nice an evening not to have a short walk."

"I may come part of the way with you," Andrew said as Bessie locked her cottage. "It is a nice night."

It was a nice night for about ten minutes. Then the skies suddenly opened, sending Bessie and Andrew running back to Andrew's cottage. Bessie stood inside the sliding doors that opened onto the patio behind the cottage and watched the rain for several minutes.

"I'm just going to run home," she told Andrew. "It isn't stopping, and I'm already pretty wet, anyway."

She could feel Andrew watching her as she hurried down the beach. Inside Treoghe Bwaane she took off her wet things and hung them in the downstairs cloakroom. It was too early to head to bed, so she curled up with a book for a short while before taking herself off to her bedroom. Once she was ready for bed, she climbed under the duvet and read for another hour before finally switching off the light. She slept soundly, waking at six feeling refreshed.

CHAPTER 9

"I hope I'm not too early," Andrew said in an apologetic tone. "I wouldn't have knocked, but I could see that your lights were on."

"I've been up for hours," Bessie assured him as she let him into her cottage. "I hope you aren't up early because you couldn't sleep last night."

"Not at all. I slept incredibly well and woke up at seven feeling better than I have in years. After a leisurely shower and breakfast, I just couldn't seem to find anything else to do to fill my time, though. When I went out for a walk, I noticed that your lights were on, so I thought I might as well just come over here."

"I'm glad you did. We can head to Peel anytime, really," Bessie told him. "We can have a walk around the quayside if we get there too early to visit Ron at his office."

"I was wondering if we should ring him first," Andrew said. "What if he's out all day showing houses?"

Bessie thought for a minute. "We want to go to Peel anyway," she pointed out. "If we wait until nine to ring him, we won't get to Peel until half nine or later. Let's just go. If he's not available, we can make an appointment for later today, or tomorrow, even."

"Is there anything interesting to see between here and Peel?"

"We could stop at Tynwald Hill if you'd like. That's where the island's government meets every fifth of July."

"I heard about Tynwald Day when I was stationed here. I'm sorry now that I didn't go along that year to see it. I didn't do anything other than work. I knew I wasn't going to be here for long, but at the time that seemed like a good thing. I wanted to be where the action was, not traipsing around historical sites or anything like that."

"You were much younger, of course. I remember wanting to do exciting things when I was younger as well. Instead, I stayed in my little cottage and simply enjoyed being where I was."

"But you lived in the US. For many people, that would be quite exciting."

"I don't remember it terribly well now," Bessie told him. "When I first bought my cottage here, I did think about moving back, though. The island felt very foreign to me, really. I'd been in the US from the age of two and didn't remember living on the island before that. Now I'm glad I stayed here, but there was a time when thought I would go as soon as I could save enough money for the journey."

"If you were trying to save money, why did you buy a house?"

Bessie laughed. "Looking back now, I suppose I didn't really want to leave the island, but I kept telling myself that I was going to go. I bought my cottage so that I could get away from my parents, as I blamed them for Matthew's death. But even then, as much as the island felt strange to me, it also felt oddly like home." She shook her head. "I know I'm not making any sense."

"I think I understand what you're saying, though. But let's head to Peel, maybe with a stop at Tynwald Hill along the way," Andrew said.

Bessie went upstairs to comb her hair and add a touch of lipstick to her lips. Andrew had only been half an hour earlier than expected, but she still felt slightly discombobulated by his arrival. He was just lucky she hadn't gone out for a second walk that morning, she thought as she found her handbag.

"Ready when you are," she told the man, who was studying the bookshelves in her sitting room.

"I may need to borrow a book or two," he told her. "I always bring books with me when I travel, but I spent a few days in hospital last month and read my way through my stockpile. I should have taken the time to get to a bookshop before I came over here, but I was too busy with other things. I did buy books in Ramsey the other day, but I'd prefer to save them for when I'm back at home, really."

"You're more than welcome to borrow anything on the shelves down here. Take a few now and throw them in your boot, if you'd like. Then you'll have them for later."

"Are you sure? I'll take good care of them and get them back to you before I leave."

"I'm quite sure, and while I'd like them back, it wouldn't be the end of the world if you kept one or two. I have far more books on my shelves than I'll ever be able to read again in this lifetime."

"I'll just borrow these two," Andrew said. "Then if I'm up early again tomorrow, I won't have to bother you."

Bessie found the man a carrier bag to put the books in, and then the pair made their way to Andrew's hire car. He put the books carefully into a small compartment in the boot. "That should keep them safe and sound."

"Just don't forget they're in there."

"No, I won't." The sun was shining on a lovely day as Andrew pointed the car southwards.

"The road to Peel cuts right across the centre of the island," Bessie told him as they went. "This road is part of the TT Course as well."

Andrew glanced at the houses which lined both sides of the road. "It seems a dangerous place to have a race."

"It's a fairly straight line, at least."

"What do the people who live in the houses do when they want to get in or out during the racing?"

"The course is a big loop. People who live inside the course can move around inside of it, but if they want to go outside of it, they have to do so at one of the crossing points. Similarly, if someone is outside, they can only get inside at a crossing point. People who live right on the course usually park their cars on side roads or in nearby car parks so that they can get to them if they need them during the racing."

"How long does the racing take? Are the roads shut for long?"

"They're generally shut all day, from early in the morning until five or six in the evening on racing days," Bessie explained. "Races usually take place on the Monday, Wednesday, and Friday of race week. There are practices as well, which shut the roads for shorter periods the week before racing and on non-race days during race week. Of course, that's all assuming the weather is good and the practices and races happen as scheduled. And that never seems to happen. When it rains, everything turns to chaos, although it is a very well-organised chaos, really."

"It sounds awfully inconvenient."

"It doesn't really bother me at all, and most island residents are used to it. Comeovers complain a lot at first, but they soon learn to adapt as well. The TT is good for the island's tourist industry. It's worth having to plan around it for the good it does the island."

"I suppose so."

"It isn't the only racing event held here, either, although it is the most famous. There is a fortnight of racing in August called the Manx Grand Prix. It's also for motorbikes and follows the TT Course, but I believe just about anyone can enter. There are other, smaller race events held around the island as well. And Tynwald Hill is just up here on the right."

Andrew slowed his car down and then pulled over to the side of the road. "It's smaller than I was expecting," he said after a moment.

"There's a car park a little further along if you want to take a closer look."

"Yes, I believe that I do."

It only took the pair a few minutes to walk from the car park to the monument.

"How do they cut the grass?" Andrew asked as he studied the stepped hill.

"I've no idea," Bessie laughed. "I've never been here when they're doing it."

Andrew walked up the steps and stood on the top of the hill. "The view from up here is lovely," he said. "I think I can see an ice cream stand."

"We haven't even had lunch yet. It's far too early to be thinking about ice cream."

"It's never too early to be thinking about ice cream. I may concede that it's a bit early to actually eat ice cream, but there's no harm in thinking about it," Andrew told her.

"Maybe we should get to Peel," Bessie suggested. It would probably be best if they were back in the car before the ice cream stand opened for business. Bessie wouldn't have been surprised if Andrew bought himself ice cream if they opened in the next few minutes.

"Okay, but I hope they'll be somewhere to get ice cream there."

"There's a small stand near the castle," Bessie assured him.

When they reached Peel, Bessie had Andrew park near the short road full of shops and restaurants. "The estate agency is just up the road," Bessie told him. "We can wander past and see if anyone is there."

They climbed out of the car and began a slow stroll up the street. Andrew stopped to look in nearly every window, which left Bessie feeling anxious. She really wanted to talk to Ron and then get out to Peel Castle. It felt to her as if Sandra was going to be a much better source of information than Ron.

There were lights on in the estate agency, but Bessie couldn't see anyone inside the building as she and Andrew walked past. When they reached the end of the street, they turned around and headed back towards the car. This time, when they reached the agency, Andrew stopped to look at some of the property details displayed in the window.

"What a lovely little cottage," he said to Bessie, pointing.

"It is lovely," Bessie replied, "and it's right on the water. It would be perfect for you."

"It does say that it needs some modernising. I wonder if they have any pictures of the interior."

"There's only one way to find out."

Bessie pulled on the building's door and was slightly surprised when it opened. There hadn't been any sign of anyone inside the shop while they'd been looking in the window, and Bessie had expected the door to be locked. As she and Andrew walked inside a loud buzzer sounded. A moment later a bald man in a dark brown suit rushed out from the back room.

"Ah, good morning," he said brightly. "I'm Ron Adams. How can I help you?"

"I was wondering if you had more photos of the little cottage in the window?" Andrew asked.

Ron frowned. "I'm not sure that I do, but I can check my files. It's a lovely little cottage, but it needs some modernising, for sure. I don't believe that the current owners have done much to it in the last few years."

He crossed to the desk in the corner and began to flip through some files on the desk. Bessie and Andrew followed him and sat down in chairs near the wall.

"Ah, here we are," Ron said eventually, "and there are a few more photos. Don't be put off by the amount of work it needs, though. It's going to be wonderful once it's been updated. You can't beat the location."

He handed Andrew a few photographs. Andrew looked through them and then handed them to Bessie.

"It's awful," Bessie said after she'd gone through them. "It's completely uninhabitable as it is. You'd need to put in a new kitchen, and it doesn't even look as if it has a loo. It simply won't do at all."

Andrew nodded. "I'm afraid my friend is correct. It isn't going to work for me."

"Why don't you tell me exactly what you're looking for and I'll see if I can help," Ron suggested. He pulled out a notebook and a pen and looked expectantly at Andrew.

"Ron Adams? Where have I heard that name before?" Andrew said, looking at Bessie.

"I believe someone might have mentioned it yesterday," Bessie said, hoping that was the lead that Andrew wanted.

"Yes, I think you're right," Andrew nodded. "It may have been Mabel Lloyd who mentioned it."

"Mabel Lloyd?" Ron repeated. "Do I want to know why you were talking to Mabel Lloyd about me?"

"We had tea in the café where she works yesterday," Andrew explained. "She was upset about an article that had been in the local paper. It seems a friend of hers was murdered a few years ago and the police are reinvestigating the case."

"That would be Jeanne," Ron sighed. "I saw the article. I sure hope the police aren't going to question me again."

"Surely you'd like to see the killer behind bars," Andrew said.

"Oh, yeah, sure, of course I would, but talking to me isn't going to help the police with that. I didn't know anything five years ago and I don't know anything now," Ron said forcefully.

"Mabel told us that you and Jeanne were a couple for a while," Bessie said softly.

"We went out for a short while, but we had a lot of problems."

"What sort of problems?" Bessie asked.

Ron stared at her for a minute and then shrugged. "She was good fun, but I couldn't trust her. Whenever I went over to her flat, there'd be a guy there. Usually it was her ex-husband, which was bad enough, but sometimes it would be some other guy she'd just met or something."

"So she cheated on you?" Andrew asked.

Ron flushed. "I don't think she was, um, well, sleeping with other men, at least not when we were together. She was just really friendly, especially with men. I always worried that one of them might get the wrong idea, you know?"

"Is that what you think happened to her, then? Do you think she was killed by some man she'd only just met?" was Andrew's next question.

"I've no idea what happened to her. The local paper had lots of theories about her ex-husband and about the guy she worked for, but they had to be careful with what they said. I suppose I was lucky that my name never appeared in any of their articles. Jeanne and I hadn't been together for years by the time she died, though," Ron replied.

"What did you think of her ex-husband?" Bessie asked.

"Kenny? He was okay. He was still sort of under Jeanne's spell in a way, but he was trying to do what was right by Sandra, too. I always hated finding him at Jeanne's because then she'd try to play us off each other. She was incredibly manipulative, when I look back now," he sighed.

"In what way?" Andrew asked.

"I'd go over after work and Kenny would be there. Jeanne would say that he'd come over to help with a leaking tap in the kitchen or something like that. Then I'd tell her that I could have repaired whatever she needed doing, which gave her an excuse to pull out her long list of little jobs that always seemed to need doing at her place. By the time Kenny and I left a few hours later, we'd have changed all of the washers in every tap, bled her radiators, rehung a door that was sticking, and paid for Chinese food for everyone for dinner." Ron shook his head. "When I'd get home, exhausted after all of that, I'd swear I wasn't going to fall for it again, but then a few days later I'd head over to see Jeanne, and Kenny or someone else would be there, and we'd start fighting all over again over who could do more for Jeanne the fastest."

"She sounds very clever," Andrew said.

"Oh, aye, she was very clever at getting what she wanted. The worst part was, we weren't even sleeping together. Somehow she always found an excuse to keep putting me off. I don't know if she was just not interested, or if she was using the promise of sex to keep me coming back, but after six months I got tired of waiting and moved on."

"And in that six months, how many other men did you meet at her flat?" Andrew asked.

"Maybe two or three," Ron said after a moment. "It was mostly Kenny who was there when I went over, but I'm sure I met at least two other guys there and there may have been three or even four. At least one of them left as soon as I arrived, but others stuck around for a while and we'd do some DIY together while Jeanne told us both how wonderful we were."

Bessie glanced at Andrew. Ron's story was interesting, but how much of it was true?

"We have wandered off topic, haven't we?" Andrew said with a chuckle. He gave Ron his name and address in the UK and then asked him about cottages for sale in the area.

"I'll pull everything we have available across the island," Ron promised. "I'll get some flyers the post to you in the next few days."

"They'll probably be waiting for me when I get home, then," Andrew said. "I'll look them over when I start to miss the island."

"If I lived in London, the Isle of Man is the last place I'd be going," Ron muttered.

"Really? Is that because you don't like the island or because you find London appealing?" Bessie asked.

"Probably a bit of both," Ron told her. "The island is just boring, that's all. I've lived here my whole life and I'm ready for a change. I thought moving to Peel from Ramsey would be interesting, but it isn't that different. London, though, London would be completely different."

"For a short while, and then you'd find yourself going to work every day and going grocery shopping and running the same boring errands, and you'd find that London is just like everywhere else, really, just larger and more crowded," Andrew said.

Ron shrugged. "That's something I'd like to find out for myself."

"Have you looked at moving?" Bessie asked.

"Yeah, of course I have, but I'm an estate agent. To be good at that job, you need to know a lot about the area you're selling. I know Peel like the back of my hand. I know who might be thinking of moving in the next six months, which couples are getting closer to splitting and selling their family home, and who's just gone into a care home, leaving their family to start fighting over putting the house on the market. I don't know anything about London."

Bessie stared at the man. Did estate agents really work at finding out all of those very personal things? She'd never really thought about it, but hearing it spelled out that way made it seem very intrusive.

"So you've no theory on who killed Jeanne Stowe?" Andrew asked, suddenly changing the subject back to murder.

"Jeanne? Oh, um, no. As I said, I've always thought she brought someone home to take a look at her central heating or something and the guy was expecting more. When he didn't get what he wanted, well, he must have been angry."

"Very angry," Bessie suggested.

"Yeah," Ron agreed.

"Well, thank you for your time," Andrew said, getting to his feet. He held out a hand to Bessie and helped her up. "Send me those property details and I'll take a good look. I'm not one hundred per cent sold on the island, but I'm still here for a few more days. I'm sure Bessie will do her best to convince me to get a holiday home here."

Bessie flushed. Such a purchase wasn't any of her business. If Andrew wanted a holiday home, that was up to him. Unable to think of a polite way to tell Andrew that, especially in front of Ron, Bessie pressed her lips together and followed Andrew to the door.

"Thank you again," he said, offering Ron his hand.

"You're very welcome," Ron replied, shaking first Andrew's and then Bessie's hand.

"That was interesting," Andrew said as he and Bessie made their way back down the street.

"Do you believe what he said about Jeanne? It was rather different to what Howard said."

"It was. I wonder who is telling the truth."

"Maybe Jeanne changed after she and Ron stopped seeing one another," Bessie mused.

"That's also a possibility. It would be interesting, therefore, to talk to James Poole. I'd also like to speak with Kenny."

"Maybe Sandra can tell us where to find him," Bessie said. "If she's working today."

The drive over to Peel Castle didn't take long. As Bessie had promised, there was an ice cream vendor right outside the stone steps to the castle.

"Perfect. Ice cream is exactly what I need right now," Andrew said.

"We haven't had lunch yet," Bessie reminded him.

"Maybe I'd better get three scoops," Andrew replied thoughtfully. "That would make the ice cream a useful substitute for lunch, wouldn't it?"

"You don't want to get lunch?" Bessie asked.

Andrew looked at her. "Right now I really want ice cream. As it is just about time for lunch, having some ice cream will probably spoil my appetite. Therefore, it makes more sense to simply have the ice cream for lunch and have lots of it, surely?"

"Or we could go and get something healthy to eat and then have ice cream when we come back."

"We could, and we will if that's what you want to do. But I'm fine with just having ice cream for lunch. I am on holiday, after all."

"You are, but I'm not," Bessie began. She would have argued further, but all of the talk about ice cream had made her hungry. And what she was hungry for was a huge scoop of strawberry ice cream. "I've never had ice cream in place of a meal," she said tentatively.

"Really? You live alone, and you have done since you were eighteen. Why wouldn't you eat ice cream in place of a meal at least once a week?" Andrew demanded.

"That wasn't the way I was raised," Bessie told him. "Ice cream was an indulgence, only for special occasions, not for every day. And it was only eaten as pudding if you ate all of your vegetables."

"Bah, I was raised the same way and my wife did the same with our children, but whenever she went away to visit her family or whatever, the children and I always had ice cream for lunch or dinner one day. It was our special thing, and we never told my wife about it. Now I live alone and I have ice cream pretty much whenever I want. Life is too short to always eat your vegetables first."

Bessie sighed. "Come on, then, let's get ice cream," she said. The sensible side of her wanted to argue, but being with Andrew made her feel younger and just the tiniest bit rebellious. A small treat would probably do her good.

Andrew got three scoops of chocolate chocolate-chip ice cream. Bessie got two scoops of strawberry with a scoop of vanilla in the middle.

"It's very good," Andrew said after his first taste.

"It really is," Bessie agreed.

They found a bench and sat and ate their frozen treats while they watched the sea splashing on the rocks. A few seals were bobbing around in the water and Bessie was quick to point them out to Andrew.

"This is a little slice of heaven," he sighed. "Ice cream, sunshine, sea, seals; this island has everything."

"Unless you're Ron and bored."

"He won't be less bored in London, just more poor," Andrew said. "I could never be bored with the sea on my doorstep."

After they finished their ice cream, they made their way up the steps to Peel Castle. Bessie knew the girl behind the ticket window and they chatted for a moment before she and Andrew took their audio guides and made their way into the castle grounds.

"I shall feel just a tiny bit rude, using this," Andrew said, "but I truly do want to see everything."

"Off you go," Bessie told him. "I'm going to visit a few favourite spots and then find a bench in the sun and watch the seals some more. Take your time and find me when you're finished."

Andrew agreed. Bessie watched as he walked over to the first marker and listened intently to his audio guide. It had been a while since she'd taken the audio tour herself, but she knew the site well. After visiting her favourite spots and hearing their history, she returned her audio guide and talked to the girl in the booth for a while longer.

"Is your friend visiting from across?" the girl asked.

"Yes, he's just here for the week," Bessie replied.

"Is he from the island or did you meet him elsewhere?"

"I met him when I was on holiday in the UK."

"Oh, that's romantic, isn't it? You met him on holiday and now he's come across to visit you. Will you be going over to see him one day, then?"

Bessie flushed. "There's nothing romantic about it at all. We became friends when we met, and when he felt he wanted a holiday, he decided to come here, that's all."

"Where does he live across?"

"London."

"Oh, you should go and visit him, for sure. There are so many wonderful museums and things to see in London. It would be a great holiday for you."

"I do enjoy a trip to London now and again," Bessie admitted, "but I haven't been there in five or six years now."

"Now you have the perfect excuse. You can go and visit your handsome friend."

Bessie smiled at the girl. "He is rather handsome, isn't he?"

The girl laughed. "He might be a touch old for me, but he's very distinguished looking."

"Not to change the subject, but someone told me that Sandra Oliver was working out here now," Bessie said.

"She is, yes. She's working in the gift shop. Do you know Sandra?"

"Not really, but I know someone who knows her," Bessie said, trying to sound offhand. "We'll definitely want to visit the gift shop anyway."

"She should be there. She's here all day today. It's her first day on her own, though, so be patient if you want to buy anything. She gets flustered easily, I hear."

"I'm told new jobs are always difficult. I can't quite imagine."

"They are. I've moved around quite a lot myself, and every time I get a new job I hate how long it takes to adjust. The last job I had, I'd only just started to get the hang of it when they closed up shop. It's better here, though. Everyone has been really nice and I've already learned a lot about Peel Castle. I've been told that I'm going to have to start learning about the other sites, too. They want to be able to move me around, which I'm not as excited about. I live in Peel and I don't like to drive too far to get to work."

"You should offer to learn about the House of Mannanan next," Bessie suggested.

The girl nodded. "Yeah, that's the next closest place, and I have to drive past it to get here every day. You'd think I'd like it better, really, but I like being outside. My little booth is covered for when it rains, but when it's quiet and the weather is good, I can go and sit outside and just enjoy myself. And it's quiet out here a lot, really."

"It sounds as if it would be an almost perfect job."

"It is at that," the girl agreed.

Andrew wandered over a short while later. "That was excellent," he said. "I loved every minute of it."

"It's a wonderful site," Bessie agreed.

Andrew returned his audio guide and smiled at Bessie. "Maybe we should visit the gift shop," he suggested.

"That's a great idea," Bessie replied.

CHAPTER 10

"Good morning," the pretty brunette behind the counter in the gift shop said as Bessie and Andrew walked in.

"Good morning," Bessie echoed. "How are you today?"

"Oh, I'm very well, thank you. How are you?" the woman replied.

"Fine, thanks," Bessie told her.

"Is this your first visit to Peel Castle?" she asked.

"Oh, goodness, no. I've been here probably hundreds of times, but it is my friend's first visit."

"We have an excellent range of books about the history of the castle and the history of the island," the woman said, waving towards the back of the shop.

"I could do with a book or two," Andrew said. The woman walked out from behind the counter and led Andrew towards the shelves at the back.

"I didn't realise you were carrying this title," Bessie exclaimed as she picked up a copy of the book containing the papers that had been given at the previous year's Manx History Conference.

"What makes that one interesting?" Andrew asked.

"Oh, I have a paper in it, that's all," Bessie said, blushing.

"Really?" both Andrew and the woman said at the same time.

Andrew picked up another copy of the book and flipped to the table of contents.

"I shall have to buy a copy and you shall have to sign it for me," he told Bessie.

"Oh, I couldn't," she exclaimed.

"Of course you can," he replied. "I'm afraid I'm going to have to insist. There's nothing better than having a book that's been signed by the author."

"I only wrote a tiny part of that book, and it's hardly a bestseller or anything," Bessie protested.

"Well, I'm impressed," the woman said. "I'd love to contribute something to the study of the island's history, but I imagine I won't be able to do that for ages yet."

"Are you in school now?" Bessie asked.

"I'm trying," the woman sighed. "I take classes at night and work during the day, which sounds manageable until I add in my three children. They're all under the age of seven and quite a handful."

"I hope your husband helps a lot," Bessie said.

The woman flushed. "I'm not, that is, we never married, their father and I. He didn't really believe in marriage, or so he told me. That was after he'd failed to tell me that he was already married when we met, of course."

"I am sorry," Bessie told her.

The woman nodded. "Yeah, so am I. He swept me off my feet and then, ah, but never mind. You don't want to hear about my problems."

"I'm always happy to listen," Bessie replied. "Sometimes simply talking about a problem helps make it seem smaller."

"But you're Elizabeth Cubbon," the woman said. She'd picked up a copy of the book and had been flipping through it. "I should have recognised you when you came in. As soon as I saw your name on the chapter in here, I realised."

"Please, call me Bessie."

"Oh, thank you. I'm Sandra Oliver. You can call me Sandra or even Sandy, although I don't really use Sandy very often. My, er, ex, he used to call me Sandy because he knew it annoyed me, but I got rather used to it over the years. Now I'm tempted to use it all the time, just to show him. Except I doubt he'd even notice." She shook her head. "I'm babbling about my problems again."

"And you're welcome to do so," Bessie said firmly. "It sounds as if you've had a difficult time lately."

"I've heard all about you, of course, and how you keep solving all those murders. I've always wondered how you find out so much about people, and here I am, telling you everything about me. It would be wonderful if you could solve the murder case that I'm tangled up in. I would happily tell you my life story if you could do that."

"If you're talking about Jeanne Stowe, everyone seems to be telling me about her lately," Bessie said.

"I never should have given Kenny Wilkins the time of day," Sandra sighed. "First he got me pregnant without telling me about his wife and then he got me tangled up in a murder investigation. I should have seen the look in his eye the day we met and realised right then and there that he was nothing but trouble."

"He never told you about Jeanne?" Bessie asked.

"Oh, he did, eventually, after I'd fallen head over heels in love with him and found out I was knocked up. When I told him about the baby and suggested that it was high time he came up with a ring, that's when he told me that he was already married."

"What a huge shock for you."

"It was. And I did the right thing, too. I broke up with him and told him I never wanted to see him again. And I didn't see him again until he turned up on my doorstep with a signed divorce decree." She sighed. "Maybe I should have insisted on getting a wedding ring right then and there, but I was so surprised that he'd actually divorced his wife for me that I didn't think marriage really mattered. I should have known better, though."

"It's easy to make bad choices when you're in love," Andrew suggested.

Sandra nodded. "And I was crazy about Kenny, I truly was. And he was so excited about the baby. He wanted it even more than I did, although I hate to admit it. He told me that Jeanne didn't want children. That was one of the reasons why they'd been having problems. He wanted our baby badly enough to leave Jeanne. I should have realised he didn't leave her for me, he left her for the baby. At the time I didn't see the difference."

"You weren't happy together?" Bessie asked.

Sandra shrugged. "I suppose, if I'm honest, that we were happy at first. Jeanne was badly hurt by the divorce, or so Kenny told me. She took up with some guy called Ron almost immediately, and I moved into the house that she and Kenny had once shared. That was uncomfortable, by the way, but it was a nice house and moving is costly, so it made sense, at least financially."

"And Jeanne moved to Ramsey," Bessie said.

"Yes, she got herself a flat up there. For a short while it was all good and then she and Ron split up and she started ringing Kenny all the time. The first time he dropped everything and ran up to Ramsey to help her with some DIY should have been a warning to me, but I felt so bad about coming between them that I didn't say or do anything to stop him."

"And then it became commonplace," Andrew suggested.

"It very quickly became commonplace," Sandra agreed. "I was getting bigger and bigger and having more and more trouble getting around and doing jobs around the house, but Kenny was off spending his nights and weekends at Jeanne's flat, repairing leaking taps and rehanging doors. Every time I complained, he reminded me that he'd kicked her out of what had been their home together and that helping her out was the least he could do."

"And did that continue until she died?" Bessie asked.

"Not exactly. Jeanne cut back on her demands when I first had the baby. I suspect she'd run out of things that needed doing, really. It was only a small flat. Anyway, for a while she left Kenny alone. She found herself another boyfriend and they were together long enough that I found myself pregnant again. But then, when that boyfriend left her to move across, she started ringing Kenny again. I was furious, but Kenny didn't see anything wrong with leaving me with the baby so that he could change light bulbs at Jeanne's flat."

"Change light bulbs?" Bessie repeated. "Surely Jeanne could manage that little job on her own."

"You'd think so, wouldn't you, but it was one of the things that she used to ask Kenny to do for her. She claimed that she had really bad vertigo and couldn't stand on a chair to change the bulbs in the ceiling lights on her own."

"Was that true?" Bessie asked.

"I've no idea, but I doubt it. I'm pretty sure Jeanne just liked having Kenny jump whenever she rang. She was very good at getting men to do what she wanted, I'm not sure how. Most of her men seemed to get tired of her demands after a while, but for some reason Kenny simply kept putting up with her for years and years."

"And that went on until she died?" Andrew wondered.

"Off and on, yes. Whenever she found a new man, she'd stop ringing as much, maybe only once a week or so if she was in a new relationship. Then when she was single again, she'd be back to ringing three or four or five times a week."

"How often did Kenny see her in the week before she died?" Bessie asked.

"Maybe once, which was less than it had been in the weeks before that last week. I was actually joking with Kenny a few days before the body was found that she must have landed a new boyfriend, actually."

"Do you know who the man was?" Andrew asked.

"I don't even know if there was a man. Sometimes Jeanne wouldn't ring for a few days or even a few weeks, for no obvious reason. I always simply assumed that she'd found herself another man, but maybe she simply didn't need any new light bulbs in those weeks. Kenny was actually starting to worry about her a day or two before the body was found, because she hadn't rung. He may have even rung her flat to check on her, I'm not sure."

Bessie nodded. "Was he terribly upset when she died?"

Sandra frowned. "He was very badly shaken up, but, well, I don't know how he felt otherwise. I mean, he was upset that she was murdered, but I've never really understood how he felt about her otherwise. I'm not sure I'm making sense now."

"Do you think he was still in love with her?" Bessie asked.

"Maybe. Let's just say that she had an odd hold over him. That's the only way I can explain it, really. He cheated, he threw her out of the house, but he never seemed to stop caring about her. It was odd, and I should have done something to put a stop to it, really."

"But you stayed together after Jeanne's death," Bessie said.

"Yeah, I was naïve and thought things would get better," the woman replied bitterly. "I'd always thought Jeanne was the biggest problem in our relationship. It turned out she was just one small part of what was wrong with our relationship. Kenny was the real problem."

"I'm sorry," Bessie said.

Sandra shrugged. "We've been separated for six months now and I'm just starting to feel as if I'm doing the right thing. The biggest problem is that Kenny is devoted, truly devoted, to the kids. He loves them far more than he ever cared about me, that's for sure. And I'm happy for them, but it means we fight about them constantly. He reckons he never gets to see them enough and I reckon he'll just spoil them even more if he sees them more often."

"It sounds as if it's a difficult situation," Bessie remarked.

"I keep thinking I should just get back with him to make life easier," Sandra sighed. "I don't really mean that," she added hastily, "but I really hate being a single mother. It's going to sound terrible, but I almost wish the police would arrest Kenny for Jeanne's murder. That would take care of the biggest of my problems, anyway."

"I am sorry," Bessie told her.

Sandra shrugged. "He might have killed her, you know. He was getting pretty tired of rushing all the way to Ramsey all the time. I told him once that every minute he spent with Jeanne was a minute he was missing out on in his children's lives. That made him really think about Jeanne's place in his life, anyway. Maybe it pushed him over the edge and he killed her."

"It's a possibility," Bessie said. "If it wasn't Kenny, who do you think it might have been?"

"Probably some other man that she'd managed to enslave. I really don't know how she did it. She wasn't even all that pretty, but once she got her hooks into a man he'd do just about anything for her. It never lasted for all that long, at least not for most men. It was just my bad luck that the effects never seemed to wear off on Kenny, I suppose."

"But he'd left Jeanne for you," Bessie pointed out.

"Except he never really left her," Sandra sighed. "Anyway, if Kenny didn't kill her, then you should look at whomever she was seeing when she died. She was never without a man for long, although sometimes she was very discreet, like if the man was married or whatever."

"Can you suggest anyone she might have been seeing?" Andrew asked.

"There was talk about her and her supervisor at the bank. His name was Nick something or other. He left the island a few years ago, though. I suppose if he did it the police will struggle to find him now."

"No doubt they'll be looking," Bessie told her.

"Yeah, maybe. Anyway, I tried really hard to not know what Jeanne was doing at any given time. I didn't want to hear about her latest troubles with men. Kenny was always talking about it when he came home from seeing her and I was always trying to shut him up." She shook her head. "I can't believe that I stayed with him for as long as I did. I even had a third child for him. And now I have to raise my kids on my own while battling over custody. What was I thinking?"

"Presumably you were in love," Bessie suggested.

Sandra laughed. "I thought I was, when I first met Kenny. When I found out I was pregnant, I was over the moon. Then I found out that Kenny was already married. I should have cut all of my ties then and there, really. I should have realised that I couldn't trust the man and cut him out of my life."

"You tried to do what you thought was right for the baby," Bessie said.

"Yeah, and now look at the mess I'm in. But you don't want to hear about all of my problems, really, do you? You're investigating Jeanne's murder, aren't you?"

"Not really," Bessie said, glancing at Andrew.

"I used to be a police inspector, so I'm fascinated by the case," Andrew told the woman. "I'm afraid I can't help but stick my nose into such things when I come across them."

"I wish I could give you more information, but I really don't know anything. As I said, I tried to avoid hearing about Jeanne whenever the subject came up. I'd be delighted if you'd have Kenny arrested, though. If he could go to prison until my baby is eighteen, well, that would be fine by me."

"I'm sure the children would miss him," Bessie replied.

"Ha! They'd miss being spoiled rotten by him, that's for sure. He simply can't say no to any of them, no matter what they ask for. We fought about money nearly all the time, because he couldn't stop buying things for the kids. Now he's on his own and he can spend his money on them if he wants, but I can still put a roof over their heads and food on the table. Maybe he'll get locked up for failing to pay his bills one of the these days, if not for murder."

"Is he still living in the house in Douglas?" Bessie asked.

Sandra flushed. "I'm living in the house in Douglas. It seemed only fair that I stay there and Kenny move out. I'm the one looking after the children, at least most of the time."

"So where is Kenny living?" was Bessie's next question.

"He's been staying with different friends," Sandra told her. "I think he's nearly run out of them, though. They all get tired of having him around after a while. I think he's staying with his brother, Jack, at the moment, but I'm not sure. I try not to talk to him when he comes to collect the children. Once we start talking, we start fighting, and it isn't good for the children to see or hear that."

"Did you ever meet any of Jeanne's friends when you and Kenny were together?" Bessie asked as an idea occurred to her.

"Jeanne's friends? No, I don't think I did. She and I only met once or twice and it was always incredibly awkward. The island is so small that it was inevitable that we'd cross paths once in a while, but I know I used to go out of my way to avoid doing so whenever possible."

"I'm sorry if talking about all of this has been difficult for you," Bessie said.

"I just hope the police finally solve the case. I'm not sure if I really believe that Kenny killed her or not, but it would be nice to finally know for sure. I think he'll feel better, too, once the killer is behind bars. Unless it's him who did it, of course."

Andrew ended up buying three books, and Bessie couldn't resist getting a copy of the book to which she'd contributed as well.

"What else do you like?" Andrew asked Bessie as they stood in the centre of the shop. "The scarves are very pretty and there is some lovely jewellery."

"The jewellery is gorgeous, but I would never wear any of it. And I have a dozen scarves and rarely wear them, either," Bessie told him.

"I was hoping to buy you a little gift," Andrew said. "Just a little something to remember me by."

Bessie shook her head. "I don't need any gifts. I'm just enjoying spending time with you, showing you around the island."

Andrew nodded, although he didn't look satisfied. Bessie paid for her book and then Andrew paid for his.

"Where did you say Kenny's brother lives?" he asked Sandra as she was putting the books into a bag.

"Oh, he's in Douglas now. He and his wife have a flat on the promenade or near to it. They don't have children, and I'm sure they're sorry now that they bought a flat with two bedrooms. If Kenny is staying with them, I mean."

"Thank you for talking with us," Bessie said. "I hope it wasn't too difficult for you. If you think of anything else that might be relevant to the case, you should ring the police. You can ring John Rockwell in Laxey at any time."

Sandra nodded. "I've seen his name in the papers a lot, too. I'll ring him if I think of anything, but I doubt I will. I've told you everything I can remember about Jeanne, which isn't much at all. But then, that's hardly surprising under the circumstances."

It only took Andrew and Bessie a few minutes to walk back to Andrew's car. "That was interesting," he told Bessie after they'd climbed inside. "But I'm starving. We need to get some lunch, I think."

Bessie gave him directions to the nearest pub. "After all that ice cream this morning, I think maybe I'll just have something light," she said as she read through the menu.

"Then we can have something more substantial for dinner," Andrew agreed.

They ordered their meal and ate quickly. As they walked back outside, Andrew smiled at Bessie. "I'd really like to speak to Kenny now."

"Me, too, but we can't really go knocking on his brother's door, can we? I think maybe John will have to follow up with him, if he's allowed to reopen the case, that is."

"Maybe we could just go and see where the brother lives," Andrew suggested. "Maybe Kenny will decide to take a walk while we're having a look."

"That would be incredibly lucky," Bessie said.

"First we need an address," Andrew told her. "Do you want to ring John or should I?"

"Maybe you should ring him. He's probably more likely to give it to you, as you're police and I'm not."

"I'm not police anymore. Maybe we should try the telephone directory before we do anything else. Where can we find a Douglas telephone directory?"

"There isn't one specifically for Douglas. The telephone company just does one for the whole island."

"So where can we find one?"

"I'm sure they'll have one at the castle, but I'd feel funny going back in to ask," Bessie said. "Let's walk over to the House of Mannanan and ask to see theirs. I nearly always know the person behind the ticket desk there."

Today was no exception. The woman behind the desk was the same one who usually worked there.

"Come to show another friend around our museum?" she asked Bessie as Bessie and Andrew walked into the lobby.

"Maybe, but not today," Bessie told her. "What I really need is to borrow your telephone directory."

"Are you going to take it away with you or just look at it here?" the woman asked as she opened the desk drawer.

"Just look at it here, thanks," Bessie replied.

"I'm only asking because we seem to have three copies at the moment. I wouldn't mind at all if you wanted to take one away."

Bessie looked at Andrew. He shrugged. "It couldn't hurt to have one, I suppose."

"If you're sure it won't be missed," Bessie told the woman.

"I'm quite sure. In fact, quite the opposite. I can barely close the desk drawer with three of them in there. I'm not sure if we were meant to share them with someone else or if the telephone company made a mistake, but we've had three for months now and I'm more than happy to see the back of one of them." She handed Bessie the book in question with a smile on her face.

"Thank you very much," Bessie said. "We may be back later in the week to take the tour."

"You know you're always welcome," the woman replied.

Bessie and Andrew headed back outside. Once they were in the car again, Bessie flipped through the book. "Wilkins, Wilkins, Wilkins, ah, here we are. J.A. and C.A. Wilkins. I assume that's Jack, although it doesn't have to be."

"Is it a Douglas address?" Andrew asked.

"Yes, in one of the large and newly remodeled block of flats. That would work with what Sandra told us." She read out the address and Andrew made a note of it in his notebook.

"Tell me about the neighbourhood?"

"It's in a building right on the promenade," Bessie replied. "I believe there are hotels on either side of it. I know it was a costly renovation and that flats in that building are very expensive."

"Do the hotels on either side have restaurants?"

"I believe so. I'm not certain, though."

"Let's go and see. Maybe we can get dinner at one or the other of them later this afternoon, while we keep an eye on the building."

"Keep an eye on the building?"

"Perhaps Kenny will decide to take a stroll."

"That seems unlikely."

"But anything is possible. Kenny is the next person we need to interview. We've had really good luck thus far with finding people and getting them to talk to us. I'm choosing to believe that our luck will continue."

Bessie thought the man was being far too optimistic, but she didn't argue. There were worse ways to spend a pleasant autumn evening than having dinner on the promenade. She helped Andrew navigate his way back out of Peel and back across the island.

"You can park anywhere along the promenade," she told him when they'd reached Douglas. "The address we want is about halfway along."

Andrew found a space near their destination. They got out of the car and then stood and looked at the block of flats that was Kenny's temporary home.

"It's far too modern-looking," Andrew said after a minute. "It doesn't look as if it belongs with the others."

"No, but I suspect the hotels on either side will soon follow suit. That's the latest trend, turning old hotels into modern flats. So many of the hotels are struggling to find guests, now that tourism isn't as popular. TT is going to be a problem one day if all of the hotels keep turning themselves into flats, though. The island's population doubles during TT, and not everyone wants to camp in a tent."

"I've been assuming that you'll be able to recognise Kenny if he suddenly walks out of the building. Do you actually know the man?" Andrew asked.

Bessie laughed. "I hadn't thought about that. Actually, no, I don't know the man. There were pictures of him in the paper when Jeanne died, though. I have a vague recollection of what he looked like five years ago, anyway."

"This is never going to work," Andrew sighed. "I don't know what I was thinking."

"Let's go for a walk," Bessie suggested. "It's a beautiful day to spend some time on the promenade."

"You're right about that. Let's."

The pair strolled along, chatting about the weather and other unimportant topics. It seemed to Bessie that they were both avoiding talking about Jeanne Stowe's murder, but it may just have been her wanting to avoid the subject. She felt as if they'd reached a dead end unless they could find a way to speak to Kenny. When they reached the Sea Terminal building, they turned around and headed back towards Andrew's car.

"Let's sit and enjoy the sunshine for a few minutes," Andrew suggested, nodding towards a conveniently placed bench.

Bessie sat down and stretched her legs out in front of her. It was the perfect day to sit on the promenade and watch the sea.

"What's our next move?" Andrew asked after a moment.

"It's getting rather late if you wanted to do any more sightseeing today," Bessie replied.

Andrew laughed. "I meant in our murder investigation. We need to find a way to meet Kenny, but we may have to be sneaky about it. Do you know where he works?"

"We should have asked Sandra that, shouldn't we? I wonder if John knows."

"He said something about having trouble finding the man, so perhaps he doesn't."

"I could ring Sandra, but that would be odd."

"Yes, we should have thought to ask her when we were there. I can't believe I didn't, actually."

"It wasn't like it was a formal interview," Bessie reminded him. "We were just chatting."

"And we've no excuse to ring up James Poole over in the UK," Andrew sighed. "Nick is in Australia or the UK, out of reach, anyway. Is that everyone?"

"What about Max Rogers? I wonder if Hugh has tracked him down."

"He was Howard's friend who supposedly had a fling with Jeanne. He might be interesting to question."

"Do you want to ring John or should I?" Bessie asked.

"I don't mind either way."

Bessie pulled out her mobile phone and dialled the number for the Laxey station.

"Laxey neighbourhood policing, this is Doona. How may I help you?"

"It's Bessie. I don't suppose John could spare a few minutes?"

"I'm sure he could. He was just out here complaining because we've run out of those little notebooks he always uses. Ordering office supplies isn't even in my job description, but I've ordered a box anyway. I'm going to hide it in my desk, and then the next time he forgets to place an order I'll give him a couple."

Bessie laughed. "I can't imagine how John's functioning without his notebooks."

"Oh, he rang Ramsey and they're sending some over. In fact, the constable from there just pulled up. Let me transfer you to John."

"John Rockwell." The voice was clipped and her friend sounded annoyed.

"It's Bessie. Have I reached you at a bad time?"

"No, not at all. Doona usually tells me when she puts you through. This time she just put you through."

"Andrew and I had conversations with both Ron and Sandra today. Now we're trying to track down Kenny and Max Rogers. We were hoping you could help with that."

"Max Rogers sells insurance from an office in Ramsey," John told her. "He should be easy to find."

"Excellent. We may have to leave him for tomorrow, though."

"And Kenny is staying with his brother at a flat on the promenade because Sandra kicked him out."

"We found out that much, but we can't exactly go knocking on their door, can we?"

"He works at Noble's. He's a lab technician there."

"Oh, dear. We can't exactly just drop in on him there, either, can we?"

"Probably not."

"We may have to think about how to find Kenny, then," Bessie sighed. "Maybe we'll try to find an excuse to knock on his brother's door, after all."

"I don't think that's a good idea. You don't want anyone to think that you're interfering in a police investigation."

"No, that's very true. I'll talk to Andrew. Maybe he'll be able to think of something clever."

"If anyone can come up with something clever, it's you and Andrew," John chuckled.

Bessie dropped her phone back in her bag and told Andrew what she'd learned.

"So, tomorrow we'll go and talk to the insurance salesman. That wouldn't be on the top of my list of favourite things to do, I must say," he said when Bessie was done.

"At least we don't actually have to buy any insurance."

Andrew laughed. "There is that. I assume Noble's is a hospital?"

"Yes, sorry. It's the island's main hospital. It's here in Douglas. I'm not sure there's any way to simply bump into Kenny there, though."

They sat together, watching the people who were making their way up and down the promenade. A couple came out of one of the hotels and began a slow stroll towards Bessie and Andrew. As they went, the woman opened her handbag and pulled a small dog out of it. She snapped a lead onto its collar and then put it down on the ground.

"I wonder if the hotel knows that they have a dog," Andrew said.

Bessie nodded, but she couldn't stop staring at the couple. As they went past her, she put a hand on Andrew's arm. "I may be crazy, but I'm almost certain that was Nick and Heather Grant," she whispered.

CHAPTER 11

Andrew stared at her for a minute. "You aren't certain, though?"

"Not one hundred per cent, but probably ninety-nine per cent. He has a very distinctive nose."

"They'll have to come back this way, won't they?"

"Unless they decide to cross the road and walk on the other side. This side is much nicer for walking, though."

Andrew nodded. "So we'll wait for them to come back and then strike up a conversation."

A few minutes later, the pair turned around and began to make their way back towards Bessie and Andrew. It seemed to Bessie as if they were ignoring one another, but maybe they simply weren't the type to chat as they strolled. When they were nearly at the bench, Bessie stood up.

"What a lovely little dog," she exclaimed.

The woman picked up the dog and held it tightly. "Thank you," she said stiffly.

"What sort is he, or she?" Bessie asked.

The woman rattled off the animal's pedigree, which meant nothing to Bessie. As she spoke, Bessie studied the man, who seemed to be ignoring the conversation.

"Nick Grant?" she said when the woman finally stopped talking.

The man jumped and then narrowed his eyes at Bessie. "Do I know you?" he asked haughtily.

"I'm Elizabeth Cubbon. I live in Laxey. I remember you from various charity events when you used to have the bank in Ramsey," Bessie explained. "Of course, I remember your lovely wife, as well," she added, nodding towards the woman.

"Elizabeth Cubbon? Oh, yes, of course," the woman said. "Everyone called you Betty, wasn't it?"

"It's Bessie, actually, and you're Heather, if I'm remembering correctly."

"Yes, that's right," the woman said.

"I thought I'd heard that you moved to Australia," Bessie said.

"We did, but after a while we decided it didn't suit us," Heather told her. "Nick's parents were the ones who wanted to try it, but they didn't like it any better than we did, fortunately."

"So you've all come back to the island now?" Bessie asked.

"Oh, no. We've settled across. No, Nick and I are just here for a visit. My sister and her husband are here, and a few of my cousins. We thought, after all these years, that we owed them all a short visit," Heather explained.

"How nice for you both," Bessie said cheerfully. "I was actually just talking about you two with a few people."

"Really? Why?" Heather asked.

"There was an article in the local paper about Jeanne Stowe's murder," Bessie told her. "The paper seemed to think that the police might be reinvestigating the case. No doubt they'll want to talk to both of you if they decide to do so."

"Talk to me?" Heather said. "Why on earth would they want to talk to me? I didn't even know the woman, and I wasn't on the island when she died, either."

"I didn't realise that. Perhaps they'll only need to talk to Nick, then," Bessie replied.

"I have nothing to say to them," Nick told her. "I barely knew the woman. She was junior staff, really. I only noticed her at all because she was coming in late a great deal in the last few months of her life."

"I spoke to Amanda McBride about that. She said that Jeanne was having problems with her car," Bessie said.

Nick shrugged. "I wasn't interested in her excuses then and I'm not interested in them now. If you're scheduled to work at nine, you should be at work at nine. Everyone has problems with their cars sometimes."

Bessie nodded and glanced at Andrew. He smiled at her. "Who do you think killed her, then?" he asked the couple.

"It was her ex-husband, surely," Heather said. "Aren't partners the first suspects when someone is murdered?"

"But they were divorced," Bessie pointed out.

"Which just gives him even more motive," Heather replied. "They must have had problems, otherwise they wouldn't have divorced, would they?"

Bessie thought about arguing, but Heather seemed to have her mind made up. She turned to Nick. "Who do you think killed her?" she asked.

"I've no idea and I couldn't care less. As I recall, she had men in and out of her life on a regular basis. That none of them seemed to stay with her for very long suggests that she was difficult. Any one of the men who wandered through her life could have killed her," he replied.

"I don't suppose you remember the names of any of the men in her life," Bessie said.

"I don't. I never spoke to her about personal matters. Amanda McBride would have been the person with whom she shared such things with if she wanted to share them with someone in the office. She must have had friends outside of work, though. Those friends should be able to tell you about the men in her life," he said.

Bessie nodded. "As I said, I have spoken to Amanda. She's still quite upset that you didn't let her ring the police on the Monday."

Nick shrugged. "First of all, it's been over five years since Jeanne died. I can't believe Amanda still cares about any such thing. Secondly, I was only doing what I thought best at the time. It seemed foolish to bother the police when Jeanne had a history of being late to work. And thirdly, as I understand it, she'd already been dead for at least forty-eight hours when the body was found. It isn't as if they might have saved her if the police had gone on Monday."

"Did you know her ex-husband at all?" Bessie asked.

"I don't believe she came to work for me until after she was divorced. I'm sure she never brought him to any of the bank's social functions. She came with a man called Ron to one or two things, and then brought someone called James to such things for a while as well. Those are the only two men I remember her bringing to events, although I'm sure there were others in her life," he replied.

"Did you have social functions often?" was Bessie's next question.

"I wouldn't say often. We had a company Christmas party, of course. Beyond that, we usually had a summer outing of some sort for employees and their families. Some departments had regular social outings, but I didn't attend those events myself. My father always insisted on a formal dinner once a year as well for all staff and their partners. That was probably where I met Jeanne's various male friends."

"How many people worked for the bank?" Andrew asked.

"At its busiest, we had around fifteen employees. When we were winding things down, that number dropped, of course."

Andrew nodded. "And Jeanne was a customer service representative?"

"Yes, that's right. She was hoping to move into the lending department, but no decision had been made on her application before she died."

"Why did she want to move to the lending department?" Bessie asked.

Nick shrugged. "As I recall, it paid a bit more per hour. There was also a more generous bonus scheme in lending and the hours were set. Customer service representatives had to work Saturdays and one late night a week. In lending it was strictly nine to five, Mondays through Fridays."

"Who was in charge of the lending department?" Andrew wanted to know.

"I was," Nick said, flushing slightly.

"So you were the one who would have been making the decision on whether to hire her or not?" Andrew followed up.

"Ultimately, yes. I had a huge pile of applicants, though. I don't even know if I would have put her on the shortlist, especially considering her punctuality issues."

Bessie opened her mouth to ask another question, but Nick held up his hand. "As fascinating as it is chatting with you like this, my wife and I have other things to do today. You'll have to excuse us."

"Of course. Sorry to keep you," Andrew replied. "Thank you for talking with us. It is a lovely little dog."

The man scowled at the animal in question and then turned and looked at his wife. "Are you ready?"

"Yes, of course, dear," she said. She looked at Bessie and Andrew and then opened her handbag. She glanced around and then tucked the dog into it before the pair continued down the promenade.

Andrew and Bessie sat back down on their bench. "I didn't like either of them," Bessie said once the pair were out of earshot.

"I didn't, either, and it's nice to be able to say that. When I was with the police, we weren't meant to like or dislike anyone involved in a case."

"She seemed quite certain that Kenny killed Jeanne."

"Or maybe she's just convinced herself of that because she doesn't want to think that her husband did it."

"Maybe. There was something odd about him."

"I found two things odd about him. The first was his insistence that he barely knew Jeanne before he told us a great deal about her. The other ties into that. He and his wife both seemed to remember the case and Jeanne awfully well. It felt to me as if something had reminded them of it recently."

"Maybe they saw the article in the local paper."

"Maybe, or maybe Heather's sister saw it and mentioned it. Nick in particular seemed to remember quite a few specific details about Jeanne, even though it's been five years since she died. Recalling that she'd applied for a different job, for instance."

"And a job working directly for him," Bessie added. "Something felt off there, that's for sure."

"I wonder if John knows that they're back on the island."

"I should ring him and tell him."

Doona answered the call again. "You know you can just ring him directly," she said when Bessie told her what she wanted. "You don't have to go through me."

"I'm always afraid I'll interrupt something important if I ring his office. Besides, it's always nice to say hello to you."

Doona laughed. "I wasn't complaining about putting the call through. I was just trying to save you some time."

"I'm not in any rush," Bessie told her. "It's a beautiful day and I'm sitting on the promenade soaking up sunshine."

"Good for you. It does look lovely outside. If I weren't having dinner with my ex-husband, I'd be tempted to go out for a walk myself."

"You're having dinner with your ex-husband?"

"Yeah. We try to get together once in a while, since we've been friends forever. Just because our marriage didn't work, doesn't mean we can't still enjoy each other's company. Anyway, his parents always loved me, so I'm having dinner with him and his wife and his parents as well. They're leaving the children at home, for which I'm grateful."

"Have fun," Bessie said, chuckling.

"I'm sure I will. Let me put you through to John."

"Ah, Bessie, what can I do for you?" John said when he picked up the phone.

"We just had a strange conversation with Nick and Heather Grant," Bessie replied. "I wasn't sure if you knew or not that they were on the island at the moment."

"Funnily enough, I just found that out. I spoke to Jefferson this morning and he told me that Nick and Heather are having a short holiday over here. Where did you bump into them?"

"We're just enjoying the day on the Douglas promenade. They walked right past us."

"Maybe you'd better run me through the whole conversation," John suggested.

Bessie did her best to repeat everything that was said. When she was done, she handed the phone to Andrew and he answered a few questions.

"I think we should meet again, maybe tomorrow night," John said when Bessie had the phone back again. "I'll see if Hugh and Doona are available. You and Andrew have spoken to nearly everyone involved with the case. Maybe you can help me put together an argument that I can make to the chief constable for reopening it."

"We'll do our best," Bessie promised. "I'll expect you all at six tomorrow unless I hear otherwise."

"I'll bring food and pudding," John added.

Bessie put her phone back in her bag. "We're having another gathering at my cottage tomorrow night," she said. "John's hoping to convince the chief constable to reopen the case."

"Excellent. Let's try to find more for him between now and then," Andrew said.

Bessie grinned. "Maybe Max Rogers will have something interesting to say tomorrow."

"I've been thinking about Kenny. There must be a way for us to speak to him."

"I have a friend who works at Noble's. I could ring her and see if she has any ideas."

"Why not? It's worth a try."

Bessie rang her friend Helen at home, but no one answered. "Helen, it's Bessie Cubbon. Can you please give me a ring when you get a chance? It's nothing urgent; I'm just seeking information," Bessie told the answering machine.

"And with that, I suppose we've done all we can for now," Andrew said. "Maybe we should think about getting some dinner somewhere."

"Maybe I should cook for you, as you've bought me lunch and dinner every day since you've been here," Bessie retorted.

"I don't want you to have to go to any trouble. Besides, I'm on holiday. I'm meant to be eating all the things I don't normally eat at fancy restaurants I can't normally enjoy."

Bessie grinned. "Douglas is full of fancy restaurants, but we aren't exactly dressed for them."

"No, that's probably true. Are there any not quite fancy but still delicious restaurants where we could get dinner?"

"Plenty. What sort of food do you fancy?"

"I could really go for a good Chinese meal, if that sounds good to you."

"There are two excellent Chinese restaurants in Douglas. They're at opposite ends of the promenade."

"So we'll get a nice long walk in, whichever one we choose?"

"Exactly. One is slightly fancier than the other, with somewhat higher prices, but the food is also better. The other one has very good food as well, though."

"Will we be underdressed if we go with the fancy one?"

"No, not at all. Especially not this time of year, when there are still lots of tourists on the island. We'll be fine."

"Let's go for the slightly fancier place with the better food, then," Andrew said. "All of this talking about food has made me hungry. Are you ready for dinner?"

"I am, actually, even though it's a bit early. We did only have a light lunch, of course."

"We can walk slowly, if you want to build up more of an appetite."

When they reached the block of flats where Kenny was staying, they stopped. "I wish I could remember what he looks like," Bessie said.

"I wonder if his brother has a dog."

"Oh, that would be handy. Assuming Kenny helps out and walks it once in a while, of course."

They stood and watched the building for several minutes, but the only person who came out was a tall blonde woman talking on her mobile phone as she went.

"We could stand here for hours and never see Kenny," Bessie said eventually.

"Or he could walk right past us and we might not even realise," Andrew added. "We should ask John to bring copies of the articles that were in paper when Jeanne died. I'd like to see some photos of Kenny."

"That's a good idea. I'll ring him later tonight or early tomorrow and ask him."

"Let's go and get dinner. I'm too hungry to care about Kenny at the moment."

Bessie laughed. "It isn't that much further down the promenade. We should be there in just a few minutes."

The small restaurant, inside one of the town's nicer hotels, was already about half-full when Bessie and Andrew arrived.

"I didn't think you'd be this busy," Bessie told the man at the door. "At least not this early in the evening."

"It's a tour bus group," he explained. "They came up to spend the day in Douglas, but they're staying in Port Erin. They'll have an early dinner here and then stop for ice cream once they get back to Port Erin."

"Can you fit us in somewhere away from the crowd?" Andrew requested.

The man gave them a table on the opposite side of the room from everyone else. Bessie opened the menu and sighed. "Everything is good here," she said. "It's going to take me ages to decide what I want."

"That's a good problem to have," the waiter suggested as he approached the table. "Will I be making things worse if I tell you about today's specials?"

Bessie nodded. "But tell us anyway," she said quickly.

In the end, she and Andrew both decided to try dishes from the list of specials. With Andrew's encouragement, Bessie got a glass of wine.

"I'm driving, so it's just fizzy drinks for me, I'm afraid," he told the waiter.

"I can get some wine in for tomorrow night," Bessie offered. "You won't be driving after our dinner with John and the others."

"I don't really drink alcohol very often," Andrew replied. "For a whole host of reasons."

The drinks were delivered only a moment later. Bessie took a sip of her wine and smiled. "This is delicious. Thank you for suggesting it."

"It feels as if it's been a very long day. I thought you deserved a glass of wine."

"I'm certainly going to enjoy it, but what shall we talk about?"

"Tell me about life on the island over the years," Andrew suggested. "It's lovely and it feels very different to anywhere else I've ever been. What was it like when you first moved back here from America?"

"It felt smaller," Bessie said after a moment's thought. "And yet larger as well. In America, we'd lived in Cleveland, which is a big city. Compared to that, the island felt small and behind the times. But because I didn't drive, Laxey felt miles away from everything. I used to take buses everywhere I wanted to go, which wasn't all that unusual in those days. Even women who did drive generally didn't have a car at their disposal. Many more people relied on public transportation then, and we didn't go very many places, either."

"What about things like shopping?"

"We had local farmers markets for a lot of things, and a small local grocers. There was a chemist's shop next door to the local doctor's surgery, as well. I didn't need to leave Laxey to find the things that I needed."

"The island has changed a lot in your lifetime, then."

"Yes, it has. I don't feel as if I've changed very much, though."

Andrew laughed. "What did you do for fun in those days?"

"I didn't go out much, really. I felt as if I was in mourning for a long while. Single women didn't go out to pubs on their own or anything like that, anyway. The church had the occasional social evening where unattached women were welcome, but generally speaking, there were very few unattached men to go around at such events. Men and women usually married quite young in those days, as well. I was engaged to Matthew at seventeen and that wasn't considered too young."

"I was married at twenty-four. My wife was twenty-one. We both encouraged our children to wait until they were older to make that sort of commitment."

"Here we are," the waiter said, putting steaming hot plates in front of each of them. "Do you need anything else right now?"

Bessie shook her head and picked up her fork; chopsticks were too much bother. Her mouth started watering as the delicious smells hit her nose.

"It looks wonderful," Andrew said.

The pair focussed on their food for several minutes.

"Delicious," Andrew pronounced. "I'm glad we chose this restaurant. It's wonderful."

"It is good tonight," Bessie agreed, "but then, I've never had a bad meal here."

A moment later a loud voice filled the dining room. "Ladies and gentlemen, it is now time to get back to the bus. Please make certain that you've settled your bill before you leave the dining room," a short woman in a bright red dress said loudly from the centre of the room.

Everyone else in the room began to gather up their things. It seemed to Bessie as if they all began talking at once, as well.

"I didn't get the bill yet."

"The bus can't leave without anyone."

"Harriet just went to the loo and she hasn't paid yet."

"I didn't get my fortune cookie."

"Where is my handbag? Jonathan, have you seen my handbag?"

"Where is the loo, then?"

Bessie looked at Andrew and they both chuckled.

"I don't think that sort of touring is for me," Bessie said quietly.

"Come on, you two, eat up. My goodness, you're way behind the others. We have to get back to Port Erin before it gets dark or there won't be time for ice cream," the woman in red said as she approached their table.

"I'd hate to miss the ice cream," Andrew said, giving Bessie a mischievous wink.

"You'll have to get a move on, then, and get the bill paid quickly, too," the woman told them. "There isn't time for either of you to go to the loo, either, so don't even ask."

Bessie opened her mouth to tell the woman that they weren't part of her coach party, but the woman had already turned and begun to walk away.

"Do you think she'll come back and shout at us some more?" Andrew asked. "If I weren't so hungry, I think I'd eat as slowly as I could, just to frustrate her."

"Surely she should realise that we aren't part of her tour group."

"She should, which is why it's such fun pretending that we are," Andrew laughed.

A few minutes later, the woman began sending people out of the restaurant. "Straight out the door and onto the bus," she told them, one after another. "We haven't time to waste. Get on the bus and find seats anywhere. You needn't worry about where you sat before. Just sit down."

"She makes bus touring seem such fun," Andrew said softly.

"Indeed."

"Are you two still eating?" the woman demanded a moment later. "You'll have to get that packaged up for takeaway. I can't wait for you any longer."

"I believe Harriet is still in the loo," Bessie said.

The woman glared at her for a minute and then stalked away towards the loos in the corner. As she pulled open the door, their waiter rushed over to them.

"I'm not sure that she realises that you aren't a part of the tour group," he said. "I tried to tell her, but she wouldn't listen to me."

"We'll tell her if she ever lets us get a word in," Bessie replied.

A moment later the woman was back, rushing an older woman out of the loo as she went. "Right, you two are the last ones. Let's go," she said sharply.

"We aren't actually with your tour group," Bessie told her, "and I'm feeling quite sorry for the poor men and women who are."

"What do you mean, you aren't with my group? Why didn't you say something when I first spoke to you?" the woman demanded.

"Do you really have time to stay here and argue with us?" Andrew asked.

Bessie hid a chuckle behind her napkin as the woman shot him an angry look and then rushed out of the room. As soon as the door shut behind her, Bessie, Andrew, and the waiter all began to laugh.

"I was talking to one of the women on the tour. They've been travelling with this guide for a fortnight now and she still hasn't learned anyone's name or even bothered to speak to any of them," the waiter said. "She just shouts at them to get them to go from place to place and then shouts out a little bit of history about each thing when they arrive at the various sites. The woman I spoke with said that they're all spending their spare time drafting their letters of complaint to the tour company."

"Which company is it?" Bessie asked.

"Not one of the ones we usually get," the waiter replied. "They're here from somewhere near Dover. I believe it's the first time the company has come to the island, and I'm not sure if they'll ever be coming back again."

"If they do, I hope they find a better guide," Bessie said.

She and Andrew finished their meal and then cracked open their fortune cookies.

"You enjoy solving life's mysteries," Bessie read her fortune.

"I suppose that's accurate," Andrew said with a smile. "Expect the unexpected," he read from his cookie. "I'm not sure I like that."

"Maybe you'll get unexpected good things," Bessie suggested.

"I certainly hope so," he replied.

The walk back to the car was exactly what Bessie needed after her large meal. When they were both in their seats, Andrew stared at the building across the road for a moment.

"I wish I knew which flat was Kenny's," he said after a minute.

"For all we know, it could be one at the back. Let's just go home."

"You're right, of course. I'm afraid I'm getting rather obsessed with this case of John's. At least it keeps me from spending all of my time thinking about Lukas's case."

"Maybe you'll have an email from him when you get back to your cottage."

"I just might. Now I'm in a hurry to get there," he laughed as he started the engine.

On the drive back to Laxey, they chatted easily about holidays they'd taken when they were younger.

"Of course, once the children came along, all of our holidays revolved around them. We did a lot of holiday parks and that sort of thing. My wife always enjoyed them at least as much as the children did. I'd have preferred to spend more time at historical sites, but the children were never interested and neither was my wife," Andrew told her.

He parked his car outside Bessie's cottage. "I'll just go and check my laptop for messages. I won't be long," he told Bessie as they climbed out of the car.

"I'll put the kettle on," Bessie replied, "and get out some chocolate biscuits."

Andrew grinned and then walked quickly away. Inside Treoghe Bwaane Bessie put fresh water in the kettle and switched it on. As she was pulling down teacups, the phone rang.

"Bessie? It's Helen Corkill, just ringing you back."

"My goodness, it seems strange to hear you calling yourself that," Bessie laughed. Helen had just recently married Peter Corkill, a police inspector with the Douglas Constabulary.

"I'm just starting to get used to it," Helen replied. "I've kept my maiden name for work, but I'm using Pete's socially. I must say it still makes me smile every time I say it."

"That's good to hear. I hope you and Pete will continue to be very happy together."

"We're working on it. It's proving to be something of an adjustment, married life, but we both feel it's worth some hard work."

"I'm sure it is. I don't want to keep you, though. I was wondering if you could suggest a way for me to meet Kenny Wilkins. I understand he works as a lab technician at Noble's."

"He does. He's actually a really good guy. Why do you want to meet him?"

"John has been talking about an old murder case, and Kenny's involved in it, that's all. Andrew Cheatham and I have been talking to some of the witnesses, trying to help John out."

"I'd heard that Inspector Cheatham was on the island. Pete would love to meet him. He's familiar with his work, of course."

"We should have dinner together while he's here. I'm sure Andrew would love to meet you both."

"Let me check with Pete and see when he's free. But you asked about Kenny. John must be looking into Jeanne Stowe's death. Kenny mentioned her to me once."

"That's the murder that John is hoping to reinvestigate," Bessie replied, "but as Andrew and I don't have any official standing, we can't just turn up on Kenny's doorstep and ask him questions."

"I'm sure he'd be happy to talk to you, though. He's still really broken up about Jeanne's death. He'd do anything to help the police find her killer. Let me ring him and see if I can arrange something. I assume you'd prefer to do this as soon as possible."

"Absolutely. Tomorrow afternoon would be best."

Bessie put the phone down and made two cups of tea. By the time she was finished with that job, Helen rang back.

"He'll meet you at two o'clock tomorrow afternoon in the café at Noble's. That's his lunch break, so he won't have a lot of time, but as I thought, he'll be happy to speak with you. I told him that it wasn't a formal investigation or anything, but that Andrew Cheatham was one of London's top criminal investigators. He's eager to help."

"Thank you so much," Bessie said. "Do check with Pete and ring me back. I'm sure Andrew would love to meet you both."

Helen promised to do that. Bessie put the phone down and found a box of chocolate biscuits. She was just piling them onto a plate when Andrew knocked on her door.

CHAPTER 12

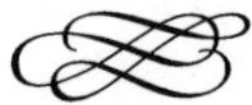

"You look as if you have news," he said as he walked into the cottage.

"I do. I just talked to my friend at Noble's. She's arranged for us to meet with Kenny tomorrow afternoon. According to her, he's eager to find out what happened to Jeanne and happy to cooperate with our unofficial investigation."

"That's good to hear."

"My friend is married to a police inspector who would love to meet you," Bessie added. "I told her you'd be happy to meet him if we can find a time and a place that fits your schedule."

"I'm always happy to meet any of your friends, no matter what they do for a living, but it's a special pleasure talking to other members of the constabulary."

"Good. She's going to let me know what works for them. Do you have news as well?"

"I do, and it isn't as good as yours."

"Your friend found Dorothy?" Bessie guessed.

"He did. Or rather he found out what happened to her. She died in a plane crash about a year after Flora died."

"A plane crash?"

"Yes, but not a commercial jet. This was a small private plane, being piloted by her fiancé. The pair were flying from London to Paris for a romantic holiday together when they crashed."

"I assume it was investigated thoroughly?"

"It was investigated, yes. Unfortunately, the plane crashed into the English Channel and there wasn't much left of it when the wreckage was found. The bodies were never recovered."

Bessie shuddered. "Maybe I don't want to hear the rest of this."

"Investigators determined that the engines had failed, but couldn't work out why. No distress call was received before the crash."

"So it was just a tragic accident?"

"If you believe in coincidences, yes. I'm not fond of them when it comes to murder investigations, though. Neither is Lukas. He's pushing for more information and might ask that the case be reopened."

"If we're right and Betty is behind all of this, how did she cause a plane to crash?"

"Before we worry about that, we have to find Betty," Andrew replied. "Or Cindy, if that's who she is. I will say that the more Lukas discovers, the more I'm inclined to believe your theory. I'm hoping to have some answers about the charity tomorrow. On the surface it looks legitimate, but there is a lot more digging to be done before I'll believe that."

"And no one knows where Betty is now?"

"Remember that she's officially Cindy," Andrew reminded her. "Lukas spoke to her mother. Her father passed away some years ago. Her mother hasn't seen her since before the fateful skiing holiday. She did tell him that she'd reached out to Cindy a couple of times, asking her to get in touch, but she's never had a reply."

"If she reached out to her, she must know where Cindy is."

"She has an address for her, yes. It's a flat in London that Cindy owns. Lukas had someone in London check and it appears that no one is living there at the moment. Lukas's friend asked around and no one in the building could ever remember seeing anyone going into or out of the flat. He tried talking to the building's manager, but the man was only friendly until Cindy's name came up. Then he shut down and refused to say anything else."

"Why would she kill the other three women? She'd already gone to prison for Betty's murder. Was it just because they knew her real identity?"

"I suspect that might be at least part of it. We may have to wait until Lukas finds her to learn the rest of it."

"I don't want you to leave the island until Cindy or Betty or whoever she is found," Bessie exclaimed. "It would be like reading a murder mystery where the last chapter is missing."

"Unfortunately, real-life crime is often like that. Remember, this case has been haunting my friend for thirty years. I promise to let you know the outcome if and when my friend finds Cindy, though."

Bessie had to be happy with that. The pair drank their tea and nibbled some chocolate biscuits while they talked about Betty and Cindy and the other women. When they were done, they took a long walk on the beach together.

"I think I'm glad I waited until September to come to visit you," Andrew said as he skirted around a pair of small children building a sandcastle. "I imagine the beach was much busier during the summer months."

"It was, indeed," Bessie agreed. "It feels almost quiet now, with only a few people around."

"I'm not sure I'd call this quiet," Andrew laughed. A group of teenagers were playing loud music from a huge portable stereo system set up behind one of the cottages. A little girl, maybe three years old, was sobbing loudly as her mother tried to get her to come inside their cottage. Beyond that, two dogs were chasing one another up and down the beach, and both were barking constantly.

"It's been much worse," Bessie told him, "but in another week or two, everyone will be gone and I'll have the beach all to myself for the winter."

"Do they ever hire out the cottages in the winter?"

"They haven't before, but I suppose they might if someone was interested."

"I may have to ring up and see about that," Andrew said lightly.

A few minutes later he walked Bessie back home again. "I'll collect you at nine and we'll go and see about some insurance," he told Bessie.

"I'm looking forward to talking to both Max and Kenny, and then sharing everything with John and the others. I hope John can reopen the case. I feel as if we're close to finding a solution."

It wasn't quite late enough for Bessie to go to bed, so she read for a short while. For some reason she simply couldn't get interested in the latest cosy mystery that she'd bought, though. Maybe it was because the two cases she was involved with were much more interesting than the fictional one the author described, she thought as she washed her face and got ready for bed. She was asleep as soon as her head hit the pillow and she slept soundly until two minutes before six.

As she locked her door behind her, ready for her morning walk on the beach, she was surprised to hear her name being called.

"Bessie? I thought you'd be out and about around now," Andrew said as he crossed the sand towards her.

"I hope you didn't have trouble sleeping," Bessie told him.

"No, not at all. I slept incredibly well and then woke up at six, wide awake and ready to start my day."

"You need a nice brisk walk on the beach," Bessie suggested.

"As it is far too early to head to Ramsey, and the fresh sea air seems to be doing wonders for my health, I'm going to have to agree with you."

Bessie headed, as she usually did, for the water's edge before turning and heading towards Thie yn Traie in the distance. Andrew fell into step beside her.

"I hope you don't mind my coming along," he said after a few minutes. "I'm sure you enjoy the peace and quiet of your morning stroll."

"I do, but you're more than welcome to join me while you're here. You'll be back in London before we know it."

"I've been thinking about seriously looking at property over here, but I hate the thought of being away from my children and grandchildren. I may have to look at moving somewhere near the sea in England, though. The air really does seem to agree with me."

Bessie felt an odd rush of disappointment and relief at the same time. She was really enjoying Andrew's company, but she wasn't sure she wanted him to move to the island. He was more than welcome to visit regularly, though, she thought as they passed the stairs to Thie yn Traie and continued onwards.

"It feels as if we're the only people awake anywhere," Andrew said a moment later.

"This stretch of beach is always quiet, even when the holiday cottages are completely booked with holidaymakers," Bessie told him. "If we keep going, we'll eventually reach the new homes that were built in the last year. They're right on the beach, and I believe someone is living in most, if not all of them."

"Are some of them still for sale?"

"No, they've all sold, but at least one was purchased by a couple from across. They intend to use it as a holiday home, I understand."

Before much longer, the houses came into view. As far as Bessie could see, all the curtains in every home were tightly shut.

"It appears everyone is still fast asleep," Andrew said.

"I suspect at least some of the residents are up and getting ready for work, but you'd never know it from out here."

"I'd have my curtains open as soon as I woke up, if I had this view," Andrew told her. "They've no neighbours behind them. They could have the curtains open while they got themselves ready for work."

"Except the beach is a public right of way. Anyone could walk past the back of their house at any time."

"Bah, then they might get an eyeful of something they weren't expecting, that's all. I wouldn't want to miss out on seeing this view, not for a second."

"Are you opening your curtains as soon as you wake up at your holiday cottage?" Bessie asked.

Andrew laughed. "Now that you mention it, no, I'm not, but maybe I should start. It is a truly wonderful view."

Bessie made a mental note to make certain she didn't glance up at

Andrew's cottage in the mornings for the rest of his stay. "I don't open mine, either, not until I've showered and dressed and feel ready to face the day. But then, I've lived with this view for a great many years. I suppose I'm rather spoiled with it, really."

"You are, but I think we all tend to take what we live with for granted. I've had friends tell me how lucky I am to have such wonderful views of London, for example."

Bessie nodded. "It's getting late," she said, after glancing at her watch. "We should head back so that we can get into Ramsey as close to nine as possible."

"I can't believe how good I'm feeling this morning," Andrew said a few minutes later as they made their way back towards home. "I haven't walked this much in a long time and I'm not even a little bit tired."

"I hope it doesn't catch up with you later," Bessie said worriedly.

"I'm sure I'll be fine. We aren't planning on doing any walking later, anyway. Sitting and talking to our various witnesses won't take physical energy, just the mental sort."

Andrew stopped at his cottage to freshen up and Bessie continued on to Treoghe Bwaane to do the same. A few minutes later they were on their way to Ramsey.

"We're best parking near the town centre and walking to the man's office," Bessie suggested as they reached the edge of the town. "He may have a small car park outside his office, but I'd rather not take up a space there."

"I think that's wise," Andrew said. "Let's leave the spaces there for proper customers."

A few minutes later Bessie found herself wondering if the man actually ever had any proper customers. His small shopfront was in between a charity shop Bessie hadn't known was there and a fish and chips shop that had gone out of business some time ago. There was a single car in the car park in front of the small strip of shops, with space for maybe three additional cars if they were all carefully parked.

Andrew drove past the building and found a parking spot on the next street. "I didn't notice if there were lights on in Mr. Rogers' office or not," he told Bessie as they got out of the car.

"There was a light on, but it might just have been a security light," Bessie replied. "We may be wasting our time."

"If no one is there, I'm sure we can find something else to do with this lovely day," Andrew said brightly.

A minute later Bessie pulled on the door to the insurance agency. She was surprised when it opened. A loud buzzer rang somewhere within the building and that noise was followed by the sound of someone running down a flight of stairs.

"Ah, good morning," a man said as he burst through a door at the back of the small room in which Andrew and Bessie had found themselves. "Good morning. How are you today?"

"Fine, thank you," Andrew said. "We're looking for Max Rogers."

"Really? Well, that would be me, so you've found him. What can I do for you, sir?" the man replied. He was probably in his mid-fifties, and Bessie thought he looked as if he'd only just finished getting dressed for the day as he'd rushed down the stairs. His shirt was only partly tucked in, his tie was off-centre, and his collar was standing up on one side.

"We recently spoke to Howard Miles about Jeanne Stowe. He told us that you had a brief relationship with Ms. Stowe just before her death," Andrew said.

Bessie was surprised to see Andrew acting as if he were conducting a police investigation. She'd thought they were going to pretend they wanted insurance, and then try to get the man talking. If Mr. Rogers asked them who they were or why they were interested in Jeanne's death, they might have a problem.

"Ah, Howard mentioned that you might be coming to see me," the man said. "Please, have a seat." He gestured towards the lumpy couch that was up against the wall. While Bessie and Andrew sat down, Max pulled a chair over to join them. "You're probably wasting your time talking to me, really. I barely knew the woman," he said as he dropped into the seat.

"But you were involved with her before her death?" Andrew asked.

"We were, well, I mean, I spent some time with her, yeah. It wasn't anything serious, though. We went out for dinner once or twice, that was about it," Max said.

"What did you think of her?" Andrew asked. Bessie found the question surprising, and judging from Max's face, he did as well.

"She was, I mean, she was nice enough, but there just wasn't any real chemistry, if you know what I mean. I liked her well enough, but after we'd gone out a few times, well, I just stopped ringing, really. I didn't like her enough to keep seeing her."

"Howard gave me the impression that you and Jeanne were sleeping together," Andrew said.

Max flushed. "I may have given him that impression at the time," he said sheepishly, "but things never actually went that far."

"Did you ever visit her flat?" was Andrew's next question.

"Oh, yes, a few times. She invited me in after I'd taken her to dinner the first time. I thought, well, that she was suggesting something, but it turned out she simply needed some help moving some furniture around. I helped her out and then she sent me on my way. After our next meal, she invited me in again, and this time she wanted my help painting her sitting room. I still agreed to take her out one more time, but, well, when she told me that she was pulling up some fitted carpets I'd had enough."

"You think she was only using you to help with her DIY?" Andrew asked.

"That was certainly the way it felt," Max said. "I mean, I don't mind helping out a friend, but it was too early in our relationship for her to be asking me to do all those things, at least in my opinion. Also, the second time, when she wanted me to help with the painting, her ex-husband was at her flat when we got back from dinner. He was already hard at work painting the ceiling. I found that odd."

Andrew nodded. "How long after the last time you saw her did she die?"

"It was probably three months, or something like that. I found another woman who was a lot more fun, but we only went out for about three months. After we split up, I actually thought about ringing Jeanne again, but then I saw in the paper that she'd been killed."

"Any idea who might have killed her?" Andrew asked.

Max shrugged. "At the time I pretty much assumed it was that ex-husband that I mentioned before. I reckoned he got tired of her having him do all that work around her flat. If it wasn't him, it was probably his partner. I can't imagine how much she must have resented his always rushing off to help Jeanne."

Andrew looked over at Bessie. "Was there anything else?" he asked her.

"I understand that Howard did a lot of DIY for Jeanne, too," Bessie said.

"Oh, aye, Mabel was always sending him over to help out her friend. I don't know why he put up with it, but then I don't understand what he sees in Mabel, either, but that's beside the point," Max said.

"Maybe Howard got tired of Jeanne's demands," Bessie suggested.

Max laughed. "If he got tired of anyone, it would have been Mabel. She was the one sending Howard to Jeanne's every night. I wondered, at the time, if she was trying to test Howard or something, maybe trying to check to see if he'd be faithful. I don't think Mabel had anything to worry about with Jeanne, though. I don't think she was interested in sex. She just wanted men for DIY."

"If Jeanne's ex-husband didn't kill her, who might have?" Bessie asked.

"Maybe some random guy she pulled who didn't realise she was only looking for help with her flat?" Max replied. "I mean, I was kind of upset when she invited me into her flat after our first dinner together and then expected me to help her and not get anything in return. She was lucky I'm a nice guy who just left after I'd moved furniture for an hour. Maybe she ran into another guy who wasn't as nice."

"Howard suggested that Jeanne went out with a number of his friends. Can you give us any more names of men we can speak to about her?" Andrew asked.

Max shook his head. "I don't know who she was involved with besides me. Most of Howard's friends are married, anyway. I mean, I'm sure Jeanne wouldn't have cared as long as the man in question was handy, but I think if any of them were looking to cheat, they'd be looking to actually cheat, if you know what I mean."

"If you remember anything that you think might help with the investigation, get in touch with Inspector John Rockwell in Laxey," Andrew told the man as he got to his feet. "Thank you for your time today."

"Oh, it was no problem. I wasn't doing anything anyway," the man replied with surprising honesty.

Andrew and Bessie walked out of the building and headed back towards Andrew's car without speaking. It was only when they were both back inside the vehicle that Bessie spoke.

"I'm almost sorry now that I never met Jeanne. She seems to have had a gift for getting men to do her hard work for her."

"Max didn't seem overly taken in by her charms."

"No, but he did move furniture and help her paint her sitting room," Bessie pointed out.

"I'm really looking forward to talking to Kenny now. As we have to wait until this afternoon for that, what shall we do with the rest of our morning?"

"How about a trip around the Manx Museum?" Bessie suggested. "You aren't getting to do nearly enough sightseeing, but the museum isn't far from Noble's."

"That sounds good, if we'll have enough time to see it all."

"We do, and there's a café where we can get some lunch, as well," Bessie said. "The museum opens at ten, so our timing should be about right. It's still quite early, really."

"I should get up at six every day," Andrew laughed.

The small museum car park was nearly empty when they pulled into it a short while later. Dan, one of the museum staff, was just unlocking the doors as they approached.

"Good morning. Welcome to the Manx Museum. How are you today, Bessie?" he greeted them.

"I'm very well. This is my friend, Andrew. It's his first visit to the island as a tourist."

"Well, then, the Manx Museum is a good place to learn more," Dan said. "Come on in and I'll set you up with the movie."

Bessie and Andrew were the only people in the small lecture theatre where the introductory historical movie was shown. When it was finished, Andrew clapped lightly.

"That was excellent," he told Bessie. "A brief but very informative history of the island. I can't wait to see what the museum holds."

Bessie was happy to show the man around the various exhibits. They took their time and reached the café at almost exactly midday. After a light lunch, they made a brief stop in the gift shop.

"You must let me buy you a little something," Andrew said. "I want to thank you for showing me around the museum."

"I don't want anything," Bessie said firmly. "I'm enjoying your company and I always enjoy a trip around the museum."

Andrew looked around for a short while and then sighed. "I really should buy presents for the children and grandchildren while I have the chance, but I'm not in the mood to shop for all of them today."

"You can always buy them things from the airport gift shop at the end of the trip," Bessie suggested. "They have all manner of things with the Manx flag or Manx cats on them."

Andrew laughed. "That's just the sort of thing they'll all expect, as well. I was thinking of getting something like jewellery for some of them, but they'll be expecting Manx flag tea towels and I'd hate to disappoint them."

It was a little bit early to head for Noble's, but Bessie knew that parking there could be difficult, so she suggested that they drive over and find a space. "We can always sit in the car and chat for a while, if we're too early," she said.

As it happened, a space opened up as Andrew turned into the car park. He slid into it and then smiled at Bessie. "That was almost too easy," he said.

"I'm told by my friends who drive that such things never happen," she replied.

"Shall we sit in the car and chat or head inside and find the café?"

"The café isn't difficult to find, but I suppose we could sit in there and have tea and cake rather than sit here."

"Cake sounds good, even though we just ate lunch," Andrew admitted.

"We did have a light lunch," Bessie said. "While I'm more excited about the tea than the cake, I won't say no to either."

They crossed the small car park and walked into the building. Bessie led Andrew down a corridor and into the café that served both staff and visitors. She smiled when she spotted Helen at one of the tables. As soon as Helen saw her, she rushed over.

"Bessie, I thought you'd probably be early," she exclaimed, pulling Bessie into a hug. "Kenny should be down in about twenty minutes."

"We know we're early, but we wanted some tea and maybe a slice of cake," Bessie explained.

"Well, you've come to the right place," Helen told her. "They have a new girl making cakes and she's very talented."

"Really? Anyone I would know?" Bessie asked.

"I doubt it, but that's her," Helen replied, nodding towards a young girl who was writing on the large chalkboard near the counter.

"It's the girl whose father owns the corner shop up the road from me," Bessie told Helen. "She moved across for a while and got a job with a bakery. Once she came back to the island, she started baking cakes and selling them by the slice in her father's shop. I didn't realise she was working here now."

"She is, and she's already proven very popular," Helen said. "I understand she sells her cakes to a few other restaurants around the island, as well, but the ones she makes here are just for us."

"Everything I tried of hers was excellent," Bessie replied. "I'm so happy we came in early. But where are my manners?" she exclaimed. She quickly introduced Andrew to Helen before they found a table in a quiet corner.

"What cakes are on offer today?" Bessie asked the waitress.

"Victoria sponge, jam roly-poly, lemon cream cake, and chocolate gateau," the woman replied.

"Chocolate," Bessie and Helen said at the same time.

Andrew laughed. "I'll have the lemon cream," he said, "and we all need tea."

The woman nodded and walked away.

"I should ring Pete and tell him that you're here," Helen said. She pulled her phone out of her pocket and then chuckled. "Or I could just wave to him."

Bessie looked over her shoulder and smiled as she spotted Pete Corkill in the doorway. Helen waved and he crossed the room to them.

"Hello, darling," he said, kissing the top of Helen's head. "I knew it was your lunch break, so I thought I'd pop over and see if you were down here."

Bessie smiled at the pair. When she'd first met Pete, she'd wondered if he ever smiled. Today, as he looked at his new wife, his smile was wide. The pair seemed perfectly suited, she thought, as Pete slid into the seat next to Helen, who quickly introduced him to Andrew.

"It's a real pleasure to meet you," he told Andrew. "I've read all of your books and found them incredibly useful."

"Thank you. Goodness knows I tried to focus on practical tips that investigators can use in the field."

"I understand you're looking into Jeanne Stowe's death," Pete said.

Andrew shrugged. "John Rockwell was kind enough to share the background on her case with me. While I'm enjoying seeing the sights around the island, I can't resist doing a bit of poking around as well. Thus far, everyone involved with the case has been very cooperative."

"After all this time, the killer probably feels quite safe," Pete suggested. "He or she won't expect you to find out anything new, not after five years."

"And I probably won't," Andrew agreed, "but maybe I can come at the old information from a new angle. If nothing else, it's proving to be an interesting mental exercise. The more of that I can get, the better."

Pete nodded. "Well, if you get tired of John's cold case, I have several dozen I would love for you to look over. Feel free to visit my office any time."

Andrew laughed. "That's a very kind invitation. I may just take you up on it one day."

Pete handed Andrew his card. "All of my contact details are on there, and Bessie has my home number if you'd prefer to use that."

Andrew dug around in his pockets and then pulled out a small notebook. He jotted down his name and a number on a sheet and then tore it out and handed it to Pete. "My home number. Feel free to ring one night when you have some time to chat. We can go over a few of those cold cases of yours. Sometimes just talking them through with someone new is all you need to shake something loose. Why, Bessie may have just cracked a thirty-year-old case for a colleague of mine."

"Really?" Pete asked. "I'm intrigued."

Andrew gave the pair a brief rundown of Lukas's case. When he was finished, Pete shook his head.

"I'm not sure I would have seen it, but once you said it, it makes sense. Betty killed Cindy and then took over her identity for some reason. Now she's gone back and killed all of the witnesses. I wonder if her mother is in any danger?"

"I hadn't really thought about that. Perhaps I should suggest it to Lukas," Andrew said with a frown.

"Considering that she seems to have murdered the other three women within a fairly short space of time not long after she got out of prison, I would think her mother is fairly safe," Pete said. "I might suggest that she stop trying to get in touch with her daughter, though."

Andrew nodded. "I'll ring Lukas tonight and discuss it with him."

"And here's Kenny," Helen said, getting to her feet.

Bessie turned and looked at the man who was walking towards them. He looked right around forty, with brown hair that had just a touch of grey in it. His hospital uniform seemed baggy and ill-fitting, but that might just have been the nature of the uniform itself. When he sat down opposite Bessie, she couldn't help but notice that he looked incredibly tired.

CHAPTER 13

Helen quickly performed introductions all around. As soon as she was finished, she got to her feet. "And now I must get back to my lovely patients. Two of them are less than lovely today, actually, and I'm sure the other girls on the floor will be happy to see me." She gave Pete a quick kiss and then made her way out of the room.

Pete watched her go and then sighed. "I need to go, too," he said. "I've a meeting with the chief constable that I'd rather not have to attend."

Bessie smiled sympathetically at him as he and Andrew shook hands. As Pete walked away from the table, Kenny spoke.

"I understand you want to talk to me about Jeanne. Helen wasn't totally clear on your official position, though."

"I'm a former London police inspector, now retired," Andrew told him. "I'm on holiday on the island, and almost as soon as I arrived, I heard about Jeanne's murder. There was an article about it in the local paper, and everywhere I went with my friend, Bessie, we seemed to bump into someone who was connected to the case in some way. The whole thing piqued my curiosity, I suppose you could say. I'm friends with John Rockwell, the local police inspector who is interested in reexamining the case. Anything that I learn will be passed along to him."

Kenny nodded. "As long as you aren't with the press, I suppose I don't mind talking to you. I just need to get some food first, if that's okay."

"Certainly. We ordered tea and cake some time ago and haven't seen the waitress since. Perhaps I should go to the counter and get you something. You look exhausted," Andrew said.

"I'm really tired today. I had my kids last night and they wouldn't go to bed. The little one wanted her mother and the other two ate too much junk food and were bouncing off the walls. It's hard work, being a single parent."

Andrew nodded. "What can I get you, then?" he asked.

Kenny shrugged. "Just tell the girl behind the counter that it's for me. She knows what I always get."

Andrew was only gone a few minutes. When he came back he gave Bessie a grin. "She's going to bring our cake with his food," he told her. "And our tea as well. She seemed to have forgotten about us."

"And poor Helen never got her cake," Bessie said.

"I told her to still bring three slices. If we can't manage all of it now, we can take a slice home with us or something," Andrew replied.

"So, what do you want to know about Jeanne?" Kenny asked.

"Who do you think killed her?" Andrew replied.

"It must have been someone random. Like maybe she started talking to a guy in a shop or something and he followed her home. Or maybe she met someone at the pub and invited him home. She did that all the time. She wasn't very smart about men, really," Kenny sighed.

"Inviting strange men home is certainly dangerous," Andrew agreed.

"Yeah, especially when you then ask them to paint your sitting room once they get there," Kenny laughed bitterly.

"Is that what she was doing?" Bessie asked.

"Jeanne was a little bit, well, odd," Kenny explained. "She simply couldn't look after her flat on her own. She needed a lot of help and she didn't understand why she couldn't simply ask anyone and everyone to provide it. She used to ring me up all the time and ask me to come over to do everything from painting and decorating to changing light bulbs or taking up carpets."

"Even after you were divorced?" Andrew checked.

"Oh, yes, the divorce didn't really change anything as far as she was concerned. She still thought that she should be my first priority."

"How difficult for Sandra," Bessie murmured.

"Yeah, I know. It was hard for her and for me. I felt so guilty about leaving Jeanne that I could never bring myself to say no to her demands, but then I'd feel guilty for leaving Sandra on her own while I was doing things for Jeanne. I felt trapped between them, really."

"And then someone helpfully killed Jeanne for you," Andrew remarked.

Kenny flushed. "I don't like the implication behind that," he said tightly.

"Here we are," the waitress said brightly. "Kenny's usual, three slices of cake, and tea all around." It took the woman several minutes to move everything from her tray onto the small table. By the time she was finished, Kenny looked less upset.

"Look, I know that a lot of people probably think that I killed Jeanne, but I didn't. I might have liked to, if I'm honest, but I'm simply not brave enough or smart enough to manage it. There were times when I was tempted to hit her, I'll admit that, but I never did, not even when she was being hugely demanding." He sighed and then bit into his sandwich.

Bessie took a sip of her tea and then patted his hand. "You were still in love with her, weren't you?"

"Yeah," he replied in a low voice. "I was still in love with her. I am still in love with her. I don't know that I'll ever get over losing her."

"But you'd left her," Bessie reminded him.

"I wanted kids really badly," he said. "It was always my dream to have five or six. I was an only child and I was really lonely. I always swore that when I got older I'd have a huge family so that I'd never be lonely again."

"And Jeanne didn't want children or couldn't have children?" Andrew asked.

"It was one of those," he replied, "but I don't know which. When we were first married, she told me she wanted kids one day, but one day never seemed to come around. Eventually I told her that I wanted to start trying, and she reluctantly agreed. After about six months, when nothing happened, I started to get upset. She went to see her doctor, or at least that's what she told me. To cut a long story short, she told me that her doctor had tested her and that if we were having trouble conceiving, it was my fault, not hers."

"Oh, dear," Bessie exclaimed.

"Yeah, exactly. I was devastated. When I met Sandra a few weeks later, I, well, I never told her I was married. I didn't worry about using protection because of what Jeanne had told me. When she fell pregnant, at first I didn't believe her that I was the father. She broke up with me when she found out about Jeanne."

"I don't blame her," Bessie said when the man stopped talking to eat. She took a bite of her cake and washed it down with tea before he resumed.

"I didn't blame her, either, but I was so excited about the baby that I left Jeanne and divorced her. In spite of all of that, yeah, I was still in love with Jeanne. Whenever she rang, I'd drop everything and rush to help her, at least until the baby came. When the baby came, well, that's when I really understood about love."

"Children are life's greatest blessing," Andrew said.

Bessie bit her tongue. There was no way she was going to argue with the man, not about something she couldn't properly understand, anyway.

"I started seeing less of Jeanne and spending more time with the baby, and with Sandra, of course. She fell pregnant again pretty quickly and I thought things were going really well. Then Jeanne's relationship ended and she started ringing me again. Even with the children at home, I couldn't resist it when Jeanne rang," he said, sounding frustrated.

"And you were still helping her whenever you could, right up until her death?" Andrew asked.

"Yeah, she was still ringing at least a couple of times a week, although she hadn't rung for the last few days before she died. At the time I thought maybe she'd found a new boyfriend, but I don't know if she had or if she'd simply not needed anything doing around her flat."

"Were you two intimate after your divorce?" Andrew asked.

Bessie blushed and took a quick sip of tea.

"No, we were not," Kenny said softly. "I can't tell you that I wouldn't have been with her if she'd offered, but she never did and I never suggested it. She was never that interested in sex, really, though. It probably never occurred to her."

"What did you think of her friend Mabel?" was Andrew's next question.

"Mabel? Jeanne met her after she moved to Ramsey. I probably only met the woman once or twice. She was okay, I suppose."

"What about her husband?" Andrew added.

"She has a husband?" Kenny asked.

"Howard Miles," Andrew said.

"Oh, Howard. I didn't realise they were married. I saw him at Jeanne's a few times. He was always willing to help her out with projects. I got the impression that he was interested in more than just friendship, but like I said, Jeanne wasn't really the type to have sex with random men. Besides, she and Mabel were good friends. She wouldn't have done anything that would have upset Mabel."

"Do you think Mabel knew Howard was interested in Jeanne?" Andrew asked.

"I've no idea. Like I said, it was just a feeling I got from the man when I saw him with Jeanne. I don't think I ever saw him and Mabel both at Jeanne's at the same time, so I don't know how he behaved when Mabel was around. And it may just have been my imagination anyway. I was, well, quite jealous of Jeanne, really. I always thought other men were interested in her."

"So you think she met someone at the pub or at a shop and took him home to help her with some DIY, but he got the wrong idea?" Andrew asked.

"I can't imagine what else it could have been," Kenny replied.

"Did Jeanne ever take drugs?" was Andrew's next question.

"Drugs? Jeanne? No, no way. I know she died of an overdose of something, the police never said what, but there was no way it was an accident or that she'd have agreed to take anything. She didn't even like to take headache tablets. Her older brother died of a drug overdose. It was accidental, but it scared her. She was incredibly careful with medications and she would never have touched anything illegal."

"What about Mabel or Howard?" Bessie interjected. "Did either of them seem like the type to take illegal drugs?"

"Not really, but maybe," Kenny said. "I mean, I barely knew them, and I never saw any evidence of anything. Whenever I saw Howard at Jeanne's he never seemed to be under the influence of anything, but there was something slightly sketchy about him as well."

Andrew nodded. "Can you think of anything else that you can tell us about Jeanne that might help with the investigation?"

"Just that I hope you find the guy and get him locked up forever. I still miss her, every single day. Every time my phone rings, I hope it's her, asking me to come over and repair something, but it never is. I know I didn't treat Sandra right and that I should find a way to make it up to her, but my heart will always belong to Jeanne, for eternity."

He finished the last of his drink and then glanced at his watch. "I really have to go. I hope I helped, at least a little bit. If you have any more questions, have Helen arrange another meeting. It felt good to talk about Jeanne. I haven't really done that in the last five years."

He jumped up and disappeared out of the room before Bessie or Andrew could reply. Bessie finished her tea and then sighed. "I feel sorry for his children," she said.

"Yes, me, too," Andrew replied, "and for Sandra."

"Yes, she couldn't possibly have known what she was getting herself into when she met him."

"He seems like a nice person, in spite of everything. He just made the mistake of falling in love with Jeanne and never getting past it."

"I think we should take another look at Sandra," Bessie said. "I can't imagine how frustrated she must have been, dealing with Jeanne and her partner's obsession with the woman."

"You could be right. I'm also curious why Howard insisted that Jeanne was promiscuous. He's the only one who has said that about her."

"Max did say that he told Howard that he'd slept with her. Maybe he wasn't the only one that exaggerated the extent of the relationship he had with Jeanne."

"Maybe, and maybe we should have this conversation somewhere else," Andrew said, glancing at the tables on either side of them that were now full of people.

Bessie got to her feet and followed Andrew out of the room. There were so many cars waiting for spaces that Andrew had trouble getting his car out of theirs. Several horns sounded behind them as more than one car tried to claim the space that Andrew finally vacated.

"Where to now?" he asked as he drove away.

"It's three o'clock. John and the others will be at my cottage at six. We don't have a lot of time. What do you think you'd like to do?"

"Are there any parks nearby with crazy golf or anything like that?" Andrew asked.

Bessie stared at him for a moment. "There are, yes," she said eventually.

"You don't like the idea? I thought you enjoyed yourself when we played at Lakeview Holiday Park."

"I did, but, well, I just thought you'd rather see more of the island's sights, that's all."

"Parks are sights," Andrew countered. "We could play a round of crazy golf, maybe get ice cream, and then watch the children running around and feel grateful that they aren't ours."

Bessie laughed. "I suppose we could do all of those things," she said.

"Tell me where I'm going."

After a moment's thought, Bessie directed him to Onchan Park. Not only did it have crazy golf, it also had a small boating lake.

Somehow Bessie was sure that Andrew would want to hire a boat and have a spin around the lake. She was correct.

"Oh, look at the little lake," he exclaimed as they walked through the park. "Let's take a boat out, shall we?"

"Why not," Bessie replied with a grin.

The lake was quite small, and after a couple of circuits it began to be a little bit boring, but Andrew was determined to squeeze maximum enjoyment out of their half-hour boat hire. "I wonder if I can start working on my crazy golf strategy from here," he said as they puttered past the course.

"I don't think you need to bother. I'm not good at crazy golf, remember?"

"Some of the holes look quite challenging, anyway."

"I've never tried it, but I'm sure it will be fun."

After they returned their boat, they paid for golf. As they walked over to the course, they passed a very harassed-looking young man who was carrying a small girl and holding hands with a slightly older boy. The boy was carrying three golf clubs and three balls, but every few steps he'd drop something. As Andrew picked up one of the balls that rolled straight at him, Bessie recognised the man.

"Bill?" she said. "I'm sorry, but you're Bill Martin, aren't you? I'm Bessie Cubbon. Liz is a friend of mine."

The man stared at her for a minute and then nodded slowly. "Of course, we've met at various things connected with the language classes that Liz takes," he replied.

"How are you?" Bessie asked, feeling concerned. The man looked as if he hadn't slept in days, even though his clothes appeared to have been slept in.

"I'm okay," he told her. "The first few days are just really difficult."

"First few days?" she repeated.

"Oh, you may not have heard. Liz had the baby. It's another girl. We're thinking of calling her Danielle, but we haven't made a final decision."

"Congratulations!" Bessie exclaimed. "I hadn't heard, no."

"Liz's mum is here, helping out. I think she's been ringing people, but she's probably only been ringing family and her own friends, rather than Liz's. I don't know if Marjorie even knows. I'll have to try to remember to ask Liz later."

"I'm so happy for both of you," Bessie told him.

"Yeah, we're happy too, but so very tired. They don't keep mums in hospital for long these days. They sent Liz and the baby home less than twenty-four hours after the baby had arrived. I know Liz is happier at home, and we've done it twice before, but we'd both forgotten how much work a new baby is."

"She cries a lot," the little boy said.

Bessie grinned. "I'm sure you cried a lot, too, when you were a baby."

"But I'm not a baby anymore," he said stoutly.

"No, you're my big helper," Bill said. "Hopefully, Liz and the baby are having a nice long nap while I'm out with the children. Then, when she has to be up in the night with the baby, she won't be as exhausted."

"Well, good luck to you all," Bessie told him. "Tell Liz congratulations from me. I'll send a little something for the baby along in a day or two."

"That's unnecessary, but thank you," Bill said. "Now we must go and get some dinner. I promised Liz and her mother that I'd feed these two while we're out."

Bessie watched as the man returned the golf clubs and balls and then walked slowly back towards the car park. "I should have introduced you," she said to Andrew in an apologetic tone.

"He was too tired to care," Andrew laughed. "I remember those first few days. It gets better, but at the time you doubt your sanity, especially after the first one, when you should know better."

The pair played a noncompetitive game of crazy golf. Bessie knew that if they'd been keeping score Andrew would have won, but since they weren't, it didn't matter. After they'd finished, Andrew insisted on ice cream from the café.

"And now we'll find somewhere to sit and watch the chaos while we enjoy our ice cream," he said.

There were benches nearly everywhere in the park. They settled on one near the large playground and ate while they watched the children playing.

"I missed a lot of this with my children," Andrew said after a few minutes. "I was always busy working. If I could go back, I'd take more time off, especially when the children were small, and really try to enjoy them. They grow up incredibly quickly, you know."

"I'll take your word for it."

"And now it's gone five and we should be getting back to Laxey, I suppose," he said after glancing at his watch.

"This was fun," Bessie told him as they walked back to the car. "It isn't something I would have suggested, but I enjoyed it."

"I'm glad to hear that. I enjoyed it very much."

"Do you want to come over to my cottage while I check my emails?" Andrew asked after he'd parked outside of Bessie's cottage. "I'm really hoping for something back about the charity that inherited Betty's fortune."

"If it won't take long," Bessie said. "The others are due in about twenty minutes."

"Assuming the computer cooperates, it should only take about ten," Andrew assured her.

Bessie sat in the small sitting area of the cottage and watched two toddlers chasing one another up and down the beach while Andrew fired up his computer.

"Finally," he said. "I have a reply from my friend in London. He says he's sorry it took so long, but he wanted to make sure that he'd dug deeply enough."

"And what did he find out?" Bessie asked impatiently.

"The charity is called RMSLE, which as far he can tell is just a meaningless set of initials. On the surface, it looks completely legitimate. It was established before Betty's death, and from what my friend could discover, it's meant to provide grants to women in need."

"What sort of need?"

"That's a good question. My friend rang the number of the charity's main office. He left a message on their answering machine but was never rung back. He was able to dig through some of their financials, though, as some things are a matter of public record. From what he can tell, various grants are awarded every year to specific women. I don't know most of the names, but I'm going to send a copy of this email to Lukas. I suspect he'll recognise them. One of the names is Cindy's, though."

"So Cindy is benefitting from her sister's death, even though she killed her?"

"It appears so. From what my friend could learn, the grants are awarded by a board of directors with sole discretion as to the use of the funds. If they want to give money to a murderer, they apparently can do so."

"It all sounds very fishy."

"Definitely. I suspect the other grant recipients may well be the other women who were on the skiing holiday."

"But I thought they were all dead?"

"They are, but maybe the board at the charity doesn't know that. Maybe Betty or Cindy, whichever sister it is, is still submitting grant requests in their names, year after year. There may not even be any board, just Cindy, writing checks to dead women and then cashing them herself"

"What a horrible thought."

"Indeed. As I said, I need to forward this to Lukas."

While Andrew typed away at his keyboard, Bessie tried to think. If the charity had been set up before Betty's death, what was her connection to it? How much advanced planning had gone into Cindy's murder, assuming it was Cindy, not Betty, who'd been killed?

"Right, we should get back to your cottage. Your friends will be arriving soon," Andrew said as he shut his laptop. "I may pop back over in an hour and see if I have a reply, though."

"I hope you get one. And I hope Lukas has found Cindy. I suspect she belongs behind bars."

"I think you're right. It's all turning out to be more complicated than I'd expected."

John was standing at Bessie's door when they reached it a few moments later.

"I'm sorry, I was just checking emails," Andrew explained as Bessie unlocked the door.

"Any news on your case?" John asked.

"Yes, although I'm not sure what it tells us," Andrew replied.

"Why not save it for when everyone is here," Bessie suggested.

"Hugh is bringing dinner," John said. "Apparently, Grace is nesting, and part of that includes cooking and baking all day, every day. When she heard about tonight's gathering, she insisted on making us a chicken casserole and a bread and butter pudding."

"How kind of her," Bessie said. She repeated the sentiment to Hugh when he arrived a short time later with pans full of the promised food.

"It isn't kindness, it's hormones," Hugh laughed. "She's been cooking and baking all week. We have three cakes, five trays of flapjacks, and a huge box of biscuits taking up space in the kitchen. I'm going to start bringing things to work to share with the other guys soon. I can't possibly eat all of it and for the first time in months, Grace isn't hungry."

"It won't be too much longer now," Bessie said soothingly. "Make sure you build up your strength. I saw Bill Martin today at Onchan Park. Liz just had the baby, and he looked completely done in."

"Oh, great," Hugh replied. "I'm already not looking forward to the first few weeks. We'll get through it, I suppose, but I expect it will be difficult."

"It will, but it's totally worth it," John told him. "When they get to be teenagers, they can start helping around the house and maybe even cooking a meal now and then."

"How are Thomas and Amy?" Bessie asked.

"Settling in at school, but slowly," he replied. "If Sue thinks she can just drag them back to Manchester whenever she decides to return, she has another think coming, though. They've been through too much already this year. I'll fight her as much as I have to in order to keep the children here for school."

Bessie wasn't sure how to respond to that. John looked far angrier than she'd ever seen him before. A knock on the door came at just the right time.

"I'm sorry I'm late. I thought I'd run a few errands, and of course they took far longer than they should have. I hope I haven't missed anything," Doona said in a rush as she entered the cottage.

"You haven't missed anything," John told her. "I was just telling Bessie that I'm determined to keep the children here for the rest of the school year. Sue still hasn't given me a definite return date. That isn't fair to Thomas and Amy."

Doona looked at John for a minute and then smiled at him. "It's been fun having them here. I'm glad they're going to get to stay longer," she said.

John nodded. "You've been a huge help with them so far. I really appreciate everything you've done. I'm going to try not to keep taking advantage of you, though."

"You haven't been taking advantage," Doona told him firmly, "and I haven't minded helping. If I start to feel as if you are taking advantage, you can be sure I'll tell you."

"I hope you will," John replied.

"Maybe we should eat," Hugh said, after an awkward silence.

"The casserole smells wonderful," Bessie said. "I can't wait to try it."

Hugh brought an extra chair in from the dining room while everyone else filled plates. Bessie poured drinks and then they all sat down together to eat.

"It's every bit as good as it smelled," Bessie said after a few bites. "Grace is a very good cook."

"She is, and I'm getting quite spoiled," Hugh replied. "She's hoping to stay home with the baby for a few years. I'm looking forward to coming home to lovely meals nearly every day."

"Maybe not when the baby is very small," Andrew said. "When my wife had our first, she kept trying to keep everything going at home as well, and it was far too much for her. I was too busy to pay attention until one night when I got home from work and found the baby crying, dinner burning, and my wife on the verge of a breakdown. Make sure Grace knows she doesn't have to be Superwoman."

Hugh nodded. "Her mother said the same thing. She's already promised to come up and help whenever Grace wants her, but knowing Grace, she won't ask. I thought I might tell her mum to just come and stay with us for a few weeks. I like her a lot, so I won't complain if she's at the house all the time."

"I'm sure you and Grace will find a way to make it work," John said, "but do take advantage of every offer of help that you get. People won't offer nearly as much with baby number two."

Andrew laughed. "That's very true, and by the time my wife had our third, even her mother had grown tired of babies. By that time we were quite used to listening to them cry, though, so it didn't seem to matter as much."

Bessie and Doona exchanged glances. "Sorry you missed out?" Doona whispered to Bessie.

"Not even the tiniest bit," she whispered back.

"I want Grace's recipe," Bessie said after she'd taken her first bite of the bread and butter pudding. "It's better than mine."

"It's my mother's recipe, actually," Hugh said. "My mother isn't much of a cook, but she has lots of recipes. I'll have Grace copy it for you, as Mum's given Grace most of them."

"I'd like a copy, too," Doona said. "Bread and butter pudding is a favourite of mine because it's fairly quick and easy, but mine isn't this good."

"Maybe it just tastes better because we didn't have to make it," Bessie suggested.

Everyone laughed as Bessie took another bite. "No, it definitely has something special about it," she said.

When everyone had cleared their plates, Doona collected them all and began to run water for washing up. Bessie put the kettle on so that they could have tea while they talked.

"That was truly delicious," Andrew said. "I'd forgotten how good home cooking can be. I generally eat in restaurants or simply make myself ready meals, as I'm on my own."

"I was doing much the same before the kids came to stay," John said. "Now they take turns making dinner for all of us. Some of the meals have been, well, interesting, and a few have been completely inedible, but mostly they've done really well. I'd like the recipes for both dishes if Grace doesn't mind. I'm sure my kids could manage them and they were good."

Hugh nodded. "Grace will be flattered to be asked."

A few minutes later Doona had the washing-up done and Bessie had the tea made. They all sat down together again.

"I suppose it's time to talk about murder," John said.

CHAPTER 14

"Should I start?" Andrew asked. "I've heard a bit more about my case."

"Go ahead," John replied.

Andrew told them all about the charity that Betty had set up before the skiing holiday. "It certainly seems odd," he said when he was done. "I've asked Lukas if he recognises any of the names of the women who've been given grants over the years. One of the names was Cindy's, however."

"Do you have any idea how much money we're talking about with these grants?" Hugh asked.

"Cindy was given five hundred thousand pounds in July," Andrew replied.

"Wow!" Doona gasped. "That's a pretty hefty grant, especially when she killed the woman who set up the charity. I'd love to know how the board makes its decisions."

"It's possible that the board is only one or two people, and Cindy may be on the board herself," Andrew said. "The charity was set up in Switzerland and it's administered from there. They're big on privacy there."

"I'm surprised you've found as much as you have," John said.

"My friend is very good at digging into things. I'm sure he'll have more information for me soon," Andrew replied.

"It seems to me that Betty set the charity up knowing she was about to kill Cindy and take her place," Doona said. "That's the only thing that makes sense, really."

"And if the other grant recipients were the women from the skiing holiday, maybe she killed them so that they couldn't take any more of the money," Hugh suggested.

"It seems as if she was paying them for their silence," Bessie suggested.

"And they kept quiet for the years she was in prison, anyway," Andrew added.

"Have you found the third girl, then?" John asked.

Andrew chuckled. "I forgot we haven't spoken since Dorothy was found," he said. "Yes, she's been found, or rather she was never found. She and her fiancé were in a plane that crashed years ago. The bodies were never recovered."

"How awful," Doona shuddered.

"Did you tell Lukas that we think that Betty's mother might in danger?" Bessie asked, recalling the conversation with Pete.

"I did. Hopefully, he'll find a way to warn her that she needs to be extra careful until he locates her daughter," Andrew replied.

"So thirty years ago, five women went on a skiing holiday, and now only one of them is still alive," John said. "One was murdered and the other three met with tragic accidents. The one who is still alive seems to be benefitting financially from the murder victim's charity. The whole thing sounds as if it's the plot of a late-night movie."

"As I told you in the beginning, the case has always bothered my friend, but he'd never followed up on it. Now that he has, he's sorry he didn't do so sooner, but at least maybe now he'll be able to get to the bottom of what really happened thirty years ago," Andrew said.

"What if Dorothy didn't really die?" Bessie asked. "Is it possible that she faked her own death? I can't see why she would have, I'm just asking."

"I suppose it's possible, as the bodies were never recovered, but that isn't that unusual under the circumstances. Maybe she faked her own death to get away from Betty," Andrew suggested.

"I would, if I'd found out that Abby and Flora were both dead," Doona said.

"Lukas is looking at all three deaths as possible murders, but there's only so much he can do after all this time. More importantly, he's looking for Cindy, who is probably Betty," Andrew said.

"And now we should talk about Jeanne," John suggested.

Bessie topped up everyone's tea and put some biscuits on the table. Even thought they'd all just eaten, everyone took a few before Bessie sat back down.

"We talked to Kenny and to Max Rogers," Bessie said. She gave them all a brief rundown of the two conversations and then answered John's questions.

"And I talked to James Poole," John said.

"You did? I don't suppose he solved the case for you?" Bessie asked hopefully.

"Unfortunately, he didn't, but he was interesting to talk to," John replied.

"What did he have to say about Jeanne?" Andrew wanted to know.

"He told me that they'd been together for about a year, but that it wasn't really anything serious," John replied. "They met through a mutual friend, Howard Miles."

"But I thought Howard said that he didn't meet Jeanne until he took up with Mabel," Bessie said. "Maybe I'm remembering incorrectly."

"If you are, I'm remembering incorrectly as well," Andrew said.

John nodded. "I have the notes from when you spoke to Howard, and when you repeated the conversation, that's what you told me he'd said. I'm going to have to speak to Howard next, I think."

"If Howard introduced them, he must have known Jeanne for years before he started seeing Mabel," Bessie said thoughtfully.

"As I said, I need to speak to Howard," John said.

"What else did you learn from James?" Andrew asked.

"Like the other men to whom you've spoken, he commented on

how Jeanne expected the men in her life to help with all manner of projects around her flat," John said. "He said it didn't bother him at first, but after a while he started to resent the demands. I got the impression that his mother wasn't as poorly as he told Jeanne. I suspect he may have used his mother as an excuse to leave the island and get away from her."

"Surely it would have been easier to simply break up with her," Doona suggested.

"He did say something about there being something magnetic about her personality. He said he would get angry with her, and then she'd come over to his flat to see him and he'd forget why he was cross," John explained.

"That suggests an intimacy," Andrew said, "but nearly everyone else has said that she wasn't particularly interested in such things."

"And James said the same," John confirmed. "He said that was another problem with their relationship and another reason why he didn't mind moving back to help his mother."

"So it's only Howard who suggested that she was promiscuous," Andrew said.

"Another issue to discuss with the man," John agreed.

"Did James have anything else interesting to say?" Andrew asked.

"Not really. He'd been questioned when Jeanne first died, but somehow he was under the impression that she'd committed suicide. I think he's spent the last five years feeling as if he may have contributed in some way to her death. I hate to say that he was relieved to hear that she was murdered, but that was the feeling I got from him after we'd talked," John replied.

"Was Howard questioned five years ago?" Bessie asked.

John shrugged. "From the notes that I have, it doesn't appear that he was, but Carl has been through the entire file and he believes that some notes may be missing. I've talked to Inspector Kelly about the case, but he doesn't recall any of the finer details, even though he only dealt with three murder cases in his time in Ramsey."

Andrew raised an eyebrow. "That surprises me, especially as this is an unsolved murder. Those tend to stay with most police inspectors, in my experience anyway."

"Yes, well, I think Inspector Kelly never quite believed that it was murder," John sighed. "He said some things that made me think that he believes Jeanne killed herself."

"I thought that wasn't possible," Bessie said.

"It's remotely possible," John conceded, "if she killed herself and then someone else came in and removed all of the evidence. I can't imagine why anyone would do that, especially as the note was left behind, though."

"What did the note say?" Andrew asked.

"I don't have a copy with me, but it was something along the lines of not being able to take it anymore, but nothing more specific than that," John replied.

"Did anyone suggest any reason why she might have been suicidal?" Bessie wondered. "We didn't ask anyone that specifically, but no one brought it up, either."

"Maybe that's something else to ask Howard," John said, making a note.

"You told us before that the handwriting was definitely hers, correct?" Andrew checked.

"Yes, according to a handwriting expert who studied it, anyway. It may be worth having someone else check it again, I suppose," John said.

"Have you seen the original note?" Bessie asked.

John shook his head. "Just a photocopy."

"Was it on a full sheet of paper, or is it possible that it was cut out from a longer letter?" was Bessie's next question.

"I'll have to have Carl pull the file and see if the note is still there," John said. "Why would someone go to the trouble of leaving behind a note and then take the medicine bottles away with them? It doesn't make sense."

"Maybe she really did kill herself, and when someone found the body he or she decided to try to frame someone else for murder," Hugh suggested.

"If that's the case, that someone did a terrible job of it," John said.

"Do you think it was suicide?" Bessie asked John.

He took a sip of tea and then nibbled on a biscuit for a moment. Eventually he shook his head. "No, I don't think it was. I think she was murdered. It feels off as suicide, for some reason."

"For what it's worth, I'm with John," Andrew said. "I think she was murdered."

Bessie nodded. She felt the same way, although she couldn't say for sure why.

"Howard has to be the number-one suspect now, doesn't he?" Doona asked. "I mean, he lied about when he'd met Jeanne, how long he'd known her, and about her, um, behaviour with men. That all makes me suspicious of him."

"I'm going to talk to him tomorrow morning," John said.

"I can't see any of the other men that we've met killing her," Bessie said. "Kenny probably had the strongest motive, but I believed him when he said he was still in love with her and never would have hurt her."

"If she did kill herself, I think he's the most likely person to have tried to hide that fact," Hugh said. "Maybe he felt as if he were responsible for her doing so and couldn't deal with the guilt."

"Aside from Kenny, I'd agree with Bessie. I can't see any of the other men we talked to being involved in any way," Andrew said. "I'm reserving judgment on Kenny for the time being."

"What about the women?" Doona asked.

"Sandra had a strong motive, but I can't quite see her as a murderer," Bessie said. "I know I shouldn't go on my instincts, but I just don't feel as if she could have killed Jeanne."

"She was dealing with a toddler and a new baby," Andrew said. "I can't see her having the time or the energy to kill anyone."

"What about Mabel?" Hugh wondered.

"She was meant to be Jeanne's closest friend. Why would she kill her?" Doona asked.

"Maybe Jeanne was having an affair with Howard," Hugh

suggested. "Maybe they'd been carrying on for years and Mabel found out."

"Except everything we've heard suggests that Jeanne wasn't that interested in a physical relationship," Andrew said.

"But maybe Howard was busy doing DIY for Jeanne and not spending enough time with Mabel," Hugh persisted.

"I'm going to talk to her after I've spoken to Howard," John said. "If nothing else, to see if their stories match."

"Perhaps Bessie and I should pay Mabel another visit," Andrew said.

John frowned. "It feels as if we might be getting close to a solution on this case," he said. "You two need to be careful."

"We won't do anything foolish," Andrew promised. "I thought we might just get another slice of cake and have another chat with Mabel, that's all."

"I suppose I can't stop you from having a slice of cake," John said.

"What about Amanda McBride?" Doona asked. "I think she's the only suspect we haven't discussed tonight."

"Let's call her a witness," Andrew suggested with a chuckle. "She's on my list, but she's pretty far down it. I can't imagine a motive for her, really."

"We could speculate about her all night," John said. "If she did have a motive, she's probably the only person who knows what it was. I may try to speak to her after I've talked to Howard, but she's not a priority."

It seemed to Bessie as if both Andrew and John were convinced that Howard had killed Jeanne. While she didn't exactly disagree, she wondered about Mabel. Perhaps they would get all of their answers soon.

"I need to go," John said, checking his watch. "I have to collect Amy from a friend's house in a few minutes."

"She'd probably be thrilled if you arrive late," Bessie suggested as John got to his feet.

"She would be, but the other girl's parents probably won't be as happy," he laughed. "Andrew, would you mind walking me to my car?"

Bessie exchanged glances with Doona as the two men exited the cottage. What did John want to discuss with Andrew that he couldn't say in front of everyone?

"I suppose I should go as well," Hugh said. "Grace will be waiting to hear what you all thought of her cooking."

Bessie insisted that Hugh take the leftover food home with him. "They're your containers, after all," she reasoned, "and Grace did all of the hard work. She ought to get to try everything."

Doona was tidying the kitchen when Bessie turned back from letting Hugh out. "We should have lunch together one day next week," she told Bessie. "I feel as if we haven't had a proper talk in ages."

As Doona only had one day off during the week, it didn't take them long to make the necessary arrangements.

"And now I must be off," she told Bessie. "I really hope John and Andrew can get both cases wrapped up in the next day or two. Ring me the minute you learn anything."

When Bessie opened the door to let Doona out, Andrew was standing behind it.

"I was just about to knock," he said with a grin. "Should I come back in or would you rather take a short walk on the beach?"

"As long as the weather permits, I'd almost always prefer a walk," Bessie said. She slid on the nearest pair of shoes and locked up the cottage behind them.

Doona waved as she pulled away and then Bessie and Andrew began their stroll.

"John is going to ring me in the morning, once he's had Howard brought into the station," he told Bessie. "He doesn't want us to talk to Mabel before that."

"I suppose that makes sense."

"We don't want to get in the way of the official investigation, but I do think we might learn something from Mabel if we ask the right questions."

"I have quite a few questions for her," Bessie said, "but I don't know that she'll want to answer any of them."

"We may learn more from what she won't answer than what she will," Andrew suggested.

"I don't know about that, but I'm looking forward to tomorrow anyway."

"I am as well. I checked my emails before I came back over to your cottage, and Lukas hasn't replied yet. I'm going to ring him in the morning, and also my friend in London. I should be over to collect you around nine, though, if that suits you?"

"I'll be ready, but what if Mabel doesn't work until one o'clock again?"

"She works from eight to five tomorrow," he told her. "I asked."

"They must think it's odd, someone ringing up every few days to ask when Mabel is working," Bessie suggested.

"This time I told them a long story about visiting last year and not having enough money with me to leave a proper tip," he replied. "It was a long and incredibly boring story, so that by the time I'd finished, whoever I was speaking to just wanted to get off the phone."

Bessie laughed. "That was very clever of you."

"I try."

Andrew insisted on walking Bessie back to Treoghe Bwaane. At the door, he gave her a hug. "If I'm up early again, I may see you on the beach."

"You'll be more than welcome to join me for my morning walk," Bessie assured him.

Feeling inordinately pleased with life, Bessie got ready for bed and then curled up with a book for a short while. She slept well and woke at six looking forward to talking to Mabel and maybe solving a five-year-old murder case.

Andrew was nowhere to be seen as Bessie made her way along the empty beach. There were no signs of movement in any of the holiday cottages, actually, and Bessie was sure that some of them were going to be empty now until the spring. She walked as far as Thie yn Traie and then turned back towards home. An hour with a good book was exactly what she needed while she waited for Andrew, she decided.

"It's already been an interesting morning," Andrew told her when she opened the door to him a few minutes before nine. "John rang. He has Howard at the station and will be questioning him soon. He's going to keep him there until after we've spoken to Mabel, just in case she says anything interesting."

"Let's go, then," Bessie said, grabbing her handbag.

They were in the car, heading south, before Andrew spoke again. "The other news is that Lukas has found Cindy. Luckily for him, she was actually trying to fly out of Switzerland. He's had her detained at the airport and will be speaking to her today."

"I'd love to be a fly on the wall for that interview," Bessie said.

"Yes, me too. Apparently she was very cooperative at the airport. He's thinking about ringing her mother and asking her to come over to see her daughter."

"I suspect Cindy might be less than cooperative if he suggested that."

"Yes, I do as well. He's going to ring me later today, or maybe send an email if he has a lot to tell me. Maybe we'll be able to close both cases today, and then I can just relax and enjoy the rest of my holiday."

"That would be nice," Bessie said. "Although I must confess that I'm enjoying our investigations."

"I am as well. It's interesting, seeing things from the outside, as it were. Of course, I'm not actually on the outside, as John knows and supports what we're doing, but I'm also not official anymore. I don't know what I'm trying to say, except that helping John has been fascinating."

Bessie laughed and then sat back and watched the scenery go past as they made their way towards Port St. Mary. "Let me know when you need directions," she said once they'd passed Castletown.

"I'm usually pretty good with finding places again, after I've been there once, but I'll let you know if I need any help."

A short while later, he pulled into the café car park. "It doesn't look busy," he said, glancing around the otherwise empty area.

"Let's just hope Mabel is feeling chatty again."

There was a man sitting by himself at a table in the corner, sipping a cup of tea or coffee, but otherwise the café was empty. Bessie and

Andrew sat at the same table that they'd occupied previously. A moment later Mabel came out from the kitchen.

"Ah, Bessie, I was wondering when I would see you again," she said. "The police haven't arrested anyone yet for Jeanne's murder, so I knew you'd be back to ask me more rude questions."

"I don't think I was rude last time," Bessie protested.

Mabel cackled with laughter. "Maybe, maybe not, but at least your handsome friend was generous when he paid me. I assume you don't actually want anything to eat or drink, being as the food is terrible and the drinks aren't any better. What do you want to know today, then?"

Bessie glanced at Andrew. He gave her a small nod.

"Different people have given me rather different views on Jeanne," Bessie began. "Some have suggested that she was rather, um, free with her favours, while others have said that she wasn't all that interested in intimacies."

Mabel laughed again. "My goodness, you're nearly beetroot from that question," she said. "As for the answer, I don't rightly know. Me and Jeanne didn't really talk about sex. Mostly I wasn't having any, but I assumed she was. She had plenty of men in and out of her flat."

"And when did Howard meet her?" Bessie asked.

"Not long after we started seeing each other," Mabel replied. "Sadly, that was not long before she died."

"That's interesting," Andrew said. "James Poole told the police that Howard introduced him to Jeanne."

Mabel stared at him for a minute. "That's not possible," she said. "He must have given the police the wrong name or something. Howard didn't know Jeanne before I introduced him to her."

"Are you quite sure of that?" Andrew asked.

Mabel nodded and then shook her head. "He would have mentioned it, if he'd met her before. I mean, they both acted like they'd never met. I never heard Jeanne mention his name before I met him. James must be confused."

"How did you and Howard meet?" Bessie asked.

"At ShopFast. I was buying frozen pizza. I'm sure I told you the story last time," the woman replied. "Jeanne and I often did our shopping together, but she'd gone off to the bakery or somewhere. Howard and I started talking and ended up making plans for dinner later in the week."

"And where was Jeanne while you two were talking?" Bessie wondered.

"I just said she'd gone off to the bakery," Mabel snapped.

"How long did you and Howard talk at that first meeting?" Andrew asked.

"It felt as if we talked for hours, but it was probably only twenty minutes," Mabel replied. "It was strange because I felt so at home with him right away. He almost seemed to know all about me, even though we'd never met."

As soon as the words were out of her mouth, Mabel seemed to realise what she'd said. She began to shake her head. "Jeanne didn't tell him about me. I mean, why would she do that? None of this makes any sense."

"Did Jeanne and Howard meet that night, then?" Bessie asked.

"No, they didn't meet until a few weeks later, after Howard and I were starting to get serious. She was really happy for me, though. I told her all about him long before I introduced them."

"I'm sure you told him about her, as well," Bessie said.

"Well, yeah, of course. She was my dearest friend. Then, once they'd met, I started having him help her with her DIY. I told you all of that, though, last time."

Bessie nodded. "Can you think of any reason why they might have pretended not to know one another?"

"None at all. There was no reason for them to do that. If Jeanne thought we might like each other, she could have just introduced him to me. I wouldn't have minded if he'd been her boyfriend first. But like I said, she never mentioned him to me, and she always told me about the men in her life."

"Did Jeanne have any family on the island?" Andrew asked.

Mabel shook her head. "They were all across, and she wasn't close to any of them."

"Parents? Siblings?" Andrew wondered.

"Her parents were both dead and her only brother died when she was a teenager. She had an aunt and maybe a few cousins somewhere, but no one that she was close to."

"What happened to her estate, then?" was Andrew's next question.

"She left everything to one of those distant cousins, but there wasn't really much to leave. Her flat wasn't worth much more than what she still owed on it and she didn't have any savings to speak of. She had a little bit of life insurance, but not much. Howard insisted, after she died, that we both take out really big policies on each other. If one of us goes, the other one will be set for life."

Bessie exchanged glances with Andrew. There was something worrying about the woman's words.

"But you didn't set them up until after Jeanne died?" Andrew checked.

Mabel shrugged. "If it was before, it wasn't much before. I don't remember the timing exactly."

"Too bad you didn't mention it to Jeanne," Bessie said thoughtfully. "She could have left her cousin a lot more, if she'd done the same."

"I may have mentioned it to Jeanne, now that you say that," Mabel replied. "Howard knew someone across who had died and left huge debts, so he insisted on the life insurance policies for both him and me. I do remember talking to Jeanne about it, actually, suggesting that she do the same. Life insurance isn't that expensive when you're young. I even told her to make me and Howard the beneficiaries, but she never followed through."

"Of course life insurance doesn't pay out when you commit suicide," Bessie pointed out.

"But Jeanne didn't kill herself," Mabel said tartly.

Bessie nodded. "It doesn't really matter, if she didn't take out the insurance anyway."

Mabel nodded. "Was there anything else? Because I should get back to work."

Bessie glanced around the room. The only customer was still reading the newspaper, seemingly oblivious to them.

Andrew stood up and handed Mabel a folded note. "Thank you for your time," he said.

"Do you think you'll actually be able to work out what happened to Jeanne after all these years?" she asked as she slid the money into her pocket.

"I'm fairly certain I know what happened to her," Andrew replied. "Now it's just a matter of gathering evidence. You've been a big help. Thank you."

"What did I say?" the woman demanded. "What do you think happened to Jeanne?"

Andrew smiled. "I'm sorry, but I can't possibly comment on an active police investigation. I'm pretty sure you'll hear something soon."

"You can't possibly suspect that I had anything to do with Jeanne's death," Mabel said.

"I didn't say any such thing," Andrew replied in a reassuring tone.

"I didn't, you know. I would never have done anything to hurt her."

"Of course not," Andrew said, "but someone did kill her and I think I know who that someone was."

Mabel nodded tightly and then turned and took a step away. When she turned back around, Bessie could see tears in the woman's eyes. "Was it Howard?" she whispered.

"As I said, I can't comment on an active investigation," Andrew repeated himself.

Mabel took a deep breath. "I never thought, I mean, I never wanted to believe, that is, I can't quite imagine…" she trailed off and looked at the floor. "He and Jeanne knew each other before I met him," she said in a disbelieving tone.

"That's certainly something we're investigating," Andrew told her.

"They were trying to kill me," she said softly.

"Maybe we should have this conversation down at the station," Andrew suggested.

Mabel shook her head. "I don't want to talk to the police. You can tell them what I tell you. Howard insisted that he never meant to hurt anyone, but I've always wondered. We were having drinks with

Jeanne that Friday night. I started feeling really sleepy after my first glass of wine. I fell asleep and when I woke up, Howard and Jeanne were fighting. I didn't understand what they were saying, but now it makes more sense. They were planning to kill me for the insurance money."

Tears were streaming down Mabel's face as she talked. Bessie stood up and handed her a tissue. She patted the woman's back as Mabel wiped her eyes.

"As I said, I believe the police should hear this," Andrew said.

"Jeanne was telling Howard that it was too soon, that if it looked like suicide, the insurance wouldn't pay. She just kept saying 'they won't pay,' and I didn't realise what she meant until just now. Howard was really angry and he kept talking about years of planning, which didn't make any sense, either, until today."

Andrew pulled out his phone. Bessie knew he had to be ringing John. She patted Mabel's back. "You need to tell John Rockwell all of this," she said softly.

"We're meant to be going on a walking holiday next month," Mabel said. "Howard has been poring over the maps, insisting that he really wants to walk on mountains and cliffs and things like that. I told him I don't like heights, but he keeps insisting."

"I'm very sorry," Bessie told her.

"I suppose I should be grateful that he hasn't already killed me," Mabel sighed. "It seems as if he's been planning it for six or seven years."

She stood still, staring straight ahead for several minutes. Bessie could only imagine what was going through the woman's mind. Every time she tried to speak to her, Mabel seemed to ignore her. Eventually Bessie stopped trying and simply stood and rubbed her back until the police car pulled up outside.

"That poor woman," Bessie said as the car drove away with Mabel in the back.

"I only talked to John briefly, but he suggested that Howard told him a very different story," Andrew replied. "Don't feel too sorry for her until you've heard his side of things."

CHAPTER 15

"Howard has actually given us two versions of events," John told Bessie and Andrew the next day. "In the first version, he and Mabel teamed up to kill Jeanne, thinking that she'd taken out the life insurance policy that Mabel had suggested to her. It's one possible solution, but it leaves a few loose ends."

"I can't see Mabel agreeing to kill Jeanne," Bessie said. "She may just be a very good actress, but she seemed genuinely devastated when she began to realise what had happened five years ago."

"You'll probably like Howard's second version of events, then," John said. "In that one, Jeanne wanted to kill Mabel. He insisted that he knew nothing about her plan, even though he did admit that he was the one who'd talked Mabel into buying all of the life insurance. He claimed he only realised what Jeanne was planning when Mabel fell asleep after her first drink that night. Jeanne had several more bottles of tablets and she wanted Howard to help her feed them to Mabel. As he tells it, he refused and then took Mabel home. He claims Jeanne must have taken an overdose herself once they were gone."

"How does he explain the missing bottles?" Andrew asked.

"He can't. He insists that the bottles were all still there when he left, along with the glasses of wine out of which they'd all been drinking," John replied.

"That doesn't explain what Mabel overheard," Bessie said.

"No, and Mabel has been working to remember as much as she can from that night. She's convinced that Howard was trying to kill her and that Jeanne intervened," John replied.

"I'm surprised he didn't try to kill her again in the last five years," Andrew remarked.

"From what we can determine, he may have been planning something for their upcoming trip. While he's never shown any interest in hiking or mountain climbing before, the entire trip was planned around both activities, even though Mabel didn't want to do any such thing," John said.

"He was probably afraid to do anything too quickly after Jeanne's death. Having Mabel die in an accident across would have been safer for him," Andrew said.

"Poor Mabel. I don't believe that she was a party to Jeanne's murder," Bessie said. "I do wonder about Jeanne, though, whether or not she was part of Howard's plan to kill Mabel."

"I don't suppose we'll ever know the answer to that," John said. "Howard has done his best to implicate her, but he may just be lying to try to save himself."

"I wonder if Mabel knows anything about the missing bottles," Bessie said speculatively. "If Jeanne died on Friday evening, isn't it possible that she went to visit her over the weekend? Maybe she found the body and took the bottles away for some reason."

"It's an interesting theory," John said. "I may just have to ask her some very specific questions."

"Maybe Jeanne really did commit suicide and Mabel was trying to frame Howard for murder," Andrew suggested.

"I'm not sure that Mabel was thinking that clearly," Bessie replied, "and I'm not convinced that it wasn't murder. I just suspect that Howard would have been more careful once he'd killed her."

"Maybe he set the scene before he took Mabel home and she went back and altered it later," John said. "As I said, I'll have to talk to Mabel again."

"Meanwhile, Lukas has been in touch again," Andrew reported. "He's had a full and seemingly honest confession."

"He has?" Bessie demanded.

"I'll read you exactly what he wrote in his email," Andrew said. "He says, 'I walked into the interview room and looked at the woman at the table. I said 'Hello, Betty,' and she burst into tears.'"

"My goodness, you'd think someone who had killed four people would be able to bluff their way out of that," Bessie said.

Andrew shook his head. "From what Lukas said, she's been waiting for someone to work it out for the last thirty years. He said she's incredibly thin and unbelievably edgy and nervous. She's been running from what she did ever since she was released from prison, apparently."

"But she did kill the other three women, didn't she?" Bessie asked.

"It certainly seems as if she had a hand in at least some of their deaths, yes," Andrew replied. "The plane crash may have been an accident, but she did admit that she'd met with Dorothy at the airport before Dorothy and her fiancé were due to leave. Whatever she said to Dorothy caused them to rush away without completing the necessary safety checks which could have been a factor in the accident."

"So she killed Cindy and then took her place?" Bessie checked.

"Yes, although she insists that it was self-defense. The fact that she had the charity already set up in case of her untimely death puts that into question, but as she's already done her time in prison for Cindy's death, Lukas isn't pushing her on it."

"Did she tell him why she killed Cindy?" John asked.

"Cindy was having an affair with Betty's fiancé," Andrew replied. "The other three women knew about it. Apparently the plan was to get Cindy to the chalet and confront her about it. Betty insists now that she never wanted to hurt her sister, she just wanted to convince her to end the affair."

"But Cindy didn't agree?" Bessie asked.

"Betty says that they got into a huge fight and then Cindy went and got the knife and started threatening Betty with it. We'll never really know what happened, of course."

"And she killed the other three to keep them from revealing her true identity?" was Bessie's next question.

"Not exactly. According to Betty, the other three women witnessed the fight and knew that Cindy had been killed in self-defense. They were all meant to tell the police the whole story to strengthen Betty's version of events when she confessed. Instead, they all insisted that they'd been asleep and missed the entire thing. When Betty got out of prison, she decided to make them pay for what they'd done to her."

Bessie shuddered. "How awful," she exclaimed.

"Lukas is looking into Betty's father's death again as well. It seems possible that the pair crossed paths accidentally and that she killed him," Andrew added. "She hinted at that to Lukas, but wouldn't answer any questions about it."

"I hope he can find enough evidence to charge her with something," Bessie said. "I'll sleep better at night knowing she's behind bars."

"As she's confessed to killing Abby and Flora, I don't think you need to worry about her getting out of prison anytime soon," Andrew assured her.

"And that makes two cases more or less solved," John said. "Mostly thanks to Bessie."

"I didn't do anything," Bessie said, blushing.

The two men laughed.

Bessie and Andrew spent the rest of his holiday sightseeing and enjoying the island. They even found time for a nice dinner with Pete and Helen. When it was time for him to leave, she felt mixed emotions. It had been fun spending time with the smart and handsome man, but it had also taken up a lot of her time and energy. Once he'd driven away, heading for the airport, she returned to Treoghe Bwaane and locked the door behind her. While she'd be happy to see the man again if he came for another visit, for today she was perfectly content on her own in her little cottage by the sea.

GLOSSARY OF TERMS

Manx to English

- **fastyr mie** - good afternoon
- **moghrey mie** - good morning

House Names – Manx to English

- **Thie yn Traie** - Beach House
- **Treoghe Bwaane** - Widow's Cottage

English to American Terms

- **advocate** - Manx title for a lawyer (solicitor)
- **aye** - yes
- **bin** - garbage can
- **biscuits** - cookies

- **bonnet (car)** - hood
- **boot (car)** - trunk
- **car park** - parking lot
- **chemist** - pharmacist
- **chips** - french fries
- **cloakroom** - bathroom
- **cuppa** - cup of tea (informally)
- **dear** - expensive
- **dust sheet** - drop cloth
- **estate agent** - real estate agent (realtor)
- **fairy cakes** - cupcakes
- **fizzy drink** - soda (pop)
- **hire car** - rental car
- **holiday** - vacation
- **jumper** - sweater
- **lead (for a dog)** - leash
- **loo** - restroom
- **midday** - noon
- **note** - paper money
- **pavement** - sidewalk
- **plait (hair)** - braid
- **poorly** - ill
- **primary school** - elementary school
- **pudding** - dessert
- **pulled** - picked up
- **starters** - appetizers
- **supply teacher** - substitute teacher
- **telly** - television
- **tills** - checkouts (at a shop)
- **thick** - not very intelligent
- **torch** - flashlight
- **trolley** - shopping cart
- **windscreen** - windshield

OTHER NOTES

The emergency number in the UK and the island is 999, not 911.

CID is the Criminal Investigation Department of the Isle of Man Constabulary (Police Force).

When talking about time, the English say, for example, "half seven" to mean "seven-thirty."

With regard to Bessie's age: UK (and IOM) residents get a free bus pass at the age of 60. Bessie is somewhere between that age and the age at which she will get a birthday card from the Queen. British citizens used to receive telegrams from the ruling monarch on the occasion of their one-hundredth birthday. Cards replaced the telegrams in 1982, but the special greeting is still widely referred to as a telegram.

When island residents talk about someone being from "across," they mean that the person is from somewhere in the United Kingdom (across the water).

"Ready meals" are prepared and chilled (not frozen) meals that can be easily reheated at home.

ACKNOWLEDGMENTS

I am especially grateful to everyone who reads and enjoys these books. Thank you for spending time with Bessie and her friends.

Many thanks to my hard working editor, Denise, who isn't appreciated nearly enough.

Thanks to my beta readers, who share thoughtful insights into ways I can improve these works.

And thanks to my family, who don't complain (too much) about sharing me with all of my fictional friends!

AUNT BESSIE TRIES

RELEASE DATE: JANUARY 18, 2019

Aunt Bessie tries to help her friends.

After Grace Watterson's baby shower, Elizabeth Cubbon, known as Bessie to nearly everyone, gets stopped by one of the party guests. Lora White is worried that someone is trying to kill her.

Aunt Bessie tries to persuade Lora to talk to the police.

The problem is, Lora isn't sure whether someone is trying to kill her or not. After hearing Lora's story, Bessie isn't certain, either. Besides, Lora doesn't want to get any of her friends or family members into any trouble.

Aunt Bessie tries to work out who might be trying to hurt Lora.

She talks to the woman's family members and neighbours, but quickly finds herself being drawn more and more deeply into Lora's life.

Can Bessie help Lora work out what's happening? Is someone truly trying to kill Lora, or does the woman simply have an overactive imagination? Is it possible that Lora is creating the incidents herself for some reason? Will Bessie be sorry that she tried to help?

ALSO BY DIANA XARISSA

Aunt Bessie Assumes

Aunt Bessie Believes

Aunt Bessie Considers

Aunt Bessie Decides

Aunt Bessie Enjoys

Aunt Bessie Finds

Aunt Bessie Goes

Aunt Bessie's Holiday

Aunt Bessie Invites

Aunt Bessie Joins

Aunt Bessie Knows

Aunt Bessie Likes

Aunt Bessie Meets

Aunt Bessie Needs

Aunt Bessie Observes

Aunt Bessie Provides

Aunt Bessie Questions

Aunt Bessie Remembers

Aunt Bessie Questions

Aunt Bessie Solves

Aunt Bessie Tries

The Isle of Man Ghostly Cozy Mysteries

Arrivals and Arrests

Boats and Bad Guys

Cars and Cold Cases

Dogs and Danger

Encounters and Enemies

Friends and Frauds

Guests and Guilt

Hop-tu-Naa and Homicide

Invitations and Investigations

Joy and Jealousy

The Markham Sisters Cozy Mystery Novellas

The Appleton Case

The Bennett Case

The Chalmers Case

The Donaldson Case

The Ellsworth Case

The Fenton Case

The Green Case

The Hampton Case

The Irwin Case

The Jackson Case

The Kingston Case

The Lawley Case

The Moody Case

The Norman Case

The Osborne Case

The Patrone Case

The Isle of Man Romance Series

Island Escape

Island Inheritance

Island Heritage

Island Christmas

ABOUT THE AUTHOR

Diana grew up in Northwestern Pennsylvania and moved to Washington, DC after college. There she met a wonderful Englishman who was visiting the city. After a whirlwind romance, they got married and Diana moved to the Chesterfield area of Derbyshire to begin a new life with her husband. A short time later, they relocated to the Isle of Man.

After over ten years on the island, it was time for a change. With their two children in tow, Diana and her husband moved to suburbs of Buffalo, New York. Diana now spends her days writing about the island she loves.

She also writes mystery/thrillers set in the not-too-distant future as Diana X. Dunn and middle grade and Young Adult books as D.X. Dunn.

Diana is always happy to hear from readers. You can write to her at:

Diana Xarissa Dunn
PO Box 72
Clarence, NY 14031.
Find Diana at: DianaXarissa.com
E-mail: Diana@dianaxarissa.com